Amy McGavin is the pen name of a Scottish wife-and-husband writing team whose real names are . . . Amy and Gavin.

The couple's contemporary romance novels are set in the Highlands. Each story is crafted with humour and heart, with a wee bit of heat thrown in.

The pair live in Glasgow with their daughter and very lively cocker spaniel. When they're not writing, they enjoy exploring Scotland's breathtaking hills, glens, and beaches, then treating themselves to coffee and cake afterwards.

To keep up to date with all their publishing news, and gain access to exclusive bonus content, join their newsletter by visiting amymcgavinbooks.com.

Newsletter

The
HIGHLAND
FLING

The True Scotsman Series

AMY McGAVIN

GRUMPY GROUSE
PRESS

ISBN 978-1-916734-03-6

Published by Grumpy Grouse Press

The
HIGHLAND
FLING

CHAPTER ONE

GRACE

The song ends and the room erupts with a cacophony of clapping hands and thumping feet. Red-faced, tartan-clad men and women cheer, laugh, and thank their dance partners. From my seat at the side of the bustling dance floor, I applaud too, swept up by the crowd's infectious energy.

When the roar subsides, the accordionist announces the next dance will be the Gay Gordons. The band, which also includes a fiddler and a drummer, are seated in a corner of the hotel's function room, by open French windows that look out onto the garden. Even though it's after ten and the sun has finally dipped below the horizon, there's still enough light to see by outside. Before today, I hadn't appreciated that summer evenings in the Highlands last an entire hour longer than in London.

"The dance floor is heaving, which is what we like to see," the accordionist says into his microphone, "but I'm sure we could squeeze a few more couples on. If you're sitting down having a breather, why not jump to your feet and join back in?"

"You heard him, sis. Grab a man and get up there!" Without

waiting for a response, my twin brother, David, follows his own advice, taking the hand of Johnny MacDonald—whose side he's barely left all night—and leading him up onto the floor.

The two of them couldn't look more different. Johnny is tall but carries himself with a hint of self-consciousness. Clean-shaven with long dark hair tucked behind his ears, he's dressed traditionally for a ceilidh, in a kilt and white shirt. My brother, meanwhile, though shorter in stature, exudes confidence. His beard is carefully groomed, and his short Afro hair is closely shaved at the sides. As anyone who's met him knows, bright colours are his trademark, and tonight is no exception: his thick-rimmed orange glasses match his orange shirt.

David and Johnny find a spot in the circle of dancers in front of Emily Thomas and Ally McIntyre, whose engagement is the reason for tonight's celebration. With a glance back at me, David impatiently beckons me up.

"I think he wants you to join in," a low masculine voice says.

I turn to see Aidan Stewart. The sight of him is as delicious to my eyes as his smooth Scottish accent is to my ears. Wavy dark-blond hair; light-blue irises flecked with gold; a tall, muscular build; and a chiselled, smooth jaw. His face is flushed, from dancing or drinking or perhaps both, and the top two buttons of his shirt are undone. He cuts a fine figure in a red kilt with crisscrossing lines of green, blue, and yellow.

He shoots me a roguish grin. "Your brother's right, of course. You should join in. As the best friend of the bride-to-be, you shouldn't be sitting on the sidelines. You should be up there, taking part."

Maintaining my composure to disguise my quickening

pulse, I reply, "In that case, as the best mate of the groom-to-be, you should dance too."

"Aye, I should." He winks at me then holds out his hand.

I take it and revel in the warmth of his skin against mine. This won't be the first dance we've shared tonight—far from it. It's hard not to feel flattered by his attention, even though Aidan's reputation precedes him. He . . . is not boyfriend material.

Aidan guides me up onto the dance floor, squeezing us in behind the newly engaged couple: Ally, a tall, chestnut-haired Highlander, and Emily, my petite, elegant best friend. Eight years ago, when I was a nervous twenty-two-year-old running my first ever yoga class, Emily was an attendee and our friendship blossomed from there. In the spring she came here to the small Highland town of Bannock for a last-minute holiday, to escape an unfortunate situation in London. She never expected to find herself a man—or a new home.

Leaning close to the besotted couple, Aidan says, "This is a cracking party, you two."

Emily and Ally turn, and I catch Ally's face tightening with disapproval. Emily has already confided in me that he feels a certain duty to protect me from his mate. Apparently, it's well known in the town that Aidan Stewart doesn't do relationships, only one-night stands. That makes him the polar opposite of me. I've always believed in forming an emotional bond before a physical one. These last eighteen months, though, I've sworn off men altogether.

Maybe it's time I finally moved on, and maybe for that I need to try something new. Tonight I'm not sure I want Ally's protection.

Trying to keep the mood light, I giggle and say, "I didn't know ceilidhs were so much fun!"

Ally and Emily exchange a look then Emily whispers something into Ally's ear, but before any of us can say anything more, the band starts up.

David, Emily, and I—the Londoners—are new to these dances, but everyone else in the crowded room seems to know them all. For this dance, Aidan positions me by his side, holding my right hand at my right shoulder and my left in front of him. When the band finishes their brief introduction to the song, all the couples in the circle walk forward.

"And now back," Aidan says, switching the position of our hands and turning me around.

We walk backwards, Aidan confidently guiding me.

"And repeat," he instructs.

Again, we walk forward, turn, then walk back.

"Now I get to twirl you around."

He raises my right hand and spins me then pulls me close to him, dropping a hand to my waist, and together we go around and around in a circle.

"You got it?" Aidan asks.

"Yeah! I like this one. It's simple."

Some of the other dances have been challenging, but this one I can do. With each repetition of the steps, I grow in confidence, and soon I'm losing myself in the dance, intoxicated by the lively music, the thumping of feet, the constant spinning. Whenever Aidan takes me by the waist, he fixes me with his baby blues, and my heart skips a beat. As we spin, I catch his scent too—a whiff of whisky on his breath, plus the smoky, masculine aroma of his aftershave mingling with the alluring hint of his sweat.

I'm warm from the dancing, carefree from the wine I've drunk. Aidan's sexy features, his enticing smell, the warmth of his hands on me, his low, gravelly voice . . .

Oh God, my senses are almost overcome, except . . . taste. I've not yet tasted him. I lower my gaze to his mouth and imagine experiencing him with my lips and tongue.

Aidan grips my waist and draws me to him again. This time I resist his blue eyes and instead look down, tantalised by the swishing and swaying of his kilt. I wonder . . . is he one of those Scotsmen who wears nothing underneath? It'd be brazen but maybe I should ask him?

Before I can decide if this is a great idea or a terrible one, the song ends. Aidan loosens his hold on me but I cling on to his fingers, refusing to let him go. I'm not done with him yet.

He raises an eyebrow. In response I lead him through the throng of people applauding the end of the dance and out into the reception area of the small, family-run Bannock Hotel. It's empty, save for us. The sounds of the party are muted here but still very much audible.

Aidan waits expectantly. Our hands remain intertwined. It's time for me to speak but what do I say?

What if I'm just being swept up by the mood of the night, this celebration of romance? But no, it's hard not to feel like I'm missing out when my best friend has found her one while my heart remains closed to love.

Aidan's stare is too intense so I glance around the reception area, trying to find the right words. My surroundings, though, only remind me of the happiness Emily has been lucky enough to find.

It was in this hotel she stayed when she came here earlier in the year, and it was at that very reception desk she met Ally, for he was then running this place along with his two younger brothers. He's since stepped back, relinquishing control of the hotel to Emily and his brothers, so he can follow his true calling: running an outdoor-activities business with Aidan.

Continuing to avoid Aidan's gaze, I focus on our joined hands. Aidan's white skin is tanned from the long summer days spent working outdoors. His colour is still much lighter than my own, but I can't help but admire how good our hands look together, linked like this.

"Are you going to say something?" Aidan prompts.

I summon the courage to meet his eye. He's grinning at me, amused by my hesitation, his expression cheeky, almost boyish.

"Well . . ." I begin.

How do I say it? I know what it is I want: I want him to take me upstairs, to the bedroom I've booked for the weekend. This could be the thing I need to move past the mental barrier I've built for myself. After clinging to the single life for so long, refusing even to create a profile on a dating app, a night with Aidan might spur me to start seeing people again. Maybe then I'll find my one, just as Emily has found Ally.

"Well?" Aidan cocks his head to the side. "As the best friends of Ally and Emily, we should probably be in there rather than out here, don't you think?" He nods to the function room.

I tighten my grip on his hand. "Come upstairs with me."

There, I've said it now.

Aidan licks his lips—those lips I'm so desperate to taste—then his gaze lazily drifts down me, taking in my silky caramel dress but paying closer attention to the parts of my body it doesn't cover: my cleavage and legs. It's not the first time tonight I've caught Aidan checking me out, but this inspection is so entirely devoid of subtlety it's practically obscene, and that sends a thrill through me.

Normally, I'm annoyed, repulsed even, when I catch men appraising my body. Tonight, though, I'm okay with it. More than that, it's what I want. I feel sure now that if anyone has the power to reawaken the part of myself I've let sleep for too long, it's Aidan Stewart.

"Ally specifically warned me to stay away from you," he says.

His words are reasonable but they don't match what his eyes are telling me: he wants me. He is, however, giving me a chance to back out. Should I take it? Am I really going to do this?

Yes, I am.

My heart pounds but I don't hesitate any longer. "I know all about your 'one-and-done policy', Aidan. We're on the same page. You live up here; I live six hundred miles away down in London. This is just . . . a bit of fun. Now hurry up! We can't be long. We've got a party to get back to."

The cheeky, boyish expression from earlier is gone, replaced instead by a raw intensity that's all man. His eyes bore into mine and I hold his gaze. Several seconds pass then, first double-checking we're alone, Aidan steps forward and swoops down, pressing his lips to my neck and inhaling deeply.

"Fuck, I've wanted to do that all night," he murmurs, planting gentle kisses on my skin. "You smell so good."

He slips a hand around my waist and leads me to the stairs. I go up them with him, my heart pounding, my body aching with desire.

CHAPTER TWO

GRACE

"And now find your way into Shavasana," I instruct.

All thirty of my students move into the final pose of the session, lying on their backs on their yoga mats, arms out by their sides, legs slightly apart, eyes closed.

I take a moment to observe the room, noting expressions of serenity on many of the faces. This is my "Rise and Shine" class, and almost everyone present will go straight from here to work. I like to think of this space as an oasis of calm in the frantic bustle of a London morning. It sets people up for the day ahead.

Talking of oases of calm, it's been nearly three weeks since Ally and Emily's engagement party in the quiet Highland town of Bannock. That place is truly a refuge from the hectic pace of twenty-first-century life, and I'm pleased, and perhaps just a little envious, that Emily has found a new home for herself there.

"Lift yourself to a comfortable seated position, then bring your hands together in front of your heart," I say. "*Namaste.*"

My students repeat the word then slowly come out of their meditative state, opening their eyes, stretching, some sighing with contentment. There are smiles and nods, to me and to each other. A few chat quietly as they gather their belongings, while others choose to savour the tranquillity a little longer.

I go over to the door and thank each person on their way out, engaging in brief small talk here and there, but when my final student approaches, the intensity of her floral perfume catches me off-guard. I try my best to hide my aversion to it, smiling politely and wishing her a good day, despite an almost overwhelming desire to gag. Thankfully, she doesn't hang about to ask a question but heads off with her mat rolled under her arm.

Wow, whatever she was wearing, it did not agree with me. Even now, the scent lingers, turning my stomach. I walk to the other side of the studio and cover my nose. Ugh!

"Morning, Grace. Oh, is everything okay?"

I glance back. Nigel, the manager of the centre, has popped his head around the door.

"Morning. And yes, everything is fine, thanks, Nigel." I beam at him, my expression of disgust gone.

"Great." He offers a slightly forced smile of his own.

Ah. Maybe everything isn't fine. I've known Nigel long enough to sense when bad news is coming.

He takes a step in. "Could I have a quick word?"

◆　◆　◆

"I'm home!" I kick the door closed behind me.

"Hey, sis!" David calls from the kitchen. "Good day?"

9

"Hmm . . . not the best, but it's your turn to cook so that's something. What are you making us?"

I doubt many thirty-year-olds share a flat with a sibling, but it works for me and David. When my last relationship ended a year and a half ago and I had to move out of my ex's place, it coincided with my brother deciding he'd had enough of his previous, rather unscrupulous, landlord. David found a two-bedroom in Finsbury Park and asked if I'd move in with him, and I haven't looked back. It's been great, actually.

"Spag bol. And . . . we have a guest!"

I'm already reaching for my slippers. No sooner do David's words reach me than my gaze falls on a pair of black women's loafers. My heart sinks. I know who they belong to.

Footsteps pad into the hallway. "Hello, Grace."

I plaster on a smile. "Hi, Mum."

I do love my mum but . . . she's hard work, and tonight I just wanted to collapse and chill.

"Aren't you going to give your mother a hug?"

I wrap my arms around her. "It's good to see you." A lie, but a white one.

She takes a step back and checks me from head to toe. "You look well," she decides.

"Thanks. You too."

Facially my mum and I are similar, but when it comes to our styles, we couldn't be more different. She keeps her hair short and pragmatic, whereas I carefully tend my shoulder-length curls every day. She prefers charcoals and blacks, even when she hasn't come straight from the office, while I never leave the house without some colour. I'm like David that way, except I rarely dress quite as vibrantly as him.

Mum and I even carry ourselves differently. She's all business, stiff and formal, whereas I'm looser, more relaxed, more . . . spiritual, I suppose.

"You said you didn't have a good day. What happened?"

It's a reasonable question and yet all I can think is that the inevitable interrogation has already begun. I hope David picked up some wine.

"Why don't we grab a seat first?" I suggest.

On the way to the living room, I glance into the kitchen and pull a face at David. He grins back at me. He'd have known fine well I wouldn't be best pleased about him springing a surprise visit from Mum on me. I wonder why he invited her over.

Once Mum and I are seated, I explain to her what Nigel told me this morning, that he's having to crank up the price of my studio rent—again.

"Well, do you know what you do when the costs of running a business increase? You put up your own prices. It's quite simple."

"Yes, but . . . when I started out, I had people from all walks of life coming along, and I really liked that. Yoga has been transformative for me personally, and I love the idea that, by teaching it, I can help others. Every time I jack up my prices, though, my classes become more and more exclusive. I don't want them to be inaccessible to folk who'd benefit from them but can't afford them."

"That's not your problem, Grace. And besides, the clients you should be focusing on are the ones with disposable incomes." She gives a smile that's more patronising than supportive. "You shouldn't be embarrassed about earning a living. There's nothing wrong with that. Just look how well David is doing with his graphic design business."

I suppress a sigh. Mum loves to compare me with my twin brother, and the comparison is always unfavourable. He's the golden child.

"These days, anyone with an internet connection and a drawing app can call themselves a freelance designer and charge a few pounds for a logo," Mum says. "David, though, has positioned himself as a professional who works with big businesses, clients who recognise his worth and pay him accordingly. That's not something to be ashamed of. Success should be celebrated!"

"Hmm. I suppose you're right."

My tone is muted. I know there's no point arguing with her: her world view is too different from my own. It's easier to just nod and agree. She's never understood that, for me, there's more to life than making money. She didn't approve of me becoming a yoga instructor in the first place.

A frown etches Mum's features. She's aware I'm saying the words but not meaning them.

"Grace, for many, the world is tough and unforgiving. As a single parent of twins, and a woman—a Black woman—I've faced more than my share of difficulties, but I've made a success of myself and raised two wonderful children. Now, when you were with Mark—"

"Oh God! Please don't bring up Mark."

Mum disregards my objection and pushes on. "When you were with Mark, you didn't have to worry about your income because he earned more than enough for both of you. You could do your yoga and have fun—plus help people, as you say—and it didn't matter how much you charged because at the end of each day you went back to your lovely home, where you never lost sleep over not being able to pay the bills and never fretted about where your next meal would come from."

Mark was a banker and had a very good salary. Mum approved.

"You had it made, Grace, and yet for some reason I will never understand, *you* ended the relationship with *him*. I would have thrown myself at a man like Mark!"

Unlikely. Mum has never had a steady boyfriend because no man has ever been good enough for her. Plus, she's fiercely independent and doesn't do compromise. But it's different for me, apparently. I should have stayed with Mark, even though that relationship was far from healthy.

And . . . this is why my heart sank when I realised Mum was here. I could have done without this tonight.

"Oi! No arguing, you two." David appears at the living room door, all smiles. "Today is a day for celebration." From behind his back, he produces a bottle of bubbly.

"Oh!" Mum beams, no doubt delighted her darling boy has some exciting news for her to praise. "What are we celebrating?"

I'm interested too. Mum and I may not agree on everything, but we both dote on David.

"Well . . . Johnny and I have been seeing each other for four months now."

David met Johnny MacDonald the first time he and I travelled up north to visit Emily, back when she was still just a guest at the Bannock Hotel. Since then, he and Johnny have been navigating the challenges of a long-distance relationship.

"I've been thinking things over," David continues, "and . . .

I've decided to move in with him. In Bannock. I'm moving up there this weekend."

The news shocks me and Mum into silence. For the longest time, neither of us says anything.

"Er . . . I was hoping for a congratulatory hug, or at least some smiles?"

"But . . . David!" I say. "You love London life. Cocktail bars, clubs, shows . . . Can you really see yourself in a small Highland town?"

He shrugs. "If it doesn't work out, it doesn't work out, but I like Johnny and I want to give it a shot. To take things to the next level, one of us will have to move, and Johnny's job is up there. As for me, being a freelancer, I can live anywhere."

"Oh, David!" Mum gets to her feet. "Of course you should give you and Johnny a proper chance—he's such a lovely young man—but I'll miss having you close by." She hugs him tight.

I hug David too. I've spent most of my life under the same roof as him, and even when we lived apart, I was never more than twenty-five minutes away from him. Siblings can be close but there's an extra-special bond between twins, and this is going to be a massive change.

"Mum's right. I'll miss you as well, but you and Johnny are great together. This . . . makes sense."

"Thanks, you two!" David relaxes then embraces us both again. "Let me pop this bottle open and grab three flutes. I'll be right back."

A moment of quiet passes between Mum and me, then she says, "Well, with David leaving, you won't be able to keep up the rent for this place by yourself. You're very welcome to move back in with me."

"No, thanks."

She raises her eyebrows. "You didn't even have to think about that, Grace."

"Sorry, it's just . . ."

I don't know what to say. How can I tell her that, growing up, I found her suffocating and hated the way she always judged me more harshly than David? How can I explain that, when I moved out, I felt the most extraordinary freedom?

Apparently, I don't have to say anything.

"Am I really so bad?" she asks.

"No! No, of course not. I just . . . like having my own space."

David returns with three filled champagne flutes on a tray. He places the tray on the coffee table then passes a glass to me and another to Mum.

"Here's to the next chapter!" He raises his flute.

I lift mine too, but when I go to taste it, the smell assaults my nose, repulsing me. "Oh no, is this corked?"

Mum frowns. "It smells fine to me." She has a sip. "Tastes fine too."

David agrees. "I like it. It wasn't a cheap bottle, by the way. It's good stuff."

"Hmm, maybe I'm coming down with something. My sense of smell has been all over the place today." I put down the glass. "I'll pass."

"Oh, Grace, that's a shame. Be sure to take plenty of vitamin C. I swear by it for fighting off colds." My mother gives me a pitying look then adds, "Anyway, so long as you're not pregnant. Ha!"

I smile weakly but a memory pops into my head. Him grunting, me gasping, our bodies connected.

I dismiss the scene as soon as it comes to me—I'm not

going to think about that in front of my family. But I remember we used a condom. Yes, we'd both been drinking, and yes, our emotions and desires were high, but we didn't forget about protection.

So . . . I can't be pregnant. I just can't. This must be something else.

CHAPTER THREE

AIDAN

"Careful, Gemma! You don't look very steady, there. Why don't you try—"

Before I can finish, the bridesmaid-to-be tumbles from her paddleboard and belly-flops into the chilly waters of Loch Bannock. The rest of the hen party burst into hysterics, the normal peace of the setting—a secluded body of water a mile south of the town—broken by the screeches of eleven rather rowdy women from Newcastle. When Gemma emerges from below the surface, she laughs too.

Thankfully, we're all in wetsuits, but they don't protect your face from the shock of the cold when you tumble in. At least Gemma's good-natured about it.

As I talk her through pulling herself back onto her board, Ally suggests to the rest of the group that, since there's a bit of a breeze now, they may want to go down onto their knees.

"Hear that, ladies? Ally wants us on our knees!" Deborah quips. She's also a bridesmaid-to-be—the maid of honour, in fact.

I smirk at her comment but Ally isn't impressed. We've

been best mates since we were babies, and our maws were best friends before us. For the longest time, Ally was stuck in a rut, dissatisfied with his life and bitter about having to run his family's hotel after the death of his parents. When Emily Thomas booked in as a guest earlier this year, everything changed. He's now set up Bannock Adventures with me, and he's a new man. The grump is gone. He's happy, more relaxed.

Or rather . . . he *was*. It turns out a group of loud, flirty hens from northern England is enough to get him worked up again.

Catching his eye, I wink at him, trying to remind him they're just having fun. Ally glowers back at me.

Bad move. He should know I enjoy a bit of teasing, and when I see someone getting uncomfortable, I can't resist testing their boundaries. Time to ramp up the double entendre.

With a few careful strokes, I manoeuvre closer to Deborah then point at her paddle. "Try gripping the shaft a little tighter."

"I'd rather grip your shaft, Aidan!" she shoots back, which of course results in more squawking laughter.

I feign surprise, pretending I didn't set that up for her, then chuckle as though I've only just got the joke. Ally scowls at me.

"Here, do you all remember what that woman with the blue hair said about Aidan?" one of the hens calls.

"Oh, yeah!" Deborah's face lights up with mischief. "Last night we went drinking in this pub called the Pheasant. When we mentioned to the woman serving us we'd booked to go paddleboarding, she told us that you, Aidan, have a reputation around town. You're a player!"

"What can I say? The stories are all true."

The hens giggle at this, a few of them eyeing me up in my

wetsuit, which I'm aware clings tightly to me and doesn't leave much to the imagination.

Ally coughs. "Aye, well, something you may not have heard about Aidan is he still lives with his maw. Almost thirty and living at home with his mummy. What do you ladies think about that?"

"Whoa, whoa, whoa!" I protest. "To clarify, it's temporary. I was away travelling the world for a few years, teaching outdoor activities all over. Now I'm back, I'm staying with her just till I get on my feet. Ally and I recently started this business, and it's doing well, so I should be in a position to get my own place soon."

I reckon that was a pretty good recovery. The last thing I want is to be a figure of pity.

"Do you know what, Aidan?" Deborah says. "We were desperate to book a stripper, but we didn't think we'd be able to in a quaint little town. However, given your reputation, maybe we can buy a dance from you as an add-on to the paddleboarding? Like a package deal?"

"I'd happily pay to see that!" Gemma exclaims.

Others voice their agreement.

I lift my paddle out of the water then stroke my chin as though giving the proposition serious thought. "Well, we were thinking of expanding into other areas . . ."

"Aye, like buying a couple of canoes," Ally grumbles. "Not stripping."

"You could strip too!" Gemma squeals. "You're more my type—darker hair, stubble, ruggedly handsome. And anyway, you're business partners: it makes sense to do it together."

The consensus among the hens is this is a brilliant idea. Ally looks more uncomfortable than ever.

Deciding he's had enough, I say, "I'm afraid Ally's a taken man. He put a ring on his fiancée's finger not so long ago."

"Boo!" Deborah objects. "Marriage and kids—that's a prison sentence. Am I right, Aidan?"

Jade, the bride-to-be, gasps. "Excuse me? Are you forgetting why we're all here? We're celebrating that I'm about to get hitched!"

At this, they all laugh, including Jade.

◆　◆　◆

I navigate the minibus along the narrow drive that winds through the sprawling grounds of the Glen Garve Resort. A huge, grand hotel situated just outside Bannock, its luxury facilities include fine dining, a full golf course, a swimming pool, and a spa.

Ally once considered it a rival of his family's much smaller hotel in the centre of town, but we're now working together. We agreed on a deal that lets the clients of Bannock Adventures use the resort's shower and changing rooms. What's more, the resort advertises our activities to their guests.

The hen party—who are still in their wetsuits and chattering away in the back—are staying here. They were able to book themselves a two-night stay, spa treatments, and the paddleboarding session all on a single phone call. It's a setup that makes things super easy for customers, and it's also a great way for Ally and me to bring in business.

I pull up outside the entrance to the leisure club, then Ally jumps out and slides open the side door.

"You'll see a laundry bin for your wetsuits inside," I tell the ladies. "If you could pop them in there once you're changed, we'd appreciate it. Thanks again for booking with us, and enjoy the rest of your stay."

The hens clamber out of the minibus, thanking me and Ally. Deborah's the last to leave, and she passes me a small, folded piece of paper.

"That was really fun, Aidan. If you're interested in some more fun . . ." She winks then steps out.

I open the paper and see she's written her number and a message: *I don't want to share you! No payment, but strip for me and I'll grip your shaft. x*

I chuckle then quickly hide the note when Ally hops back in.

The parking space for the minibus is a wee way off, so—acting nonchalant—I drive us there, then Ally and I return to the leisure club on foot. We head inside and into the men's changing rooms.

"Well, that was a nightmare," Ally gripes. "I don't know if we should accept bookings from hen parties going forward."

"Are you kidding me?" I sit on a bench and remove my boots. "It was a laugh! Besides, we're not in a position to turn down clients, and there were twelve of them—we made a good bit of money from a single booking."

"Of course *you* enjoyed it. Hanging out with a group of loud women who want to book you as their stripper is probably a dream of yours. Which reminds me . . . you're not meeting up with her."

"What do you mean?"

"Deborah—I saw her give you her number. Thought you might slip into her room tonight, did you?"

Opening my locker, I flash him a sly grin.

"It's not happening, Aidan. She's a client. You can't sleep with her. It's unprofessional."

"Er, excuse me, Ally, but you got to know Emily when she was a guest at your hotel. That's no different."

"It's completely different! As you said, I *got to know her* when she was a guest. *Then* I slept with her. And now I'm marrying her. There's nothing wrong with that. But you? You do things differently. You see a woman you like, you sleep with her, then you never so much as look at her again. That could get us some very nasty reviews online, so it's not happening. You're not sleeping with her or any other client, for that matter."

I sigh then unzip my wetsuit and start working my way out of it. Ally's already got his top half out. He angles himself away from me then tugs the suit down and over his feet. Like me, he goes commando underneath.

Ugh, it doesn't matter how many times I put one of these on, they're always a nightmare to get off. Eventually, though, I manage.

"Teaming up with the Glen Garve Resort may be the best thing we ever did," I say, deciding to drop the Deborah chat. "After freezing your balls off in a loch, nothing beats a hot shower, does it?"

Ally wraps his towel around him then peers into my locker. "I'm looking forward to my shower, aye. But as for you . . ."

"Hey, what are you doing in there?"

A perk of working with the resort is I get a permanent locker, rather than one you put a coin in and borrow for a few hours. I always like to be prepared so I store a few different things in it.

"Ah, perfect!" Ally pulls out a T-shirt and some shorts. "You'll need these for your jog." He throws them my way.

I catch them and, since my towel is still in my locker, hold them in front of my crotch. I'm not exactly modest—a changing room is for getting changed, after all—but I am confused, and I'd rather not have my dick out while trying to understand what's going on here.

"What are you talking about?" I ask Ally.

"I'm talking about the very long jog you're going to go on to get all that sexual energy out of your system."

I groan. "Hold up, mate! How about I just give you my word I won't sleep with any of the hens. All right?"

"Like you gave me your word you wouldn't sleep with Grace?" Ally smirks as if he's put me into checkmate, which he kind of has. "Do you remember I was worried it'd make things awkward and stop Grace from wanting to come and visit? Well, guess who hasn't been back since the engagement party?"

"Jesus! That was only three weeks ago. She's hardly going to travel up every weekend. And besides, it was her idea, I swear!" I recall how Grace looked that night—silky dress, corkscrew curls, luscious lips—and can't help but grin. "Anyway, it's not my fault Emily's got such a beautiful friend. How could I say no?"

"You couldn't, apparently, which is why I'm sending you on a jog to ensure it doesn't happen again. Track yourself on the app, and don't bother coming back until you've done at least ten miles. I'll be monitoring you."

"Mate!" I protest. "Are you being serious?"

I shift my weight from foot to foot. I was sure I'd be getting laid tonight. I've not been with anyone since Grace, due to focusing all my attention on the business, and I've been getting restless. This is a spanner in the works.

"Aye, I'm being serious. Now get your stuff on and go!"

CHAPTER FOUR

GRACE

The small town of Bannock is nestled in the beautiful green valley of Glen Garve. Stone buildings line both sides of its main street, which is narrow, having been established long before motor cars. The odd private home sits between businesses such as the gift shop, the Otter's Holt; the café, the Coffee Bothy; and the pub, the Pheasant. The Bannock Hotel, where Emily now lives and works, is also on the main road.

David drives us past these places then turns right down a side street that runs parallel to the River Garve. The cutest cottages flank this lane, their stone exteriors brightened by doors and window frames painted in vibrant colours, as well as by the blossoming flowers in their modest but well-maintained gardens.

My brother pulls up outside the fifth home along on the left. The cottages on this side back onto the water and must have the most gorgeous views from their windows.

"Well, this is Johnny's place."

I can't believe it. "It's like something out of a storybook."

"It really is special," Mum agrees. "What a delightful little town this is! I can't wait to explore it more."

The champagne the other day wasn't just for celebrating David's news. I think it was also intended to loosen me and Mum up so we'd agreed to help him with the move. Of course, I didn't touch the drink, but I was hardly going to miss today. It's a major milestone in my twin's life.

Admittedly, there were times during the ten-hour car journey here I regretted my decision. Stuck in a small box on wheels, I couldn't escape Mum's probing questions or her unwanted advice. But despite the journey dragging on forever, we're here now and it's still light, thanks to the long Scottish summer days.

I get out and do a few stretches, my body stiff. Mum inhales the crisp, refreshing air and lets out a contented sigh. This is my first time seeing Johnny's cottage but it's her first visit to Bannock.

From the back seat, she and I grab the gifts we brought to mark the occasion, but we leave everything else in the car for now. David clicks open a small wooden gate then leads the way to a green door and bangs the brass knocker. He grins back at us excitedly.

The door opens and Johnny's handsome face lights up when he sees David. But, taking in me and Mum, his smile falters. "Grace! And . . . Viola!"

"Hi, Johnny." Suddenly uneasy, I glance at my brother. "Er . . . David, you did tell Johnny that Mum and I were coming, didn't you?"

Johnny doesn't rush to assure me he was expecting us, which tells me he wasn't. Great. Not exactly what you want after travelling all day.

"Surprise!" David says brightly, throwing his arms wide.

A moment passes. Then another. Johnny's brow furrows with confusion. A knot tightens in my stomach.

I'm all too familiar with my brother's flair for the dramatic, but surely even he wouldn't . . .

"Oh God. David, tell me Johnny knows you're moving in with him?"

From the way Johnny's eyes widen at my words, I'm going to take that as a no.

I grab David's shoulder. "What are you thinking? You can't move in with someone without speaking to them about it first!"

"Now, now! Let's all stay calm." Mum's tone is mild but she wears a tense expression. "David, this does seem a little . . . irresponsible. Johnny, I'm incredibly sorry about this."

David holds up his hands in a placatory manner. "Hey, let me clarify! Johnny and I have been talking a lot, and Johnny, you've said on several occasions you wished we lived in the same place. Right?"

"Er . . ." Johnny blinks his blue eyes. "Aye." He looks dazed.

"You told me your cottage feels lonely when it's just you in it. You said I light it up whenever I visit and you hate it when I have to leave. Your exact words were, 'I wish we could live together.' Remember?"

"Aye." Johnny bites his lip and nods. "I remember."

David's enthusiasm finally wavers. "Oh, crap. Have I messed this up? I thought you'd be happy. Everything has been going so well, and I was so sure you'd be pleased I decided, what the hell, I'll surprise him. But I've obviously misjudged the situation. I'm so, so sorry."

David takes a step back, forcing me to do the same.

His throat bobs. "This is really awkward, especially with my mum and sister here. If you'd rather just end things and never see me again, then—"

"What? No! This . . . is amazing." The corners of Johnny's lips twitch into a smile. "It's a bit of a shock, but . . . a good shock. A brilliant shock." He reaches for his boyfriend's hand.

David inhales a shaky breath then throws himself into Johnny's arms. "You had me so worried!"

My knot of anxiety unravels as Johnny—who's literally the sweetest guy—hugs and kisses my brother, who's also lovely and wonderful but has, at times, been known to be "a bit much". I'm so glad this didn't end up being a disaster.

"Where are my manners?" Johnny says. "I've left you all on the doorstep. Come in, come in!"

He beckons us inside then embraces me and Mum. "It's great to see you both."

"And you, Johnny." The relief in Mum's demeanour mirrors my own. "What a beautiful home you have!"

The living room and kitchen are open plan, with wooden beams, tartan soft furnishings, and a wood-burning stove that must be so cosy in the winter. The whole place has a rustic charm.

"It really is stunning." I go over to the window and peer out at the river flowing by, rippling and glimmering, a family of ducks bobbing in the water. "Inside and out."

"Thank you. I've seen some great wildlife out there."

David surveys the interior. "It is a nice home, but now that I'm going to be living here rather than just visiting, we may need to switch things up a bit. For example, don't you think some purple would really make this part of the room pop?"

"David!" I reprimand, laughing despite myself. Sometimes I honestly can't believe him. "Johnny's only just getting used to the idea of you moving in. I wouldn't talk about redecorating quite yet."

"I can't help it." David shrugs. "I've got a good eye for these things."

Johnny chuckles and gazes at my twin with what I can only describe as adoration. As much as I'm going to miss David, I'm so glad these two have found each other.

"Oh, before I forget, I got you this." I hand Johnny the wrapped box I'm carrying. "It was to thank you for agreeing to take my brother in. Trust me, if I'd known you hadn't actually agreed, I'd have got you something bigger."

Johnny smiles and opens the present. It's a jigsaw puzzle of Tower Bridge, the Shard standing tall in the cityscape behind it. "Aw, this is lovely! Thanks, Grace."

"I thought it'd be nice for you to have a bit of London up here, plus it'll pass some time on a rainy day."

"I got you boys a little thing as well," Mum says, "but please, open it later."

It's no doubt something pricey. With her everyday expenses, Mum watches the pennies, but for a special-occasion gift? She likes to splash out. As judgemental as she can be—towards me, especially—she can also be incredibly generous.

"Thanks, Viola." Johnny places the items on the kitchen work surface then, from a cupboard, takes out a bottle of Glen Garve whisky and four glasses. "We'd better celebrate David's move with a wee dram, eh?"

"That would be lovely," Mum agrees.

Johnny starts to pour then suddenly stops. "Hang on a minute—sleeping arrangements! I'm so sorry but, Grace and Viola, as I didn't know you were coming, I've not got anything organised."

"Relax!" David walks over and pats his partner's back. "Mum can take the spare room—I'll set it up. As for Grace, she wants to catch up with Emily. If there's an empty room at the hotel, I'm sure she'll be welcome to it. Otherwise, she'll be fine on the sofa for a night."

"Oh." Johnny looks at me for confirmation. "Is that all right?"

I smile and nod. "Yes."

Emily doesn't yet know I'm in Bannock this weekend. Given my trip was arranged last minute—David having only sprung his news on me two days ago—David suggested I keep my visit a secret and surprise her on arriving here. I'd agreed, not realising he was also going to keep it a secret from Johnny.

"Okay, great." Johnny finishes pouring the whiskies and hands them out. "Well, here's to David's move to Bannock being a success!"

We respond to his toast by raising our drinks, but when I go to taste mine, it's like the champagne all over again. The whisky's sharp, smoky smell hits me, stinging my nostrils and turning my stomach.

Trying hard to maintain my composure, I put down my glass. "Sorry, but after a day spent in the car, I'm feeling a little light-headed. Is it okay if I step outside?"

"Of course." Concern etching his features, Johnny shows me to the back door.

To the rear of the cottage is a small garden with a rowan tree whose branches stretch over the river. Beneath the kitchen window, a wooden bench provides the perfect spot from which to enjoy the view.

"Is there anything I can get you, Grace? Some water or . . . ?"

I shake my head and take a seat on the bench. "I just need a minute. Thanks, Johnny. You go back inside. I'll be right in."

Johnny does as I ask, but David comes out in his stead and sits beside me.

"How are you doing?"

"Fine. A bit of fresh air will sort me out."

He gives me a sideways glance. "Grace?"

"Yeah?"

"Do you remember that thing Mum said the other day? You couldn't be . . ."

"I'm not pregnant, David," I assure him. "I feel funny after the journey up, that's all. After Inverness, there were so many twisty roads. I could do with a walk but I don't want to leave you when we've only just got here. We need to celebrate your big move."

"Don't be ridiculous—you've spent all day with me! Why don't you surprise Emily then go for a stroll together? Oh, and ask if she has space in the hotel. You'll be more comfortable there than on the sofa. C'mon, let's go get your bag."

He leads me around the cottage then grabs my bag from the boot. It's small and light, containing just enough for a night away.

"I'll say your goodbyes for you. Take it easy, okay? If the hotel's full, I'll see you later on. Otherwise, let's catch up in the morning. Love you, sis."

We hug.

"Oh, and Grace? Go straight to the hotel, yeah? I don't want you wandering around by yourself if you're not one hundred per cent."

I laugh. "You're sweet but I promise you I'm fine. Enjoy your night."

CHAPTER FIVE

GRACE

The name Main Street implies a level of activity unknown to this sleepy town. Reaching it, I glance to my left towards the Bannock Hotel then hesitate and check behind me. David has gone back into Johnny's cottage: I'm not being watched.

I turn right and go over an old stone bridge that crosses the river. I *am* looking forward to catching up with Emily, but first I need to make sense of at least some of what's going through my head.

The town continues on this side of the water. I pass a peaceful, pretty church and walk on until I come to a public footpath that leads into a wood. Yes, David warned me not to wander by myself, but I'm okay physically—I just need some mental space to think things over.

I follow the path, leaves rustling in the gentle breeze, evening sunlight filtering through from overhead. I let my outstretched fingers graze against the rough texture of trees I pass. Whiffs of wild flowers tickle my nose, their aromas surprisingly strong but not affecting me the way the whisky did.

This heightened sense of smell . . . I told David with absolute conviction I'm not pregnant, but the truth is, I don't know. Yes, Aidan used a condom, but what if something happened? What if it ripped?

I didn't realise until Mum's comment the other day, but my period is a little late. By itself, that doesn't mean anything: it wouldn't be the first time I've been irregular. But combined with my nose's strange sensitivity, well . . . pregnancy is a possibility. I've been trying to deny it to myself but I can't ignore the signs forever.

I could have got a definitive answer yesterday. It was on Thursday that David announced his news to me and Mum, and today is Saturday. I had all day Friday to get a pregnancy test and find out for sure but . . . I didn't.

Out of the corner of my eye, I notice movement. A red squirrel scurries up a tree then disappears from view. I stop in my tracks, a smile tugging at my lips. Grey squirrels are a familiar sight around London's parks but I've never seen a red one before. That was special.

The encounter provides me a momentary reprieve, but my mind soon returns to the matter in hand. I walk on.

Why didn't I test yesterday? It's so stupid but . . . I think it's a bit like that thought experiment, Schrödinger's cat. Until you check the box, the cat can be both alive and dead, but once you look, it's either one or the other.

If I take a test and the result is positive . . .

It won't be. I'm sure I'm not pregnant. And yet . . . am I actually sure? My head is telling me I can't possibly be, but my gut is saying something else.

A less-trodden path breaks off from the main one, meandering past Scots pines, silver birches, and oaks, leading deeper into the woods, further from the town. I take it. I'm in no rush to get back. By escaping civilisation for a while, maybe I can also escape the possibility that something could be growing inside me. When I return, I'll force myself to finally face this, but I'm not ready quite yet.

Time passes, and I wander on. At some point I'll have to turn around—the further from Bannock I go, the further I'll have to walk back—but I want to avoid reality for a little longer.

The ground slopes up, the incline getting progressively steeper. I plough on, feeling the strain in my leg muscles.

Why the hell did I have sex with Aidan? I'd been doing just fine since ending things with Mark. I'd been putting all of my energy into taking care of myself, not worrying at all about men, and it'd been good for me. When I was with Mark, I was so focused on keeping him happy, I somehow missed that it was one way, that my well-being wasn't as high on his list of priorities as his was on mine.

These last eighteen months have been exactly what I needed, so why did I decide it was time for a change? Am I so weak that I risked the satisfying life I'd established for myself for one fast and frantic tumble with a man who sleeps with a different woman every weekend?

But even as I try to tell myself how content I was, an image of Ally and Emily dancing at their engagement party comes to me. The way they gazed at each other . . . their love was clear for all to see. I think too of how Johnny, after his initial shock at my brother's surprise announcement, took David in his arms and kissed him.

My best friend has found her forever partner, and it seems my twin might have too. More than that, they've both found a new home, and just look at this place! The surrounding scenery is stunning, the town itself so full of charm. Last year, if someone had said that one of us—either Emily, David, or me—would end up living here, we'd have all guessed it would be me. I've no doubt about that. My personality is the most suited to rural life, isn't it?

Yet it's Emily and David who have moved here and found love, while I have to go back to London tomorrow.

And not only that, but . . . oh God, could I be carrying Aidan Stewart's baby?

Out of nowhere, a wave of dizziness hits me. Trees spin around me; the woodland floor rises and falls beneath me. I lean against an oak and take deep breaths in and out. Closing my eyes, I listen to the wind whistling through the leaves and the trickling of a nearby stream. The ridges and grooves of the bark help stabilise me, grounding me to the earth.

The sensation subsides. What the hell was that? Okay, I think it's time to head back.

I open my eyes and survey the steep slope I've climbed. At least the start of the return journey is downhill.

I begin my descent but the going is harder than I expected, the terrain uneven in places, outright treacherous in others. Coming up, I didn't once worry about slipping, maybe because I'd have just fallen on my face. Going down, though, it's all I can think about. It's a long way to the bottom, and unhelpfully my legs feel wobbly, which is typical when now, more than ever, I need a steady base.

I more or less get the hang of things and am nearing the halfway mark when the dizziness hits again. Crap! I grasp at a branch for support and make the mistake of giving it my full weight. There's a loud snap, and the next thing I know, I'm tumbling forward, my heart jolting, my right ankle twisting painfully. I crash and roll down the slope, twigs snapping, the forest blurring around me.

Finally I come to a stop, breathless, dirty, cut, and grazed. I groan. Falling down a hill? I'm such an idiot.

With some difficulty I twist myself onto my back, and for a while I just lie where I am, catching my breath. Eventually I lift my head and try to survey the damage. My quicker-than-intended descent has left me looking quite a state, but the roll hasn't caused me any significant injury—only the odd scrape here and there. The initial trip is another matter: my ankle is throbbing. I must have gone over it badly.

I pull myself up to a seated position and cradle my injured leg. After inhaling and exhaling three times, I try to get to my feet but pain shoots through my ankle. Gritting my teeth, I slump back to the ground. There's no way I can put any weight on it.

Great. I'm stranded in the middle of a forest with a twisted ankle. I'll have to call someone for help. How do I even explain to them where I am?

I open my bag and look through it: toothbrush, pants, socks, top—all the essentials for a night away. But . . . no phone.

Shit. I was playing with it on the drive up. I can visualise exactly where it is: in the pocket of the passenger door. When David got me my bag, I didn't think to grab it.

Unease creeps over me.

Remember your breathing exercises, Grace. Find your centre.

I don't panic but instead give myself ample time to calm my thumping heart. Then, once I've relaxed, I try to get up again.

Nope! It's agony. I settle back onto the forest floor.

Right, what are my options?

One: scream for help. I give that a go. There's a commotion

in the treetops as several birds take flight, but otherwise there is no response to my cry.

Okay, what else can I try?

There are sticks about. Lots of them. If I can find one big enough, maybe I can use it for support and hop and hobble my way back to Bannock.

Rather inelegantly I crawl through the woods, searching for something more significant than a twig, but even moving on my hands and knees is painful. This is a disaster! If only I'd gone straight to see Emily like David told me to. Then I wouldn't be in this predicament.

I try calling out again, just in case, but my second attempt is no more successful than my first.

Angry, panicked tears sting my eyes but I hold them back. Self-pity won't get me out of this.

As I continue my hunt for the perfect walking stick, low sounds reach me from somewhere nearby. Something is moving fast through the woods with a steady, purposeful gait.

No, not something, someone—those are human footsteps. A jogger?

"Help!" I yell. "Over here! I've fallen."

The footsteps start coming my way. I keep calling out, guiding the person to my location, and soon a tall, broad-shouldered man in shorts and a T-shirt appears. Relief washes over me—until I look up at his face.

Oh no.

I shake my head. "Uh-uh. Forget it. Anyone but you. Jog on! I'll be fine."

"Grace Adefope!" Letting out a disbelieving chuckle, Aidan Stewart lifts the bottom of his T-shirt to wipe his brow, revealing his toned abs in the process.

To my great annoyance I can't help but glance at them, and absurdly, despite everything—despite my situation and Aidan being the last person I wanted to see—a thrill shoots through me. With his muscular figure, blond hair, blue eyes, and easy grin, he's infuriatingly attractive.

"What are you doing here?" Aidan comes closer. "I didn't know you were in Bannock. Ally actually had a go at me earlier, saying I'm the reason you've not been back since the engagement party, and yet here you are!"

"It's a long story." It's not that long but I've no wish to talk to this guy. "I fell but I'll be okay. Thanks for your concern. Don't let me interrupt your jog."

He scoffs. "You'll be okay? So why were you calling 'Help!', and why are you sitting on the ground? What's the matter? Where does it hurt?"

I sigh. "I went over my ankle but I'm sure it'll be fine. It probably just needs a bit of time and then I should be able to walk again."

Smirking, he kneels beside me. "C'mon, let me help."

"Oh, and you're a doctor, are you?"

"Well, I'm an outdoor instructor, and for that I've done first-aid training, so . . . I'm far from the worst person to have found you. Actually, I'd say you were pretty lucky it was me who came along."

"Lucky!" I splutter. "Of everyone who lives in Bannock, you're the last person I'd have picked."

"Oh? Is this because we had sex?"

Jeez, this guy has no tact. How come in romance films, the male leads always know just what to say, but in real life men are so . . . disappointing?

"That may have something to do with it," I reply primly.

"The way I remember it, you weren't complaining at the time, so I don't know why you're suddenly being so mean to me."

I've half a mind to slap him for that. I wasn't "complaining at the time"? The cheek!

He flashes me a quick grin. "Anyway, your ankle, can you describe the pain? And would you like to peel up your leggings so we can take a look? Or I could—"

"I'll manage!" I carefully lift them, revealing my swollen ankle, which is already bruising.

Briefly I explain to Aidan what happened and how it feels. When he asks if it's tender to the touch, I rush to put my hand there before he can. "Yes!" I wince.

Aidan checks things over for a little longer then gives his judgement. "You'll need to get this seen to. It may just be a sprain but it's best to be sure. Right, let's get you to Bannock then I can drive you to hospital."

"And how am I going to get to Bannock? I can't walk."

He gives me a funny look. "Well, I'm going to carry you, obviously."

I shake my head. "No, absolutely not. How about, instead, you jog to Johnny MacDonald's cottage? My mum and brother are there: they can come and help. Or maybe you could go get Emily and A—"

"I'm not leaving you here by yourself," he interrupts. "If you'll just let me . . ." He reaches out to pick me up.

"I'm not sure about this!" I blurt, halting him. "Besides, I . . . am not the lightest." My cheeks burn with shame.

Practising yoga daily keeps me pretty toned, but despite my best efforts, my body remains naturally soft in certain places. As for my thighs and bottom, they're never going to be small and dainty like those of my petite best friend, Emily.

Unperturbed, Aidan places one arm around my back and slides his other under my legs. "You carry your bag and I'll carry you, okay?"

With horror, I wait for him to attempt to lift me then give up with words such as "Well, that isn't going to work" or "I'll have to try a firefighter's carry." Instead, he raises me in his arms with an ease I'd never have expected.

"You can hold on to my neck, if you like," he offers.

I've no idea how to respond to that suggestion. I want to touch Aidan as little as possible, but would it make things easier for him if I did? Aidan doesn't wait for me to decide but starts walking, so I keep my hands to myself.

Even so, I'm pressed up against his damp T-shirt, and his sweat engulfs my sensitive nose. It's not an unpleasant smell; it doesn't set me off. No, Aidan Stewart is a player who's perfected the art of wooing women, and somehow even his sweat smells good. And—

A memory flashes into my head. He was sweaty that night in the hotel—from the dancing, and from the intensity of what passed between us. I'd kept on my dress, him, his kilt. After eighteen months without sex, the encounter had overwhelmed me and set all my senses ablaze. Although well used to hook-ups, Aidan had been caught up in the passion of the act too. We were only away for a few minutes, and yet we'd both come, and hard. In fact, it was the sensation of him losing himself inside me that had tipped me over the edge.

Now that I'm back in his arms, a warmth spreads from my core at the recollection. I can almost taste the sweaty saltiness of his lips on my mouth again. And damn, the way he's holding me snug against his firm pecs is enough to make me want to—

Grace, get a grip!

I shake these thoughts away. They're not helpful. The only emotions I should be feeling right now are mortification that I'm being carried by Aidan Stewart and . . . concern that I may be pregnant with his baby.

No, hang on, I don't want to think about that either.

"Are you sure you should be doing this?" I say, trying to focus on something, anything, else. "Didn't you break your wrist a few months back?"

The very first time I met Aidan—on my first visit to Bannock, before the engagement party—his arm was in a cast.

"All healed now," he assures me brightly. He doesn't even sound out of breath. How can he so effortlessly march through a forest with me in his arms?

As if to prove how easy he finds it, he strikes up a conversation, telling me how his and Ally's business is doing and then asking me to share the "long story" that brought me to Bannock today.

I don't understand how he can chat away with me in such a relaxed manner, and I'm not just meaning because of the physical strain he's under. Doesn't he find it awkward that we were intimate and now we've been thrown together like this? Apparently not. Maybe it's different for him, being so used to one-night stands.

Whatever the reason, he's his usual charming self, and this gets to me.

"You can stop trying so hard!" I snap, my tone uncharacteristically harsh. "You've already slept with me, and as everyone

40

knows, you've got a 'one-and-done policy', so this isn't going to lead to anything."

I want to put him in his place but he chuckles.

"I can't help it. You can't turn this charisma off!"

I groan. "You know what? Put me down. Just . . . leave me here."

"Oh, and you'll wait for the next jogger to come along and rescue you?"

"Exactly."

"Right . . . except this isn't some London park with a daily footfall of thousands and thousands of people. This is the Highlands. No one else may come this way again today. You're lucky I did."

"Even so, I'm asking you to put me down, so if you could just—"

"You're funny, Grace," Aidan says with a cheerful grin. "I like that. But I'm not leaving you alone in a forest with an injured ankle."

Indignant, I swat at his chest. "I told you to put me down!"

"Och, wheesht, lass! I'd appreciate it if you didn't wriggle quite so much. I'm taking you to Bannock and that's that."

◆ ◆ ◆

We reach the town without Aidan needing to stop for a single break. His arms must be killing him but he doesn't complain. He marches along the pavement in a determined fashion.

The day is wearing on but it's still light, and although Bannock is quiet, there are some people about. Unsurprisingly, a woman being carried like a bride attracts attention.

An old man hails Aidan from the other side of the road and

asks if everything is okay. Aidan assures him things are under control. Soon after, a passing car slows and the driver, a kindly woman, winds down her window and checks if there's anything she can do to help. Like the man, she addresses Aidan by name, which boggles my mind. I suppose that's the nature of small-town life: everyone knows everyone. Aidan thanks her for her concern but tells her we're good. What he doesn't realise is, far from being good, I'm dying—of embarrassment.

"My car is just a little further," he says to me, approaching the bridge. "I'm parked outside my maw's and she's opposite the Bannock Hotel. As a kid, it was great: I could leave my front door, nip across the road, and be in Ally's place in just a few seconds. I practically grew up in the hotel."

This entire time, he's chatted away to me like it's perfectly ordinary I'm in his arms. I just don't get him.

"Aidan, thanks for getting me to Bannock, but we're not going to your car and you are not driving me to the hospital. I'm sure it's nothing. I probably just need to rest."

"Maybe, but we'll get it checked out, to be safe. As the one who found you and carried you here, I feel a certain responsibility to ensure you're taken care of."

"You can't . . . kidnap me!" I spot Johnny's cottage on the other side of the river and point to it. "Take me there! If I need to go to hospital, my brother can drive me."

No sooner do I suggest this than I remember the celebratory whiskies Johnny poured. David won't be able to get behind the wheel, and even if he could, Mum would insist on coming along and I can't think of anything worse. If the doctor wants to do an X-ray, they'll ask me if I could be pregnant. What would I say? I could make Mum stay in the waiting room, but she always knows when something is up, and she's an expert at sniffing out information. She'd find out somehow.

"On second thoughts, let's go to the hotel. I want to see Emily, and Ally can drive me to the hospital if I need to go."

Emily never learnt to drive but I'm sure she'd keep me company in the car. Yes, that'd be infinitely better than going with Aidan.

"Grace, it's honestly no bother. I'm quite happy to—"

"Nope! Thanks, Aidan, but take me to the hotel, please."

He glances down at me and a smile plays on his lips. "You've got a funny way about you, you know that? It's cute."

I've got a funny way about me? What does that mean?

"Please don't tell me I'm cute. And are you going to take me to the hotel or not?"

"Aye, I am. And I didn't say you were cute—I meant your manner is cute."

Thankfully, before too much longer, we reach our destination, a charming old building with eight guest bedrooms over three floors, plus a few extra rooms for the McIntyre family. It also has a small restaurant, a tiny bar area called the snug, and a function room. It was in the function room that the engagement party took place, and it was in one of the bedrooms that Aidan and I—

Yeah, I'm not going to think about that right now.

Aidan carries me into reception, which is empty. There's no one behind the desk.

"Hello?" he calls. "Anyone about?"

After a brief pause, Lewis McIntyre appears from the restaurant. The elder of Ally's two younger brothers, he's the new manager. He has the same chestnut hair and tall, strong figure as the eldest McIntyre, but while Ally has a certain ruggedness to his features, Lewis has almost model good looks. He's dressed smartly in a shirt and trousers.

He takes in the sight of me in Aidan's arms and raises his eyebrows. "Er . . . Grace? I didn't realise you were visiting."

"Where's Emily?" I demand.

Lewis's expression suggests there are a number of questions he'd like to ask, but he replies, "Upstairs, in her and Ally's room."

"Let's go!" I command Aidan.

He heads for the stairs.

"Whoa!" Lewis holds up his hands to stop us. "Er . . . the thing is . . . since the restaurant was starting to quieten down, I told Emily I could handle service and she could sign off for the night. The next thing I know, she and Ally are heading upstairs, hand in hand, giggling away to each other. I think they may be . . . you know . . . having some private time." His cheeks redden.

It's at this moment the third McIntyre brother, Jamie, makes an appearance, strolling in from the snug. Leaner than his two brothers, and also a little taller, he sports a perpetual mischievous grin. "What's all this commotion, then? Oh, hi, Grace. Back in Aidan's arms already? What's going on, Aidan? You don't normally go back for seconds!"

I shoot daggers at him. He's always like this. He's not even funny—just mean!

"Knock it off, Jamie," Aidan says.

Jamie grins.

"Look," I say, "I'd wanted to speak to Ally and Emily. Aidan thinks I need to go to hospital, and I thought they'd be able to take me."

"*I* can take you," Aidan mutters.

I ignore him and push on. "But Ally and Emily are . . . unavailable, so one of you boys will have to drive me instead. Preferably you, Lewis."

"Er . . ." Lewis scratches the back of his head. "I'd love to help but we've still got a few customers in the restaurant. I can't really abandon them, I'm afraid."

Smirking, Jamie adds, "And although I was only your second choice, I'm out as well. There are some folk drinking in the snug—I need to keep an eye on them. But . . ." His grin widens. "I hear Aidan's free to take you."

I let out a long, exasperated sigh. It seems the cards are stacked against me today. "I can't believe I'm saying this but . . . okay, Aidan, you can drive me."

He beams. "Great! Now that's sorted, Jamie, grab us some ice from the snug, please. And Lewis, get me a bandage from the first-aid kit. Grace, you're a yoga teacher, right? That's perfect: you shouldn't have any issue raising your foot up onto the dashboard. It's a bit of a drive to the hospital so we should do what we can to bring the swelling down on the way."

"A bit of a drive"? Remembering the endless winding country roads on the journey up, I suspect that's an understatement. I'd hoped to avoid Aidan during this flying visit. Instead it looks like I'll be spending more time with him than with anyone else.

Just my luck.

CHAPTER SIX

AIDAN

A loud rapping at the door. "Aidan, it's time to get up! In fact, it's long past time to get up. It's after nine o'clock!"

With a groan, I force open my heavy eyelids and squint at the bright light streaming in through a gap in the curtains. "Maw, what is it?"

I'm grateful she's letting me stay here while Ally and I nurture our fledgling business, but is it too much to ask that she let me sleep in on a Sunday morning?

Without waiting to be invited, Maw comes in, to the bedroom that's been mine my whole life. A couple of years shy of sixty, she's given up dyeing and has let her hair go grey, but her blue eyes sparkle with a youthful energy and never more so than when she thinks she's about to hear some juicy Bannock gossip.

"Well? Out with it! I heard you were a hero yesterday, rescuing Grace Adefope from Bannock Woods and driving her to the hospital. I want to hear the story from the man himself."

Maw's the chef at the Bannock Hotel's restaurant. No doubt either Lewis or Jamie filled her in.

I yawn. "Maw, we had a long wait at the hospital—I didn't get back till late. Plus, yesterday I did a ten-mile jog *and* carried Grace quite a distance. I'm knackered! If I'm a hero, shouldn't I get to sleep a wee bit longer?"

"Nope!" She perches on the edge of my bed. "Not only am I desperate to hear the full story—and don't you dare leave out any details—you need to get up because we're going to go to Johnny MacDonald's cottage and welcome David to Bannock. I can't believe I didn't know he was moving here! I wish I'd had a chance to organise something to mark the occasion. But it's the weekend—what awful timing!"

Saturdays and Sundays are when Maw is busiest, since on those days the restaurant opens for lunch as well as dinner.

I rub at my eyes. "Er, am I missing something? Why do you feel the need to 'mark the occasion'?"

"Well, David met Johnny through Emily and Ally, didn't he?"

"Aye. And . . . ?"

"And if Ally's mother and father were still alive, they'd have given David a proper welcome. But they're gone, sadly, and since Mairi and I were best friends, it falls to me to do something in their place. I'd rather have prepared a meal, but the least we can do is pop round and hand in a wee gift."

I close my eyes and pinch the bridge of my nose. "Honestly, Maw, any obligations you feel to be hospitable are tenuous at best. But aye, sure, if you want to hand in a gift, go ahead. As for me, I'll no doubt bump into David before long so I'll just say hi to him when I see him. Grace may be at the cottage, and she was getting a wee bit tired of me yesterday, so I won't go around and bother her. I'm going to lie here a while longer."

Last night there had been a marked difference in Grace's

behaviour between the drive to the hospital and the drive back. On the way there, I'd chatted away to her, even teased her a little, enjoying how easy it was to rile her up. Considering she's a yoga teacher and is supposed to be an embodiment of inner calm or whatever, it's amazing how quickly I can push her buttons.

At the hospital there had been good news. The doctor confirmed it's just a sprain and the best thing Grace can do is keep up the RICE therapy: Rest, Ice, Compression, Elevation. Despite this, on the way back, she wasn't herself. I'd hoped for some more repartee. I don't know why, but I kind of like winding her up. Instead, even though she was beside me in the car, it was as though she were elsewhere in her head.

We actually spent most of the drive home in silence, and that's unusual for me—I'm never short of chat around women. I suppose she'd had a long day of travelling, and maybe I was getting on her nerves a bit.

Anyway, aye, I think she deserves a break from me today.

"Son, listen to me, you're going to get up, fill me in on what happened last night, and come with me to Johnny's place. It's just good manners."

"But—"

"I hope you've got something on because these covers are coming off." Maw grabs my duvet.

I do too, frantically. "Maw, I sleep naked!"

"Well, then, I'll give you two minutes to pull on some clothes. If you're still in bed when I come back, I'm whipping this off. No time extensions will be granted!"

She leaves and I let out a long, exasperated sigh. I really need to move out.

◆ ◆ ◆

Maw raps the brass knocker of Johnny's cottage. She's carrying a box of shortbread and a bottle of red wine. I've pulled on a light-blue shirt and jeans.

It's David who answers the door. "Elspeth! It's so nice to see you. And Aidan!" He hugs us both then ushers us inside.

From the sofa, Johnny raises a hand in greeting. There's no sign of Grace but there is a woman who just has to be her maw. She gets up from her armchair and offers a small but friendly smile.

"This is my mum, Viola," David says. "And Mum, this is Elspeth Stewart and her son, Aidan. If I remember right, Aidan shared quite a few dances with Grace at the engagement party."

He shoots me an amused grin. As Grace's twin, I'm sure he knows exactly what Grace and I got up to that night.

Viola comes over and gives Maw and then me a firm, business-like handshake. "Very pleased to meet you both."

"It's just wonderful that David's moving up here," Maw gushes. "He's such a lovely young man. But you'll miss having him nearby, Viola. When Aidan went travelling around the world, I missed him dearly." She squeezes my arm.

"Oh, I will miss him, but it's reassuring that he's moving to a place where the people are all so friendly and welcoming."

Maw's face lights up, pleased as punch by this compliment.

Viola turns to me. "Grace is up too but she's staying at the Bannock Hotel to catch up with Emily. You may like to pop in and say hello, Aidan?"

"Oh, don't worry, I saw her last night. I was the one who drove her to the hospital."

Viola's brows knit together, creasing her forehead. "I'm sorry, I'm not sure I follow. What do you mean you drove her to the hospital?"

CHAPTER SEVEN

GRACE

"That was quite the adventure you had yesterday," Emily says with a conspiratorial smile. "I still can't believe it was Aidan who rescued you."

We're in the Bannock Hotel's cute little restaurant, which is just big enough for nine tables. The walls are adorned with paintings of rolling green hills and misty lochs, and the carpet is, of course, tartan. The scent of freshly brewed coffee wafts through the air, mingling with the aroma of hot breakfast dishes being prepared in the kitchen. Silverware occasionally clinks against plates, the sound resonating over the gentle murmur of other guests' conversations.

"Oh, don't!" I say. "It was mortifying, him carrying me like that."

"Well, I'm just glad he found you. You need to be more careful, okay?" Emily reaches across the crisp white tablecloth and takes my hand.

She looks different now from how she did when she lived in London, her outward appearance mirroring the internal transformation she's gone through. In the past her brunette hair would always be straightened, and she was never seen without flawless make-up and a designer outfit. In contrast, nowadays she embraces her natural curls together with a more fresh-faced approach, complemented by relaxed and comfortable clothing. Ironically, despite no longer caring so much about how she's perceived by others, she looks more incredible than ever. I don't know what her secret is—maybe it's just her happiness shining through.

Normally, Emily would be waiting on the hotel's guests, showing them to their seats and talking them through the breakfast offering, but today Ally has stepped back into his former role so she can catch up with me.

"How's your ankle?" she asks.

"It's still pretty tender but I had some paracetamol when I got up. It'll be fine—I'll just take things easy for a while. I'm exhausted, though, so sorry if my chat isn't the best. I didn't sleep very well."

"Oh no! Grace, I work here now: I want all our guests to wake up feeling refreshed. Was it your ankle that bothered you? Or was it something else?"

I assure her it was my ankle, but it wasn't. It was the other thing the doctor and I discussed at the hospital that played on my mind all night, keeping sleep from coming.

Jamie comes over to our table, a cheeky grin already playing at his lips. "Morning, ladies! So, how does this work, Emily? Tomorrow do I get to sit while you take my order?"

She offers a saccharine-sweet fake smile. "I suppose. If you can find someone to cover for you, just as I found Ally."

He drums his fingers on his leg. "Hmm . . . that's a pain. Obviously, I need to get myself a girlfriend. Talking of romance"—he turns his attention to me—"how did yesterday with Aidan compare to the night of the engagement party?"

I roll my eyes. I've little patience for Jamie's humour in general, but today? Today he's treading on dangerous ground.

"Your silence says it all!" Jamie winks at me. "Anyway, what can I get you two to drink?"

"Coffee, please," I say. "And if you know what's good for you, maybe cut out the jokes this morning. I'm not in the best mood."

"I can tell! I hear yoga is a great stress reliever—you should try it sometime."

He just can't help himself.

"How do you work with this guy?" I whisper to Emily, loud enough for Jamie to catch. "Doesn't he drive you up the wall?"

Emily nods emphatically. "And not only is he my colleague, soon he'll be my brother-in-law. What am I getting myself into?"

"She loves me really," Jamie assures me. "Anyway, Emily, are you for a coffee too?"

"I'm actually going to pass on a hot drink this morning. I'll just grab some juice for myself."

"All right, I'll go get your coffee, Grace, then I'll be back for your hot-food order." Picking the menu off the table, he holds it in front of Emily's face. "Have a wee look! We've got some nice things on here."

She sighs. "Are you as annoying to actual guests as you are to me and Grace? Because if so, you and I will be having a chat later."

With another wink, Jamie leaves. Emily goes over to the continental-buffet area and pours herself some orange juice.

There's a fine spread: cereals, pastries, fresh fruit, yogurts. On top of that, Lewis is a brilliant breakfast chef, a role he's continued with since taking over as hotel manager. I know from experience the cooked options are to die for, and yet . . . I'm not sure I can eat anything, hot or cold. Just the thought makes me nauseated. I'm tense and my nerves all over the place. I'm still trying to get my head around what the doctor told me.

Jamie comes back with a pot of coffee and fills me up. Emily, taking her seat again, orders the vegetarian breakfast, while I ask for a potato scone and some scrambled eggs—a small portion. We'll see if I manage any of it.

After Jamie leaves, Emily leans across the table and says in a low voice, "I have some news. I wasn't planning on telling anyone yet, but seeing as you're here, it makes sense to tell you in person rather than wait and tell you over the phone. The thing is . . . well, your coffee smells really good but I'm actually off caffeine at the moment."

She watches me expectantly, but my sleep-deprived brain doesn't understand why she's delivering such mundane news in such a dramatic whisper.

And then things click into place.

"You . . . you're pregnant?"

A smile breaks across Emily's lips and a chuckle bubbles up from her chest. "Yes!" She glances about her then lowers her voice again. "I'm at the very early stages. My period is only a couple of days late, but I took a test and it was positive."

I glance down at my black coffee. I shouldn't be drinking the stuff either—I hadn't even thought.

"Well, aren't you going to say something?" Emily's brow furrows.

"Sorry. It's just . . . a bit of a shock. But it's wonderful news, Emily. Congratulations!"

Her eyes soften and the tension in her forehead vanishes. "Thanks. Apart from you and Ally, no one else knows yet, including his brothers, so keep it to yourself, yeah? But I had to tell you. You and I tell each other everything."

Oh God. She just had to say that, didn't she? Normally we do tell each other everything. The day after her engagement party, it didn't even occur to me *not* to confess to her I'd slept with Aidan. Now would be the perfect opportunity to admit that I, too, am pregnant, but I can't bring myself to. The words won't come, like they didn't yesterday when I got back to the hospital waiting room and Aidan jumped up to ask me about my ankle. With hindsight I wish I'd blurted the news out then—dumped it on him the same way the doctor dumped it on me—but I didn't. I kept it to myself.

And now I find myself doing the same thing again. The truth is, although we're both pregnant, we're in very different circumstances. Emily's found the love of her life. She's moved to a new, wonderful home and has a brand-new job that she's incredibly passionate about. Together with Lewis, she's making big changes around the hotel, modernising some of its tired decor and bringing in additional revenue via the newly finished function room.

As for me? The man who got me into this situation doesn't do relationships and only ever sleeps with a woman once. My brother has just moved out of the flat we share, and I have to find a new place, which won't be easy, given London prices. And if I'm being honest with myself, my job isn't exactly fulfilling me the way it once did, especially as I have to put up my fees yet again, which will push away people who genuinely benefit from what I do.

Of course, there's also an even bigger difference between us. Emily is excited there's a baby growing inside her, whereas I . . . am not sure what to think. I'm still considering my options.

No, I can't spoil Emily's happy news by revealing what's happening with me, so instead I force a smile and say, "Well, how are you feeling? Any morning sickness or is it still a bit early for that?"

◆ ◆ ◆

Even though Johnny's cottage is only a couple of minutes' walk away, Emily insists Ally drive the two of us there. She won't hear of me going on foot, given my sprained ankle. When Ally pulls up to let us out, Emily instructs him to carry me from the car inside, and that's where I draw the line. I make it clear that will not be happening.

I've had more than enough of being carried by men for one weekend. Besides, the doctor said there's no need to avoid walking altogether and, in fact, gradually putting some weight back on my ankle is an important part of the healing process. So, with a hand on Emily's shoulder for support, I navigate my way along the garden path without any help from Ally. He turns the car then lingers in the lane, waiting to check we get in okay. It's sweet but I shoo him away. I hate being treated like an invalid.

Emily reaches for the knocker, but before she can use it, the cottage door is flung open. Mum stands in the doorway, arms crossed, brows knitted together in a deep frown, eyes fixed on me.

"Grace Adefope! How could you not tell us? This family does not keep secrets from one another."

A chill creeps up my spine. How on earth does she know? Things rarely remain hidden from Mum for long, but apart from the doctor, I've not spoken to a soul about my pregnancy.

"When were you going to inform me you were at the hospital last night?" she demands. "And how is your ankle now?"

A quiet sigh of relief escapes my lips. Mum is not, in fact, aware of the pregnancy. I'm puzzled, though, how she knows about my injury.

"Oh . . . Mum, I'm sorry, but I left my phone in David's car yesterday, and when I got back to the hotel, it was late and I didn't want to disturb you."

I also couldn't bear facing my mum or brother straight after receiving such staggering, life-changing news. My decision to avoid my family came at a cost, though. Lying awake in bed last night, all I'd wanted to do was scroll through advice sites and read about how other women coped after finding themselves in situations like mine. Instead I'd been completely removed from the world, with no device on which to access the internet and only my own thoughts for company.

I actually enjoy a digital detox every now and again, but not when I'm craving the reassurance the World Wide Web can uniquely provide, by connecting us with others across the globe with experiences similar to our own.

"How did you know about the sprain?" I ask Mum.

Before she can answer, David appears behind her, his bright smile showing off his perfectly white teeth. "Morning, Grace. And hello, Emily!" He places a hand on Mum's shoulder.

"Rather than interrogate them on the doorstep, why don't we invite them in and let them take a seat?"

We go into the cottage and Emily wraps her arms around David, squeezing him tight.

"Grace told me you've moved up here. That's amazing!" She hugs Mum too. "And it's great to see you, Viola."

"You too, Emily. You're looking very well. Life in Bannock obviously suits you."

Johnny stands and gestures for me and Emily to sit. "I'll go pop on the kettle." He heads to the kitchen area.

Mum checks her watch. "That would be lovely, thanks, Johnny. We can have a quick tea but then, David, you'll need to take me and Grace to the airport."

To thank me and Mum for joining him on the long drive up yesterday, David booked us seats on a flight back to London. By road the journey takes ten hours, but by plane just an hour and a half.

After he drops us off, David is going to hang on to the car, which he and I actually bought together. I could do with fewer outgoings, though, and between insurance, parking costs, and petrol, being a driver isn't cheap. David has insisted on giving me some money to make up for my loss of the vehicle, and he'll continue to pay rent for a while too, given he moved out with only two days' notice. I wish my financial situation were such I could tell him I don't need his cash, but the truth is I do, so I gratefully accepted.

"All right, let's hear it." From the sofa, I turn to Mum, who's in an armchair. "How did you know about my ankle?"

"A lovely woman—Elspeth, her name was—came around earlier to welcome David and give him a present. Her son was with her and he asked after you. When he mentioned a hospital visit, I'd no idea what he was talking about, so he explained he'd carried you from the woods to his car and driven you to see a doctor. I was flabbergasted! I'm glad it was him who found you, though. What a pleasant, well-mannered young man."

Emily, who's beside me on the sofa, tries to catch my eye, no doubt so we can share an in-joke at this description of Aidan. I don't acknowledge her. If she knew about the being growing inside me, she wouldn't find it funny either.

"Anyway, are you okay now?" David is perched on a foot-stool, leaving the other armchair free for Johnny.

"I'm fine. I might need to get creative with my yoga classes this week, but I'll manage."

My answer fails to wipe the concern from David's expression. "It's just . . . yesterday, you said you weren't feeling very well, remember? And then, in the woods . . . what happened, exactly?"

Ugh, this is the thing about being a twin. I love it, but it's incredibly difficult lying to someone who knows you so well.

I don't quite meet his eye. "I tripped. That's all. Look, I went to a hospital and a doctor checked over me. I'm okay! There's nothing to worry about."

He nods, apparently accepting my assurances, but once again I'm holding back information. I hate this secrecy. I normally tell David and Emily everything. It's taking all I've got to keep my voice level and to resist the urge to fidget with my hands.

"It's a relief you're okay, Grace," Mum says. "Now, a date for your diary! Elspeth was upset she didn't have a chance to prepare a meal for us all to celebrate David's move here. However, since Aidan and Ally are both turning thirty in October, she invited you and I up for a lunch then. As weekends are busy at the hotel, it's on a Monday and sadly I have a work commitment I can't get out of, but I said you'd attend."

"Mum!" My tone is incredulous. "You can't say yes to things on my behalf. I have a job too, you know."

She waves a hand dismissively. "Well, no doubt you'll be able to swap classes with one of the other instructors. It's a joint celebration and Ally is your best friend's fiancé, while Aidan rescued you last night then drove you to the hospital. I'm sure you can arrange your calendar so you can make it."

Argh, she's so meddlesome! I'm not a child and my life isn't hers to control.

Emily looks my way hopefully. "Please come to the party! I barely saw you this visit and already you're leaving again. I miss you. Let's have a proper catch-up next time, yeah?"

Inwardly I sigh. I don't have the strength to argue. "Fine! I'll come back up for Ally and Aidan's birthday lunch."

CHAPTER EIGHT

GRACE

The number-four bus inches along Seven Sisters Road. It's late on a wet October afternoon and outside pedestrians with umbrellas and hoods up hurry by, their gazes downcast as they brace themselves against the relentless rain.

Summer is but a memory. It's been over seven weeks since David moved to the sleepy town of Bannock. I've left the flat we shared and found my own place, which is where I'm returning to now.

The bus is busy, with all the downstairs seats taken and a number of standing passengers. I was lucky enough to secure a spot near the back, and when I'm not looking out the window, my gaze is drawn to the woman opposite me. It's evident she is pregnant and a lot further on than my twelve weeks.

The last thing I want to do is stare but the sheer size of her belly is almost unbelievable to me. It's not as if I've never seen a woman who's nearly full-term before, but before I fell pregnant myself, I wouldn't have paid any more attention to an expectant mother than to any other stranger on a bus, except to give up my seat if no other was available.

Now, though, there's a connection between us, even if she doesn't realise that as I'm not yet showing. She and I are going through the same process, and I'm naturally intrigued—and concerned—about what is to come, especially since it seems that what is to come is my belly growing to a size I can scarcely comprehend.

The woman's partner has an arm protectively slung around her shoulders. He notices me watching her so I avert my gaze and open my handbag. Carefully I take out a photo that was captured just half an hour ago. Handling it like a fragile ancient artefact, and keeping it well away from my damp coat, I stare with wonder at the grainy black-and-white image of my baby.

My baby! This is the child growing inside me. Ultrasound is far from a new technology, but it really is amazing that we can see the tiny little person at this stage, when he or she is only the size of a plum.

My emotions have been all over the place in recent weeks, and I've constantly been questioning whether I'm a fool for going through with the pregnancy. But when I heard the beating heart and saw the image on the screen, I knew I'd made the right decision for me. I'm having this baby. I'm going to be a mum!

I'm not deluding myself—I know this won't be easy. In the waiting room at Whittington Hospital's antenatal clinic, I was the only woman there by herself, without a partner, a parent, or even a friend to accompany me. That's because I've not yet told anyone my news. I was putting it off until after the scan, but now that's been and gone, I'm still not sure I can do it. Not today anyway. Maybe tomorrow.

Raising a baby as a single mother will be a massive challenge, and although I'm anticipating the difficulties already, the reality of it will still no doubt come as a shock. But every time I feel overwhelmed by what I'm putting myself through, I remind myself that Mum did this before me, all by herself, and she gave birth to twins. As much as I want this baby, I was relieved when the sonographer confirmed there's only one little being in my womb.

Mum may not be perfect but she does have the most incredible can-do attitude, and I reckon I need to push aside my self-doubt and adopt a bit of her confidence. If she can do it, I can do it. I've always wanted to be a mother, and sure, this isn't quite how I imagined it, but this is how it's happening and I'm going to own it. My child will be just as loved as any other kid.

The bus comes to a stop and the pregnant woman and her partner stand.

"Congrats!" Smiling, the woman nods at my scan picture. "And don't look so worried. You've got this!"

"Thanks."

I want to say more—offer her well-wishes for the upcoming birth—but she's already getting off. It was such a short and simple interaction, and yet just what I needed. A confidence boost.

The sensation is, unfortunately, fleeting. New passengers get on, including a fifty-something man who takes one of the vacated seats opposite, and whose stench of tobacco and stale body odour turns my stomach.

Maybe it's rude to be so repulsed by an individual's smell, but it's something I have no control over. This could end very badly, so I press the stop button and put away the picture. Praying I can get off before long, I bow my head and place a finger against my nostrils. I don't want to puke right here on this busy rush-hour bus.

When the doors open, I hurry out. I don't waste time reaching inside my handbag for my umbrella. Instead I let the rain strike me as I take slow steps along the pavement, urging my stomach to settle itself, no more wishing to vomit out here, in front of passing cars and pedestrians, than on the bus. Nausea has been a frequent visitor in recent weeks, and as I've discovered, the term "morning sickness" is very much a misnomer. It can come on any time of day.

On this occasion, thankfully, my stomach calms and the sensation fades. Breathing a sigh of relief, I put up my brolly then set off for my flat, facing a longer walk than I'd expected, having got off three stops early.

◆ ◆ ◆

My new home is . . . compact. That's one way of putting it. Bloody tiny is another. It's a studio flat, with the bed so close to the kitchen I could almost prepare my meals while lying down. There's little in terms of living space—just a small table with two chairs—and the only other room is the bathroom. Although can you call it a bathroom if it doesn't have a bath? Anyway, whoever fitted a toilet, wash-hand basin, and shower in that glorified cupboard must be a master of Tetris.

It's not a lot to look at, this place, but it's mine. Or rather, it's the landlord's, but it's mine so long as I'm renting it. It's clean and it's got everything I need. Personally, I'd prefer to be self-sufficient than live with strangers in a house-share, especially given the morning sickness and my regular need to pee, and since in six months I'll have a screaming baby. No one would thank me for that.

It's the arrival of my future flatmate that worries me the

most. *I* can just about manage here but it's not somewhere to raise a child. Then again, how much space do babies really need? This place will be fine for my pregnancy and the first year or two. After that . . . I'll just have to deal with it when it comes.

I make myself a herbal tea then settle on my bed, my back against the headboard, and turn on the TV. The wall-mounted screen is a little close for comfort, and the bed is no sofa, but it's fine. Some nights the walls close in on me and I'm desperate to go out, but today—between exhaustion and the rain—I'm content to stay in. In a while I'll switch off the television and read my book instead, but right now I'm too tired to concentrate. Pregnancy really takes it out of you.

Suddenly the buzzer goes.

Weird. I'm not expecting a visitor.

Getting up, I put my tea on the table and lift the entry phone. "Hello?"

"Grace, it's your mother. It's very wet so let me in, please."

Mum? Ugh, today of all days. I just wanted to relax after the hospital visit.

"Oh . . . of course." I press the button that opens the door downstairs and take a few deep breaths, calming myself. Then I turn off the TV, grab a cardigan from my limited hanging space, and tug it on, tying the belt firmly. It's stupid—I'm not showing yet—but the extra layer of protection offers me some comfort.

Before long Mum knocks on my flat door. I'm on my way to open it when I remember the scan photo. Crap! It's lying out on the work surface. I snatch it up and hide it under my pillow, then I let her in.

"Mum! This is a surprise."

"Yes, well, it occurred to me that if I kept waiting for an

invitation, I'd never see your new place, so I thought I'd just drop by." She steps in and casts a critical eye around. It only takes her a few moments—there's not a lot to see. "Have you been had? This flat isn't much bigger than a box! I should be insulted you'd rather live here than with me."

Grinding my teeth, I close the door behind her. I'm on edge. Mum is like Sherlock Holmes: from the most trivial of details, she can reach a conclusion before anyone else. I may not be showing yet but that doesn't mean I can let my guard down.

"This place has everything I need," I say. "I'm quite happy here."

"Hmm. Well, let's have a look at you, then." Mum holds me at arm's length and does her usual thorough examination of me. "This is the first time I've seen you since we went to Bannock together. Not for want of trying on my part, but apparently you've been busy. Have you lost weight?"

How can she even tell through my cardigan?

"Have I? I hadn't noticed."

I *have* noticed. Losing weight in the first trimester isn't uncommon, thanks to morning sickness. As for Mum's comment about me being busy, I do feel bad that I've been avoiding her—especially with David having moved away—but I reckoned the easiest way to keep my pregnancy a secret was to see as little of her as possible.

I'll have to tell her at some point, but not today. No, I'll start off with Emily or David to ease myself into things. I need support from the first people I tell, not judgement.

"You're not skimping on food to save money, are you?" She shifts her gaze to my tiny kitchen area.

"Of course not!"

"What do you use to prepare your meals? A microwave—is that all you've got?"

I go over to a kitchen cupboard and, from it, pull a portable two-ring stove. "I've got this too. I put it away when I'm not using it because there's not much space on the work surface."

There's not much cupboard space either but I don't mention that. I don't need to—it's obvious.

"No oven? Grace, this setup is hardly ideal. And you don't even have a washing machine!"

"There's a laundrette close by."

There is, but on parenting forums I've seen mums talk about how babies go through multiple outfits a day. Not being able to machine-wash clothes at home is going to be a pain.

But it's fine. In this compact space I have more than many people in the world do. I'm grateful for that.

"Take a seat, Mum. The kettle has just boiled. Tea or coffee?"

"A coffee would be lovely."

She sits at the table and, from her bag, pulls four wrapped presents. "This one is for you." She places it aside. "It's just a little thing. That's good because if I'd opted for something bigger, you wouldn't have had anywhere to put it."

I ignore that comment and open the cupboard over the sink. Luckily, there's a jar of instant coffee I took with me from the old place. Since Emily mentioned she was off caffeine, I've been avoiding it myself.

"The other presents are for you to take up to Bannock," Mum goes on. "Something for Elspeth, for being a gracious host, and small gifts for Ally and Aidan, the birthday boys. You can say they're from both of us."

I fill her mug with boiling water. "Oh, Mum, I know I said

I'd go up for the lunch this Monday, but I've been thinking about giving it a miss."

"Nonsense! Is this about money? Because if so, I'll pay your fare."

"No, it's not that."

But Mum's purse is already out of her bag and in her hands. She removes some notes.

"Mum, no! Thank you, but I don't need a handout. I'm a grown woman—I can pay my own way." I put her coffee on the table.

"Well, in any case, I'll just leave these here." She puts the cash down. "Please go up for the party? It'll be good for you to see David and Emily."

"Mum, like I say, I wasn't planning to—"

"Why don't you want to go?"

I don't have an answer for that—at least, not one I can tell her—so I let out a quiet sigh and sink into the other chair.

I take a long sip of my tea. "All right, fine. I'll go but I don't need your—"

"The money is a gift. If you don't want to spend it on your fare, it can be your laundrette fund, seeing as you don't have a machine of your own. And I insist. It's yours now."

I shake my head but I know from experience it's easier to accept than to argue. "Thanks," I murmur.

I realise I don't sound grateful—and yes, she is trying to be nice—but she's got this way of making me feel like I can't look after myself. It's always annoyed me but now it really gets to me because if I can't look after myself, how am I supposed to look after a baby?

CHAPTER NINE

AIDAN

Today is my thirtieth birthday. To mark the occasion I'm viewing a property, a secluded house a ten-minute drive from Bannock, accessed via a dirt track off the main road. Although it'll require a fair bit of love and care, it's a beautiful place with more than enough space inside for a bachelor like me. In fact, if I moved here, I'd need to think what to do with a few of the rooms. It comes with some land too, plus it's nestled at the edge of a forest and surrounded on all sides by nature.

It's long past time I moved out. The business is bringing in some money now, and I'm entering a new decade of life—that's the kick up the arse I needed to sort out my living arrangements. As much as I love Maw, I can't go on staying with her.

Earlier the estate agent, Finlay Cochrane, showed me around, but I'm now taking in the property by myself while he waits outside. He has assured me there's no rush.

I gravitate back to the kitchen, which is the largest room and the one in which I reckon I'd spend most of my time. There's a cosy living room at the front, but the kitchen has the view of the forest and it's a stunning sight. As well as a window above the sink, there are French windows leading onto the garden, with a tired sofa facing them. That'd be a nice spot to chill and read a book or scroll on my phone, occasionally glancing up at the trees, on the lookout for wildlife.

The previous owner couldn't take a lot of his furniture with him as he's moved into a much smaller retirement flat, so the property comes with a fair bit of his old stuff. Some of the items have seen better days and would need to go eventually, but the kitchen is home to a beautiful oak table. I'd definitely keep that.

Like the sofa, the table would be a nice place to sit, in the morning with a coffee, reading the news on my tablet, or for dinner with guests. I could make something for Maw and my sister, Iona, when she's up visiting. Plus, Ally has confided in me that Emily's expecting a bairn so I could have them over on other occasions. I'm sure they'd appreciate someone preparing them a meal and there's plenty of space for a high chair.

And when it's just me, it's not as if I'd live like a hermit. At the weekend I could go into Inverness and pick up a lass then bring her back here. We could drink wine, chat, flirt, maybe get up to a bit of mischief, eventually have sex by the crackling wood burner . . .

Aye, that's what I need. Since I got home from my travels, living with Maw has seriously cramped my style. For my sex life more than anything else, I desperately need my own place.

I open the French windows and head out into the garden, which has a gate at the end that takes you straight into the woods. Aw, it's just perfect. The wilds have always called to me—that's where my passion for outdoor sports comes from. But although in Bannock I grew up surrounded by country-side, I love the idea of living *in* nature, not removed from it the way you are in a town. Here, that's what you get. There are no other houses about—just a beautiful landscape.

As well as the woods, there's the River Garve, which passes close by. Some days I could catch a fish for my dinner, and I could get into foraging too. I love the idea of going back to some hunter-gatherer basics.

By the wall of the house, there's a log store. Every year before winter, I'd need to chop plenty of wood and fill that up, then drive to the shops and stock up the cupboards too. The snow could render the track off the main road impassable, possibly for days at a time. Some people would hate being stranded and cut off from everything, but for me, there's a sense of adventure about the idea.

Anyway, even if my car got stuck, I could hike to Bannock. The evening Ally sent me on a jog—the same jog on which I found Grace Adefope sprawled at the bottom of a hill—I came out this way. The public footpath that links the towns of Bannock and Duntreath passes the property, just a short distance into the forest, although far enough in that the trees provide some privacy. Walking, it'd take about an hour to get to my maw's, door to door.

Aye, this place ticks every box. It's time to go have a chat with Finlay.

I head around to the front of the house, where Finlay sits in his car, checking his phone. Glancing up and spotting me, he comes out, grinning widely. He was two years above me at school and is tall with ginger hair and a friendly manner.

"Well, what are you thinking?" he asks.

"I love it," I say honestly. "Now I need to see if I can sort out a mortgage."

Because the house is remote, the price is a lot less than what you'd pay in Bannock itself. And because it needs a bit of modernisation and upkeep, it's more affordable still. But I like the idea of putting my own stamp on the place, and I could do with a project to keep me busy in the evenings, especially as Ally will soon be a husband and a da and will have little time for hanging out outside of work.

Each to their own, but settling down with a wife and kids isn't my scene. But pottering around here and turning it into somewhere really special? Aye, that sounds a pretty damn brilliant hobby.

The one difficulty could be that Bannock Adventures is still new. Even if I can prove I've got enough coming in to make the monthly payments, banks are wary of start-up businesses. Hopefully, I can find some sort of solution. I can't live with Maw indefinitely.

Finlay claps my back. "Keep me in the loop with how the mortgage hunt goes, okay? But for now, if you're done here, I'll lock up then we can head off."

We only took the one car out: Finlay's. We know each other, and Cochrane and Munro Estate Agents is just down the road from my maw's. It'd have been silly for us to both drive.

"Actually, I'm going to walk back, by the woods. Get more of a feel for the surroundings, you know?"

"Are you sure you don't want a lift?"

"I'm sure. Speak to you soon, all right?"

I leave Finlay and the house and set off into the trees, joining the public footpath. I've only gone a short way when my phone pings with a message.

Nice! I have reception out here. That's a bonus.

I check and see it's my sister, who works as a vet down in Glasgow.

IONA

I come back up for your birthday and you're not even here! Maw doesn't know where you are either. Said you left while she was in the bathroom.

AIDAN

Aye, timed it that way deliberately. I hate how she asks me where I'm going every time I leave! Keep this to yourself but I was at a house viewing. I love Maw to bits but I need my own space.

IONA

That's exciting! I suppose if you can't treat yourself on your birthday, when can you?

AIDAN

Fancy buying it for me with that big vet salary of yours?

IONA

You wish. Anyway, you won't want to hear this, but better now than when everyone is gathered for lunch. Da called and asked me to tell you happy birthday. I'm tired of being the middle person, Aidan.

AIDAN

Aye, well, he's got my number.

IONA

True, but he says you never answer his calls or reply to his messages.

AIDAN

I wouldn't say NEVER but . . . okay, fair point.

IONA

With you being thirty now, and it being a new decade and all that, maybe it's time for some changes in your life? A bit of forgiveness, for example?

AIDAN

😔 All right, I'll give Da a call. But . . . not today.

CHAPTER TEN

AIDAN

"There he is—finally!" Iona bounds up to me and wraps me in a hug. "Happy birthday, bro!"

Like me, Iona is blonde and blue-eyed, but style-wise, we couldn't be more different. She's got on large glasses—a callback to the seventies—and a green dress decorated with illustrations of badgers, otters, and weasels. I'm not sure if you'd describe her look as geek chic or just eccentric, but either way, she owns it. Always has.

"Hey, you! I'm desperate to know, where did you find a mustelid dress?"

She glances down at her outfit then beams. "*Mustelid?* I'm impressed. You know your mammal families."

I wink at her then step further into the Bannock Hotel's restaurant, which is where we'll be doing the birthday lunch. It's the usual setting for joint McIntyre and Stewart family celebrations, and since it's closed to patrons on Mondays, we've got the place to ourselves. Several tables have been pushed together to form a single long one we can all get around.

Pleasant smells waft through from the kitchen, where Maw

and Lewis are no doubt hard at work. In the restaurant itself, the only others here so far are Ally, Emily, and Cat.

"Good to see you, Cat." I sling an arm around her and give her a squeeze.

Catriona is the youngest of the four McIntyre siblings and the only girl. Strands of auburn hair frame her delicate, almost elfin face, which is adorned with a nose stud. Confident and with a reputation as a bit of a party animal, she has her three older brothers wrapped around her little finger—Ally, especially. She's in teacher training down in Glasgow and shares a flat with my sister.

"Hey, Aidan. Getting old. How does it feel to be thirty?"

"Great! But Emily's shooting daggers at you so maybe check who's in the room before describing thirty as old." In a stage whisper, I add, "She's a bit sensitive about having a toy boy. Ally is still in his twenties, after all, even though he's trying to hijack my big day and make it a joint party."

Maw's face appears at the kitchen door. "Ally's birthday is in six days! This lunch is just as much for him as it is for you. It's only because of the way the days fell this year we're doing it today."

And with that, she's gone again, back to preparing the lunch, which she's told me will be pumpkin soup followed by steak pie, with a veggie option for Emily and Johnny.

I grin at Ally then give him a hug and a back slap. "Good to see you, mate. And you, Emily."

"Oh, yeah? I'm a year older than Ally, Aidan. A year! That doesn't make him a toy boy or me a cougar."

Ah. Note to self: don't tease a pregnant woman. It's just asking for trouble.

Thankfully, I'm saved by Jamie, who wanders in carrying a

large picture frame covered with a drape, immediately attracting everyone's attention.

"Oh, hi, Aidan. Happy birthday." He nods to a painting of a loch hanging on the wall. "Would you mind taking that down for me?"

"Er, okay," I say, puzzled. "What have you got there?"

"All will be revealed in due course." He wiggles his eyebrows mysteriously.

"What are you up to?" Ally demands.

He has good reason to be suspicious. Jamie is the joker of their family.

"Can't a guy do a nice thing for his big brother and his big brother's best friend?" Jamie hangs the mystery picture using the hooks I make available then adopts an angelic expression.

"When do you ever do nice things?" Ally mutters.

"Hello, everyone!" David Adefope strides into the restaurant, his lively demeanour cutting through any tension.

He's followed by Johnny and Grace, and damn, Grace looks good, which is no surprise since she always looks good. Her shoulder-length spiral curls bounce around her high cheekbones as she walks. She's in a loose-fitting cream woollen jumper—a sensible choice for autumn, and yet, on her, it's somehow sexy.

Wow. Normally, once I've slept with someone, my desire is sated and my attention drifts elsewhere. I like that—it's safe. Every so often, though, I crave more and that's how it is with Grace. It's for occasions like this I have a simple but strict rule: never have sex with a woman more than once. No exceptions.

Helpfully, when I carried Grace from Bannock Woods, she made it clear she had no wish to revisit our engagement-party shenanigans. Unfortunately, despite her lack of interest, and despite my sexual policy, my body hasn't got the message. Warmth is already spreading through me as a result of her presence.

"What's this?" Jamie nods at Johnny. "A MacDonald at a McIntyre and Stewart party?"

Ally clips his brother over the back of the head. "Welcome, Johnny! Please ignore Jamie—we all do."

Johnny's older brother, Robbie MacDonald, is the same age as me and Ally, and he was the town troublemaker when we were growing up. I never got on with him, but Ally and Robbie had a bitter rivalry that at times became pretty unpleasant. That's all in the past now, though. The MacDonalds work at the Glen Garve Resort, and Ally agreed to put old grievances to bed when he and I began our professional relationship with them.

Besides, Johnny couldn't be any less like his brother anyway.

Johnny brushes off Jamie's comment, and he and David start the hugs and greetings, while Emily skips over to Grace, takes her hand, and squeals her hello.

I slink over to say hi too. "How's the ankle?"

Grace's jaw tightens and a flicker of something—exasperation?—crosses her face. "Oh. Aidan. Fine, thanks. Here, this is for you. Happy birthday." She passes me a present.

"Thanks! What is it?"

She shrugs. "Don't know. My mum bought it. Wrapped it too. I'm just handing it over."

Phew, that's some serious animosity. I'm not sure what I've done to provoke her ire.

"All right, well, I'll let you two catch up." I put the gift in the corner of the room. I'll open it later.

Maw appears at the kitchen door again. "Oh, good! Everyone's here. Are Lewis and I okay to serve the starters?"

"Actually, Elspeth, before we eat, I'd like to say a few words," Jamie announces.

Maw claps her hands together. "Lovely! Come on out, Lewis."

Lewis emerges from the kitchen and sneaks a quick glance at Iona before redirecting his attention to Jamie, who's moved to stand by the drape-covered picture.

Jamie clears his throat, a hint of mischief playing at his lips. "First, I'd like to remind everyone that, as well as a birthday celebration, this lunch is our way of formally welcoming David to Bannock. Welcome!"

Those of us closest to David pat his back, and he beams, delighted by the attention.

Jamie goes on, "But we are, of course, also here to celebrate a major milestone in the lives of Ally and Aidan. They've now been on this earth for thirty years, so I thought we should reflect on some of their finest moments."

He removes the drape to reveal a collage of photos of me and Ally, from when we were gummy bairns, through our childhood and teenage years, to more recent times.

"Oh, would you look at that!" Maw puts a hand to her heart. "What a thoughtful gesture, Jamie."

We all crowd around to inspect the pictures, and I quickly realise they aren't so much of our finest moments as our most embarrassing. There's the inevitable snap of us in the bath together as toddlers, with nothing left to the imagination. Then there's one of us as tweens, posing in shirts and with styled hair, our serious expressions emulating the boy bands of the day. TV singing competitions had been all the rage, and we'd been certain we'd be the next big thing. Our complete lack of musical talent hadn't deterred us in the slightest.

Our gangly, spotty, ugly-duckling stage is represented by a disproportionately high number of images. We turned out all right in the end—I don't think it's vain to say we're both pretty good-looking now—but man, you wouldn't have guessed it from some of these pics. Questionable haircuts and poor fashion choices are also captured. And then . . .

"Oh God!" Cat wails. "Jamie, why did you include that one?"

We all follow her pointing finger to a picture taken from behind. It shows Ally and me in kilts. We're lifting the backs of them to moon the camera.

"Bloody hell!" Lewis grumbles. "I don't want to see your bare arses."

"And, er, not just their arses." David points. "Ally, I believe that's one of your testicles."

I lean closer and snigger when I see David's right. Unlike me, Ally's legs are slightly open, and something is peeking through. Definitely a ball.

Red-faced, Ally tears the photo down. "Jamie! The bath pic is one thing—I was just a bairn—but I was nineteen in this! What were you thinking?" He lunges at his brother.

Jamie deftly dodges, laughing.

"Oi, come here!" Ally growls.

"Nah, you're all right."

"Boys!" Maw protests. "Can't we have a pleasant meal for once?"

"Elspeth's right, and actually, I've got an announcement, which might make up for Jamie's crummy one." Emily takes Ally's hand, squeezes it to calm him, then shifts her focus to me. "If you don't mind? I don't want to take the attention off you on your birthday."

"Go on!" I encourage. "It's about time you told everyone else your news."

"What news?" Maw is suddenly on high alert, her expression animated with eager anticipation.

"Well . . ." Emily glances at her fiancé. "Ally and I are expecting a baby."

"Oh, that's just wonderful!" Maw exclaims.

Cat squeals, clapping and delightedly hugging the pair. "I'm going to be an auntie! You two have made me so happy. Thank you, thank you, thank you!"

Everyone else joins in with the congratulations, the room erupting with excited chatter. Only Grace stands back, not hurrying to embrace Ally and Emily, but then she, like me, already knew.

Actually, wait a minute, where's Jamie? No sooner do I wonder this than he reappears, carrying a bottle of champagne. "This calls for a proper celebration," he declares.

Ally eyes the bottle suspiciously. "That's our most expensive wine. Are you buying that as a gift for us all, or is the hotel paying for it?"

"Shh!" Jamie shakes his head. "Always worrying about money, and you'd got so much better recently. Just relax and enjoy the moment."

"The hotel's paying for it, then," Ally mutters.

Lewis and Cat fetch champagne flutes then Jamie pops the bottle and fills the glasses. He passes them out, except to Emily, of course. When he tries to give one to Grace, she refuses.

"I'm doing a detox but I'll take something soft. Give me whatever Emily's going to have."

"Oh, go on!" Jamie encourages. "Your best friend is pregnant. That deserves a toast. Diets and health kicks can wait."

"I'd really rather not."

"Grace, you never turn down bubbly!" Emily laughs. "Don't tell me you're pregnant too?"

It's obviously a joke and yet Grace freezes like a deer caught in headlights. Emily's smile falters, and all conversation trails off as everyone notices how flustered Grace is getting.

"No," she says, far too late. "I'm not pregnant." But her eyes well with tears. "I . . . I have to go. I'm so sorry."

She makes a hasty exit. David hurries after her, followed by a very confused Emily. A heavy silence settles over the room.

"Fuck," Jamie says eventually. "She's definitely pregnant."

Most eyes turn to me.

"What? Why are you all looking at me?"

"Aidan," Ally murmurs, "you were the first person Grace had slept with in a long, long time. And . . . I don't know that she's been with anyone since."

"Shit." My blood runs cold. But . . . we used a condom. Surely . . . ?

I gulp. "You don't think . . ."

"Son?" Maw's mouth hangs open.

I don't have any words.

"Well, we can't drink to Emily if she's not here so here's a new toast instead." Jamie holds his flute aloft. "To Aidan, on the occasion of his thirtieth birthday, and on learning he's to be a father!"

No one else raises their glass. Ally thumps his brother.

I'm too stunned to react. This cannot be happening.

CHAPTER ELEVEN

AIDAN

I've left the hotel and gone across the road to Maw's. I needed a bit of space from everyone.

I'm lying on my bed, staring up at my phone. I've opened the contacts app and found Da's number, and my thumb is hovering over the call button. Normally, Da's the last person I want to talk to, but for some reason, right now I want to hear his voice.

I slide a hand behind my neck and rub it, then I hit the button. He answers on the fourth ring.

"Aidan?"

"Hi, Da."

"Son, happy birthday!" His deep tone radiates warmth. "Thanks for ringing. It's been too long. Thirty years old, eh? Ha! I can't believe it. I still remember holding you for the first time in the hospital. How do you feel?"

"Aye, I'm doing all right." My voice is monotone. "So . . . er, it looks like you may be becoming a grandfather."

The line goes quiet for a few seconds.

"What was that, son?"

I repeat myself.

"Why . . . that's fantastic! I didn't even realise you were with a lass. I'm so out of the loop."

"No, you're not. I'm not with anyone. It wasn't exactly planned. Just like Archie, eh?"

Archie is my half-brother. My da and my maw split up eleven years ago, but Archie is fifteen. I'm sure you can see the problem. It turns out Da wasn't doing a lot of long hours at the office in Inverness. He had another life going on.

"Well . . . congratulations, son, if that's the right word. And, you know . . . I still regret the way everything happened."

"Aye. Anyway, Iona said you wanted to speak to me so I thought I'd give you a call and fill you in. I still need to find out more myself, to be honest. I don't have a clue what's going on."

At first, ringing Da had seemed a good idea but now I want off the phone again. "So, I'm going to go but—"

"Can we meet up at some point? Talk face to face?"

"Aye, at some point. Anyway, I've got to go. Speak to you later." I end the call.

I get about a second to myself before my bedroom door opens.

"Was that your father on the phone?"

"Aye." I'm not in the mood for speaking to Maw either. "Look—"

"A grandchild, Aidan!" Her eyes glisten. Somehow her expression is both happy and furious.

"I couldn't have asked for a better birthday present." My tone is deadpan. "You're going to be a granny, assuming she keeps it and it's definitely mine. Congratulations."

"Son!" She strides over to me, picks up a paperback from my bedside table—a comedian's autobiography I've been

84

glancing through—and raps my arm with it. "This is not how this was supposed to happen!"

"Ow! Maw!" I rub at where she struck me. "We don't hit people to rebuke them. I'm not sure I'll be leaving my kid with you."

This earns me another whack.

"Aw, come on!" I complain. "Are you done yet?"

"No! I toiled for hours over that lunch and you ruined it."

She goes for a third blow but I intercept this one and pluck the book out of her hands.

"I'm sorry, Maw, but please, calm down!"

"Calm down? Just look at Ally and Emily! Such lovely news—engaged and with a baby on the way. *That's* how you do things. Not"—she waves at me—"like this! And even if you have got it all wrong, why are you lying here moping instead of talking to Grace?"

"Oh? And what do you suggest I say to her?"

"You've never been scared of chatting to lassies before. I'm sure you'll think of something."

I shake my head. "I reckon I should just give her some space."

"Pass me that book. I want to hit you again."

"Bloody hell, Maw! All right, I'll go chat to her."

"Good. And you be nice, okay? Think before you speak. You may be feeling sorry for yourself, but remember, this is a lot harder for her. If you're about to say something foolish, picture me whacking you with that book then bite your tongue. Don't be an eejit!"

◆ ◆ ◆

I find Grace in the Bannock Hotel's garden, which is around the back of the building. She, Emily, and David are sitting on a bench that Ally had installed earlier this year to commemorate his mother and father.

"You shouldn't have been going through this all by yourself." Emily, whose face is etched with worry lines, is holding Grace's hand. "You can tell me anything. You know that, right?"

"And me," David adds. "I'm your twin!"

Grace nods, wiping her eyes. "Thanks. I don't know why I can't stop crying—I'm glad you both know now."

As I wander over, all three look up.

"Hi." I raise a hand in greeting. It's a bloody stupid way to start but I wasn't sure what else to say.

"We'll leave you two to it." David squeezes his sister's arm then stands. "Aidan." He inclines his head and pats my shoulder as he passes.

Emily gets up too. "When you want us to come back, just shout," she tells Grace. "We won't go far."

They head into the hotel and I edge closer to the bench.

"Is it okay if I sit?"

She nods so I do.

"So . . ." I don't know where to begin.

"It's a lot to take in, isn't it?" Grace stares ahead, dabbing at her eyes.

"Aye. It is."

"I've not slept with anyone else, just in case you were wondering."

"Right."

There goes any hope this is all some big misunderstanding and it's actually another guy's baby.

Shit. What to ask first? What I want to know more than anything is if she's planning to keep the baby, but even without Maw's warning, I'm aware that'd be an insensitive first question. I'd also like to ask her about the condom but that's not a great place to start either. Besides, why would she know any more about that than me? Maybe it tore—that's something I should have checked for afterwards. But we were drunk and in a hurry to get back downstairs . . .

"How have you been feeling?" I ask instead.

"Not great. The morning sickness has been pretty bad and it's been lonely keeping this to myself. I'm also . . . scared."

Her words hurt me—a sharp, physical pain in my chest. I'm surprised by my reaction, but I really don't like the idea of her being alone and afraid.

I want to reach out and comfort her, just as Emily and David used touch as well as words to soothe her earlier. But I'm out of my depth: when it comes to the opposite sex, flirting is the only tool I've got. Unless I'm trying to get a woman to my bed, I don't know how to act around her. Besides, I got Grace pregnant—I'm not sure she'd want me putting my hands anywhere near her.

I keep them on my lap. "I get why you're scared. It's a big deal. How far along are you?"

"Fifteen weeks and two days." She turns to me, her dark-brown eyes watery. "And if you weren't aware, they count it from your last period, not from conception. I'm just telling you in case you do the maths, realise we had sex thirteen weeks ago, and try to claim it can't be yours."

"Oh." I nod. "Right." I don't know what to say to that, but honestly, I'd no idea that's how a pregnancy term was measured. Every day is a school day.

"I'm a week further along than Emily," Grace adds.

"Aye? That's kind of . . . funny. There were only six days between me and Ally, and now I'm due to become a da a week before him. That's pretty crazy."

We lapse into silence for a while. There are probably a thousand different things I should be asking—this is such a massive, life-changing event—but my mind has gone blank. I'm at a loss what to say.

"I'm keeping the baby." The words come out of the blue, unprompted, answering my unspoken first question. "And I know you're not cut out to be a father, Aidan. I'll be doing this by myself."

I scratch my cheek. "Aye, well, Emily and David live here so you'll be coming to visit, and Bannock isn't big enough for us to avoid each other. Like it or not, Grace, I'll be a part of the bairn's life."

I give her a moment for this to sink in then add, "I suppose we just have to be sensible about this. If there are things you need from me, tell me. Like . . . what about child maintenance? Honestly, I don't know how that works or how much it is, but whatever I'm supposed to pay, I'll pay."

Obviously, I don't mention that with the business still being new, and with my plans to move out, it's not exactly the best timing. Instead, remembering what Maw said, I try to think about things from Grace's point of view.

"I'm sorry you felt you had to keep this from Emily and David. Have you told anyone in London, like your mum?"

"She's the last person I want to tell."

"Oh."

Subtly glancing at Grace's belly, I imagine the being growing in there—half me, half her. A sudden current of panic tugs at me but I resist its pull. I can't be selfish about this. As Maw pointed out, this is harder for Grace than it is for me. And yet . . . this just isn't how I saw my life going.

"We should probably get to know each other better," I say. "I mean, seeing as we're having a baby together."

"I'm travelling back to London tonight." She says it dismissively, like it makes my suggestion an impossibility.

Despite my nerves, I smile. "Damn, if only there were a way to talk to someone who's in a different place than you."

Grace snorts. "Are you really suggesting we try long-distance dating?"

"Whoa, whoa, whoa!" I throw my hands up in protest, my nervous smile twisting into a grin. "Who said anything about dating? No offence, but I was just meaning . . . chatting."

She doesn't respond straight away, her forehead crinkling as she considers this. "I suppose we could talk," she says eventually. "I'm glad we clarified it's not dating because I've no interest in that. I've decided to focus all my attention on myself and the baby." She glances down, a hand sliding to her belly.

"All right, cool. We'll talk."

This child won't have a traditional family but I reckon they might just be lucky to have Grace for a mother. She already seems to care deeply about the bairn, even though she won't meet them for another six months.

CHAPTER TWELVE

GRACE

I'm in my usual spot in the flat, sitting on my bed, back against the headboard. It's the middle of November, so rather than sitting on the duvet, I'm under it, with the covers pulled up to my armpits. The heating is on but I'm cosy like this. I've been devouring a romantasy novel all evening—it's so good—but reaching the end of a chapter, I wake the tablet beside me to check the time.

Seven fifty-eight. Two minutes until my call with Aidan.

I set aside my book then open the device's camera in selfie mode. I take out my scrunchy and redo my hair, fixing my spiral curls atop my head. Should I put on some lip gloss?

No, that'd be silly. I'm not trying to impress him—I'm only doing these calls because he asked. Although . . . I have come to look forward to them. Since I was in Bannock, we've spoken once a week and today will be our fifth call. I'd suspected Aidan might lose his initial enthusiasm but no, he's surprised me. And actually, our chats are fun and make me feel like I'm not entirely alone on this journey.

I come out from under my duvet then grab my pillows and

prop the tablet on top of them. No sooner have I moved into a cross-legged pose than it rings.

Eight o'clock. Right on time, as always.

I tap to accept and Aidan appears against a background of a stunning sandy beach. The water is a deep blue and the sun is blazing in the sky. He grins at me then turns and shields his gaze, as if checking out the view.

I roll my eyes but can't quite suppress a chuckle. "Wow," I say drily, playing along. "I didn't realise the beaches in Scotland were like that at this time of year. And at night!"

"It's bonny, eh?" He faces me again, his eyes sparkling, their colour enhanced by the sea and the sky. He taps a button and the background disappears. "Ha! Believe it or not, I'm not actually at the beach, just my maw's place. That was my wee way of introducing today's topic: travel!"

For each of our calls, Aidan has come up with a theme to guide the conversation, in case it trails off, I suppose. After all, apart from our best friends being engaged, we don't know each other very well. We've never let the topic constrain us, though, and anyway, Aidan has this way of putting me at ease so that talking with him feels effortless and natural. As a pick-up artist, calming a woman's nerves is probably one of his skills.

"Travel?" I scoff. "That's hardly fair! You spent years travelling the world. I've not visited nearly as many places."

"Well, it can be places you've been or places you want to go. It can even be places that don't exist. Always wanted to receive a letter from Hogwarts? Now is your chance to tell me about it."

"Ha! I may not be a seasoned traveller but don't worry, I've got some material. I shouldn't need to resort to fictional locations. Anyway, you go first, travel man."

Aidan and I swap stories. He tells me about teaching

outdoor sports in faraway places like New Zealand and Australia, while I share some memories of holidays in Europe. I recount one of my favourite tales, about the time David attempted a bit of Spanish in a bar while chatting a guy up and got *años* and *anos* mixed up.

"It was an easy mistake to make," I say, "but instead of asking the man how old he was—or literally, how many years he had—David asked him how many anuses he had."

Aidan throws back his head and barks out a laugh. "Ha, brilliant! I take it that scared the guy off?"

"Actually . . . no. It got the two of them talking and led to a holiday romance."

"Wow!" Aidan scratches his chin. "I consider myself an expert of the pick-up line but that's a new one for me. Next time I'm on the prowl, I'll try asking a woman how many anuses she has and let you know how I get on."

I shake my head, stifling a smile. It's a stupid joke and yet somehow, thanks to his charm, Aidan gets away with it.

"Of all the places you've visited, where was the most beautiful?" I ask.

"Hmm, it's cheesy, but honestly? The Highlands." Aidan shrugs. "I loved travelling but nowhere won over my heart more than home."

"That *is* cheesy but it's nice you live somewhere you love so much, and Bannock is pretty special."

Aidan nods. "Anyway, how have you been feeling this week?"

"I'm doing well. The morning sickness has stopped and my appetite has returned. My energy has too—I'm less tired in the evenings."

"You're eighteen weeks now, right? Are you showing yet?"

"If I wear something tight."

"Really? Can I see the bump?"

"Er . . ." I glance down at my loose-fitting hoodie. I could lift it up—I've got a top on underneath—but would that set a dangerous precedent? We agreed at the start these chats would be purely platonic, and I'm not sure I like the idea of removing clothing on Aidan's command.

"Hey, it's my son or daughter you're growing in there. Go on, show me!"

I tilt my head to the side. I've half a mind to tell him that if he wants to see my belly, he'll have to flash me his abs. Thankfully, I catch myself. No, that would not be appropriate. Between his attractive features and charismatic manner, it would be all too easy to develop feelings for Aidan. I have to be careful to maintain the boundaries we've established.

"Please!" Aidan pleads. "I'm missing out by being up here. If I were in London and saw you in a tight top, I'd see your bump, so really, it's only fair you show me on video." He pauses then adds, "Although, obviously, don't do anything you don't want to do. I'm just saying I'd like to see it, if that's okay."

"Oh, all right." I stand and adjust the tablet so I'm side-on to Aidan. A little self-consciously, I pull my hoodie up, exposing the lower part of my now curved and protruding stomach.

"Wow, you really are showing!"

"Thanks for that." I tug the hoodie back down then return to the bed. "It's still a small bump. It's only going to get bigger."

"Hey, I didn't mean it as a bad thing. You look good! Pregnancy suits you."

I bite the inside of my cheek to stop myself from smiling.

Keep it together, Grace. Don't let a simple compliment break down your walls.

"Is our pregnancy scandal still the talk of Bannock?" I ask, moving the conversation along, not wanting to dwell on how nice it felt for Aidan to say I looked good.

"Of course, but that's what small towns are like. Have you told your maw yet?"

My stomach tightens. "Nope."

He frowns. "Just as well I'm not a judgemental guy or I might have something to say about that. As you said, the bump is only going to get bigger. You won't be able to hide it forever."

"Well, it's a good thing you're not a judgemental guy because I wouldn't want you sticking your nose in and telling me how to handle my mum."

He smirks and holds up his hands in defeat. "Noted! Although I think I've found my topic for next week's call: family!" He winks.

"Oh, yeah? Bring it on! So long as you're prepared to answer some tough questions about your family."

"Ha! It'll clearly be a more contentious topic than travel, but since we've got five getting-to-know-you calls under our belts, I reckon we're ready for some more challenging subjects."

"Agreed. And for the week after that, we could go even more controversial, like . . . former partners!" I wince. "Oh, wait, it has to be something we can talk about in an hour, doesn't it? That might be difficult for you as by all accounts you've slept with more women than I've read books—and I'm a voracious reader."

Aidan chuckles and runs a hand through his hair. "You know, Grace, on first impressions you're a sweet lass, a yoga teacher who's in touch with nature and full of love for all around her. Now I've got to know you better, though, I've discovered you can be feisty when you want to."

We lock eyes and there's a mischievous glint in Aidan's gaze. To my great annoyance, my heart rate quickens.

He's the first to look away, towards the corner of his screen. "Our hour's almost up."

"Same time next week?"

"Aye, or we could continue talking? I'm game for bending the rules if you are."

The rules he's referring to are ones I came up with before our first call. I told Aidan I was happy to speak to him once a week for an hour max. I think it's important for us to have clearly defined boundaries.

"No, let's stick to what we agreed, yeah?"

Aidan's smile falters—just for a moment, but infuriatingly, that fleeting glimpse of vulnerability tugs at my heartstrings.

"Having said that," I add, unable to help myself, "my next scan is coming up. If you and Ally have bookings you can't get out of, that's fine. Plus, I know it's a long way to travel for an appointment so there's no obligation, but if you like, next week, instead of a video call, we could meet in London? You can see the baby on the monitor, and we should be able to find out whether it's a boy or a girl."

"Really?" Aidan sits up straighter, his grin back to full force. "I'd love that."

I'm touched by his eagerness. I just hope I don't regret this.

CHAPTER THIRTEEN

GRACE

GRACE

Where are you?

After going by myself to my last scan, I was looking forward to having Aidan with me today. But he's nowhere to be seen, and once again, I'm the only expectant mother in the busy waiting area who hasn't brought along someone for support.

AIDAN

Not far! Count to 1000 and I'll be there.

GRACE

I'm not counting to 1000! Anyway, I'm pretty sure I'm next. They'll be calling me any minute.

AIDAN

All right, I'll count for you. 1, 2, 3 . . . actually, scrap that, here I am!

Aidan strolls in, bag slung over one shoulder, phone still in his hand. His azure-blue eyes search the room until they meet mine then his lips curve into a smile. He strides over, his long jeans-clad legs eating up the space between us. Just for a moment my heart melts at the sight of him, but before he reaches me, I harden it again.

"You're cutting it fine!"

He shows no sign of being bothered by my tone. In fact, he looks truly pleased to see me, and the way his gaze sweeps over every detail of my appearance sends a ripple of self-consciousness through me. If I'm honest with myself, there's a spark of excitement too. I don't entirely dislike his attention.

"Aye, well, I did come from the Highlands for this. It was a bit of a trek. Anyway, I had you down as a hugger!" He throws his arms wide.

"Grace Adefope?" a voice calls.

"Here!" I stand. "All right, Aidan, that's us. Let's go."

I use the interruption as an excuse to avoid a hug and follow the woman who called my name. She introduces herself as Ruth and explains she'll be our sonographer for the appointment.

As much as I want to concentrate on the present moment, I can't help but worry about Aidan. It was hard enough resisting his charm on the video calls; I hadn't appreciated how much more difficult it would be in real life. He's only just arrived and already his magnetic presence is threatening my resolve. But that's what he does—he picks up women—and I can't be taken in by it. It wouldn't be fair on me or the baby.

Ruth leads us into a dimly lit room then indicates for me to lie on the bed. Aidan takes the nearby chair, sitting so close to me I can smell the Highlands off him, like he's just strolled through a forest.

Pulling some blue paper from a dispenser, Ruth comes to my side. "Can you lift your top for me, Grace?"

Pretending Aidan isn't right next to me, watching everything, I tug up my white smock-style top, revealing my lower abdomen.

"Good, and bring your leggings down a little more. That's it."

My cheeks warm as the top of my bikini line is exposed. Ruth tucks the paper into my leggings to protect them from the cold gel, which she applies next.

I glance at Aidan and see he's observing the proceedings with interest, although I do catch his gaze briefly shifting to my breasts. They've grown since I got pregnant and apparently he's noticed. Of course he has.

Ruth moves the ultrasound probe over my belly, concentrating on the screen. There's just a long enough wait for me to worry there might be a problem, but then she smiles.

"There we go!" She adjusts the monitor so Aidan and I can see the black-and-white image. The rapid and steady thump of a heartbeat fills the room.

Aidan leans in for a better view. "Wow, so that's our bairn?"

Ruth titters. Surely she's not blushing because of Aidan's smooth and melodic accent? "That's your child, yes."

A large warm hand finds one of mine and squeezes it. I glance at Aidan in surprise but his attention remains fixed on the screen. Has he even realised he's touching me, or is he so wrapped up in the moment he doesn't know what he's doing? I'm not sure I should allow it, but then again, we are having a baby together. Shouldn't we be able to hold hands as we look at an image of our child?

Ruth points out all the major organs and takes measurements. I don't withdraw from Aidan's touch.

"Everything is as it should be at this stage. Would you like to know the sex?"

"Yes," I say.

"All right, but just so you're aware, we can never confirm it with one hundred per cent certainty. That's our little disclaimer! If you choose to paint the nursery one colour and buy lots of clothes in that colour, and then the baby isn't the sex you were expecting, you don't get to sue us, I'm afraid. That being said"—her lips twitch into a smile—"I'm pretty sure you're having a girl."

My heart flutters. Aidan's strong hand squeezes mine again. I turn to him, and this time, our eyes meet. He grins and I do too.

◆ ◆ ◆

It's already dark when we leave the clinic and there's a chill in the air.

"That was really something." Aidan walks by my side. "Hearing her heartbeat, seeing her up on the screen, it made it all seem so . . . real."

"Real and a bit scary, right?"

"Oh, absolutely terrifying, and I'm not the one who has to carry her for another five months or push her out. How are you doing?"

"Yeah, scared, but excited too."

I cross Magdala Avenue, a narrow tree-lined street with cars parked along both sides. Aidan follows.

"This is where I get the bus." I nod to my stop then glance at his rucksack. "Have you booked into a hotel? I wasn't sure if you were going straight back up to Bannock, but if you've got time, we could grab something to eat and have our next getting-to-know-you chat in person?"

I know it's important to respect the boundaries I've set, but I can do dinner. Aidan travelled all the way down here, after all.

Confusion creases his forehead. "Ah. This is awkward. See, when you invited me here, I thought . . . well, I thought I'd be staying with you. So no, I've not booked into a hotel."

"*What?*" I sink onto the bus shelter's bench, taking this in. "Jesus, Aidan! You can't just assume you'll be staying with someone."

"Sorry. Obviously, I misunderstood."

I shake my head. "How long are you going to be in London for?"

"Er, I've not bought my ticket back yet. Outdoor activities are seasonal and this is the off season. Unless you're into skiing, of course, but that's never been my thing. Ally and I have a couple of guided winter hikes booked, but in general I've got time on my hands so . . . I thought I could help out with a few things—you know, stuff the bairn will need?"

"There's really not a lot you can do before the baby comes, and I'm sorry, but my place is a box. It's barely big enough for one person, let alone two."

"No room on the sofa?" he asks hopefully. "I did a fair bit of sofa surfing when travelling. I'm used to it."

"I don't even have a sofa!" I fidget with my hands. This situation is making me deeply uncomfortable.

"Oh . . . right. How about the floor, then?"

He gives me a puppy-dog look. Jeez, isn't he supposed to be a player? How does a man with as much experience as him in the bedroom pull off such an endearing expression? I blame his baby blues.

I grimace. "I really don't like you springing this on me. You should have asked me beforehand."

Doesn't he understand why I've been putting limits on our interactions? I only agreed to one call a week. I can hardly go from that to letting him stay with me!

And yet it's dark and cold, and he doesn't have anywhere to go. Maybe he could find a hotel room online? Then again, he did come all the way down here for the scan, and it was a long journey from Bannock. Isn't offering him a bit of floor space the least I can do?

Oh God, I'm such a pushover. I'm probably going to regret this, but I say, "I doubt you'll be comfortable, but if you want to sleep on my floor, you can—*for one night only*. From tomorrow, if you plan to hang about in London, you'll have to find somewhere else. All right?"

Aidan's answering smile cracks through the defences I'm hurriedly trying to re-establish, weakening my knees. I'm glad I'm sitting down.

"Deal."

CHAPTER FOURTEEN

AIDAN

"Wow, you weren't lying when you said your flat is small." I kick off my shoes and place the Japanese takeaway bag on the table. Kneeling, I tap the laminate floor. "So, this is my bed for a night or two?"

"For a night!" Grace pulls on a pair of fluffy pink slippers. "And I did warn you there wasn't much room."

"You did, although I notice it's a double bed." I wiggle my eyebrows at her.

She's only just closed the door but she opens it again. "Good luck finding a hotel. Bye!"

I chuckle and raise my hands in surrender. "I'm only kidding. The floor looks perfect."

Forming a V with two fingers, she points at her eyes and then to me. She closes the door, washes her hands at the kitchen sink, then sits at the table. Plucking her bowl of ramen from the bag, she removes the lid and inhales deeply. "Ah! It smells amazing. When you're tired, it's so nice not having to cook."

At first we'd planned to sit in at a restaurant, but Grace was flagging so we agreed on takeaway instead—my treat.

I wash my hands too then take a couple of glasses down from a shelf and fill them. I join her at the table, which is tiny with hardly any space under it, and I've got long legs.

"Aidan! Please don't brush up against me. I don't want to play footsie with you."

"Sorry, it's just . . . a bit cramped." I push my chair back. "There. Better?"

She nods, collecting her chopsticks from the bag and passing me mine too, along with my ramen. "Better. Although now I feel bad because you're too far from the table, and that'll make eating difficult. Oh, come back to where you were. If our knees touch, it's not the end of the world. I mean, you've put your penis inside me before, so—"

"Bloody hell!" I splutter. I'd just taken a big gulp of water and it goes down the wrong way. Coughing, I pat my chest. "Shit, I'm sorry, but I wasn't expecting you to say that. It took me by surprise."

Grace's lips curl upwards. "It was a bit blunt, wasn't it? Then again, I'm pregnant, and in a few months I'll have to push out our baby. That's hardly going to be glamorous so why beat about the bush? Your penis *has* been inside me."

"Er . . . aye, you're right, it has." I scratch behind my ear, my cheeks warming.

I don't get embarrassed about sex—it's far from a taboo topic for me—and yet Grace's casual references to my cock catch me off-guard. But soon the initial shock fades and that's when laughter bubbles up in my chest. I can't contain it: it bursts out.

"Oh God, please tell me you're not some immature schoolboy who giggles every time the sex-ed teacher says 'penis'?"

"I didn't think I was! I'm a thirty-year-old man with a well-developed sense of humour. And yet . . . you keep on saying it, and it keeps on making me laugh."

She shakes her head. "So much for your reputation as a ladies' man. This is the real you, isn't it? No maturity whatsoever. I'm not even surprised. Anyway, scoot back in and eat your food."

Letting out a final chuckle, I do as she instructs, drawing closer to the table again, our knees inevitably touching. But it's fine. In fact, the incident has broken the ice. It wouldn't have been relaxing to spend the evening at a distance from her, careful never to accidentally brush against her. It's better to be as we are now, laughing and not worrying about the odd bit of contact. After all, aye, we've agreed things are to be platonic between us, but friends can still hug and show affection through light touches, right?

I lift the lid of my ramen and steam rises in soft curls, its spicy scent tickling my nose. "This does smell incredible. And, mmm, it tastes good too."

I can get by with chopsticks but Grace is defter with them than me. She's also not self-conscious about slurping the hot broth so I don't hold back either.

"Talking of good food," I say after chewing down some noodles, "my maw said when she was pregnant with me, I'd go wild in her belly whenever she ate chocolate. Have you noticed anything like that?"

Grace shakes her head. "No. I haven't actually felt her move yet, so it was a relief when the sonographer told us everything is okay. Most mums feel movement by twenty-four weeks so it should be coming soon."

"Oh, right. And is that when I'll be able to feel her kick?"

Her eyebrows snap up. "You're assuming I'll let you put your hand on my belly, are you?"

I nudge her leg with my knee. "Won't you? I'd like to feel our baby."

"Hmm." She nudges me back. "Let's cross that bridge when we come to it. Anyway, it's normally a few weeks more before others can feel the movements."

I take some more ramen. "Do you remember the sonographer's warning about making everything pink?" I glance around the tiny room. "What colour *will* we paint the nursery?"

"Oh, don't!" She stamps on my toes with a soft, fluffy slipper.

"Ow! Maybe I'd be safer back where I was."

"Probably, but you deserved it. I'm already worried about how I'll cope with a baby in here. I could do without you stressing me out even more."

It's clear she's genuinely upset about it so I immediately switch gears. "Sorry, I was only teasing. Look, you'll be able to fit a cot over there, and babies don't need much space anyway. Sure, you get a lot more for your money in the Highlands, but you're paying to be in London, in the midst of everything. You're in a nice spot. You and the baby will be just fine here."

"Do you really think so?"

"Aye, I do."

Her shoulders lower and her brow smooths. "Good. Anyway, talking of babies, are you ready to move on to today's topic?"

I blink. "What do you mean?"

"You haven't forgotten, have you? On our last call you said we'd talk about family this week. Sure, we're seeing each other in person rather than by video, but I reckon we should stick to the schedule. Does that work for you?"

I drink some broth, mulling this over, then grin. "All right. Let's do it."

"Great. I'll ask the first question. Hmm, okay, I'll start with an easy one. You and Iona are pretty different. What was it like growing up with her?"

"We got on well, but aye, we're opposites in some ways. When I was a teenager, Maw was always trying to get me to take my exams more seriously. She wanted me to spend less time outdoors and more time reading and revising. But Iona always had her head in a book, so Maw was forever suggesting she put it down and try experiencing the world first-hand. When Iona wasn't reading, she was hanging out with Lewis."

"As in Lewis McIntyre, Ally's brother?"

"Aye. The pair of them were inseparable growing up, the same way me and Ally were. Everyone thought they'd end up together—it seemed inevitable—but instead they're barely even friends now. I'm sure something happened between them to cause a rift, though I've no idea what. Iona and I talk about a lot of things but not relationships. She doesn't want to know who I've been sleeping with, and I don't pry into her love life.

"Anyway, what about you and David? Having a twin is a pretty special connection, isn't it?"

Grace nods and sets aside her chopsticks, done with her food. "It is. As a child, I was never lonely because my brother was my friend. We've always been close. I doubt many people would move back in with a sibling in their late twenties, but that's what David and I did almost two years ago and it worked well. When he moved to Bannock, it was a massive change and I really do miss him."

Grace talks a while longer about David, happy memories mainly, although she confesses her mother has always been harder on her than him and that has come with its challenges.

"That's why I haven't rushed to tell her, even though David is constantly on at me, saying I need to. It's like, in Mum's eyes, David can do no wrong but I can never do anything right. I can already picture her disappointment when she finds out. She'll make me feel awful—I know she will—so . . . it's easier to keep it a secret. Of course, I'll have to tell her at some point, but right now I don't need negativity and judgement. Pregnancy is hard enough without her making it harder."

"Shit. I'm sorry." For a moment I hesitate, then I reach out and squeeze her shoulder.

I half expect her to slap my hand away or at least tell me to keep it to myself. Instead she accepts the gesture as it was intended, as an offering of support.

"Well, seeing as you're to become a father, let's talk about dads. Mine has never been a part of my life. How about yours?"

"Och, I grew up with my da, but he's now in Inverness with his new woman and my half-brother, Archie."

In a matter-of-fact tone, I tell her about how Archie was born while Da was still living in Bannock with me, Maw, and Iona. None of us, I say, had any idea Da was keeping secrets from us.

That's not quite true but I rarely share the whole story. I decide to keep a few details to myself, at least for now.

◆ ◆ ◆

Yawning, Grace comes out of the bathroom in fluffy pink pyjamas that match her slippers, plus a silk headscarf.

It's only just gone nine, but Grace is tired and I had to get up at the arse crack of dawn to travel down from Bannock. We agreed to hit the hay early.

I tugged off my jeans and socks while Grace was brushing her teeth, and now her gaze trails from my T-shirt down to my boxer briefs.

"Jesus, Aidan! Don't you have pyjamas?"

"Hey, I'm trying my best to be proper here." I scratch my arm. "Normally, I sleep naked."

She pulls a face. "How considerate of you. But really, come on, they don't leave much to the imagination." She waves in the direction of my crotch.

"Are you being serious?" I laugh. "Sorry I'm not some genital-less Ken doll! And I don't think I've worn pyjamas since I was twelve but maybe I'm missing out. Yours look cosy." I hold out my arms. "Night-time hug?"

"Nope. That bulge isn't going anywhere near me, thank you very much. We agreed this would be platonic." She grabs one of the pillows off her bed and throws it my way. "For you. And here, have these too." She takes a couple of thick blankets from a cupboard and drops them on the floor.

"Cheers." I sort them into a makeshift bed then settle into it. I try to get myself comfortable but I'm not sure that's going to be possible. Her floor is cool and hard.

"Will you be all right down there?" There's a crack in Grace's voice, a hint of concern.

"If I say no, do I get to jump in with you?"

"Forget it. Night, Aidan." She switches off the light.

CHAPTER FIFTEEN

GRACE

The darkness of my flat is interrupted only by a faint sliver of light sneaking in through a gap in the curtains from a lamppost outside. I don't know how long I've been lying here on my bed but I've still not slept. On the floor Aidan changes position yet again.

"Will you stop tossing and turning?" I whisper. "You're keeping me awake!" I held my tongue for as long as I could but I can't take it anymore. I've got work tomorrow.

"Oh, shit, sorry," he murmurs. "I thought you'd fallen asleep ages ago." More quiet shuffling. "It's just . . . I can't get comfortable. And it's cold down here."

I don't reply straight away. Eventually I say, "Please don't misinterpret this but it *is* a double bed. You can come in so long as you understand it's only to sleep. Nothing else, all right?"

Aidan sits up. I can just about discern his outline in the dim room.

"Are you sure?"

"Yes, but if you give me any longer to think it over, I might change my mind."

That's all the encouragement he needs. He stands, pads over, then slips under the duvet.

"Bloody hell!" I squeak when his bare leg brushes mine. "You really are cold."

"Aye, and you're all lovely and warm." He's on his side, facing me. "And your jammies are just as soft as I thought they'd be. Can I snuggle up to you?"

"Right, back on the floor, now!"

"I'm only joking. I'll keep my distance, I promise." He turns his back to me and settles. Within minutes his breathing becomes slow and steady.

Has he drifted off already? No way. I'm jealous. I've never been able to nod off that quickly.

I fixate on the silhouette of Aidan's strong shoulders as they rise and fall with each breath. Once I'm sure he's in a deep sleep, I wriggle closer, tucking my knees up behind his so we're touching, just. I close my eyes and relax.

I'm loath to admit this, and I'd never tell Aidan, but as much as I've thrived on being independent the last couple of years, the truth is there's something comforting about a man's presence in my bed. It makes me feel . . . safe.

With my body nestled against his, sleep finally finds me too.

◆ ◆ ◆

When I wake up, a weak morning light is spilling into the room. I rub at my bleary eyes then freeze when I hear a man's guttural grunts. Turning my head, I see Aidan is no longer in the bed beside me.

More grunting, low and primal. The floor creaks.

Oh God. Given Aidan's large number of former partners,

he obviously has a high sex drive. But surely he's not "seeing" to that, is he?

With a mixture of trepidation and, I'll admit, curiosity, I peek over the side of the bed, only to spy Aidan's boxer-brief-clad arse going up and down. His back is bare and taut, his T-shirt discarded, his broad shoulders and biceps contracting and flexing in a steady rhythm. With every upward push, a deep growl escapes his lips.

"Oh! You're doing press-ups."

He sinks to his knees then shifts into a seated position, stretching his long legs out in front of him, slightly apart, and leaning back on his hands. There's a rosy hue to his cheeks, and his chest and abs glisten with sweat. For a moment I'm transported to the engagement party, memories of our entwined bodies flooding my mind.

"Morning," Aidan says between breaths. "Aye, just doing my pre-breakfast workout." His face scrunches up. "Wait, what did you think I was doing?"

"Oh . . . er . . ."

I can't stop my eyes from drifting to his sculpted underwear. I objected to them last night and I stand by my comments. They're obscene! I mean, everything is *right there*, behind a very thin layer of material, and yet he's not self-conscious in the slightest. Am I just a prude?

Aidan follows my gaze then looks back up at me, his mouth twisting into a grin. "What did you think I was doing?" he repeats, more insistent this time.

"Nothing," I mumble.

He climbs to his feet and does a few stretches in front of me. "Say it, Grace!"

I'm still on the bed so his bulge is now at my eye level. He's playing with me. Clearly.

I turn away, heat creeping up my neck. "I'm not saying it, and could you *please* put that thing away?"

"You're too easy to wind up." Aidan chuckles. "Be honest with me: you thought I was masturbating, didn't you? You have such a low opinion of me."

"I . . . er . . . how about you go for a shower then put some clothes on? Please!"

"Aye, or maybe we could do our bit for the environment and shower together? We've only got one planet, Grace."

I glance at his grinning face then look away again. I know he's teasing but blood still rushes to my cheeks. "Could you pass me something so I can throw it at you? All I've got here is a pillow and that's not hard enough."

"Ha! All right, I get the message. I'm going to the bathroom. No need to get violent."

He leaves, and moments later the water turns on. Aidan hums to himself while he washes. I get up and make the bed then fold the blankets I gave him last night. As I do, I remember there's no lock on the bathroom door. It'd be the easiest thing in the world to walk in on him right now. I sent him away so I didn't have to be near his almost-naked body, but was that because I didn't want to see it or because I was worried about the effect it was having on me?

Aidan is an attractive man and he's in great shape—there's no point denying that. And while we've already slept together, that was fast and intense and offered no opportunity to properly explore and appreciate his physical form. Heat floods through me as I imagine going into the bathroom. How would he react?

He doesn't seem to know the meaning of modesty so I'm

sure he wouldn't shy away from my gaze. No, he'd let me admire him for as long as I liked. More than that, he'd invite me to remove my pyjamas and join him under the water—he's already joked about it. Sex in the shower with Aidan . . .

Desire courses through my body and my limbs tremble with a jittery energy. God, what is wrong with me? I have to put a lid on these feelings. They're what got me into this situation. I'm excited about becoming a mother, but I have to be more careful from now on. My daughter deserves to have a positive relationship with both her parents, and she should see us interacting in a mature, amicable way. That's only going to happen if we keep this platonic. Aidan is a womaniser—he doesn't do commitment. If we bring sex back into this, things will only get messy.

I pop on the kettle then slide some bread into the toaster and look out butter and marmalade. I set the table for two and am just placing down a pile of toast when Aidan comes out, a white towel wrapped around him, his wet skin glistening, his hair tousled and damp. A droplet of water trickles from his chest down to his abs then disappears from view. A waft of my own mint shower gel hits me.

"Sorry, I'm just grabbing some fresh clothes." He reaches for his bag, his muscles flexing enticingly.

Jesus.

"I've moved on to a morning tea since I got pregnant," I say, trying to distract myself. "Would you prefer a coffee?"

"If you don't mind, that'd be perfect. I'll pop these on then be right out."

A minute later he emerges in jeans and a T-shirt. I've just sat at the table and he joins me.

"Oh, wow! Marmalade, nice. London's most famous bear would approve."

I can't help but giggle. "You've got some funny references, Aidan. You know that, right?"

"How so?"

"Well, you've got a reputation as a ladies' man. I'm not sure mentioning beloved children's characters really fits with that image."

He tuts and shakes his head. "I don't see why not. Who doesn't love Paddington? Those stories were great. We'll need to read them to our wee lass."

My heart flutters, though not with desire, as earlier, but with something else altogether.

It won't be easy navigating parenthood with Aidan. For a start, we live on opposite ends of the country—that alone complicates things. But although I'd never have expected it, Aidan may actually make an okay dad. I won't know until the time comes, of course, but there's been the odd hint here and there. His insistence on the video calls. His attendance at the scan. And . . . his familiarity with Paddington Bear.

I didn't grow up with a father figure in my life but maybe my daughter will. I'd like that.

Aidan grabs a piece of toast, spreads on butter, slathers on marmalade, then munches on it. "Mmm, so good."

"The coffee is just instant, I'm afraid."

"That's okay." He takes a swig. "Anyway, a question for you: have you always snored or is that a pregnancy thing?"

"Excuse me?" I nearly choke on my tea. "I don't snore!"

He pulls a face. "Right, except . . . I just slept in the same bed as you and you were definitely snoring."

"Well, I . . ." I don't know what to say so instead I kick him under the table.

"Ow! You're vicious!" Aidan's loud laugh echoes around the small room. "Don't get me wrong, it was quiet, lady-like snoring. Very cute."

I scowl at him. "I can only assume your chat is better when you're picking up women. Otherwise, it's a miracle you're not a virgin."

"Ha! Good one." He grins happily. "You're pretty fun, Grace. I enjoy hanging out with you."

"Yeah? Well, you won't be able to for much longer." I glance at the clock on the wall. "I've got classes today and need to go soon. What are your plans?"

"Oh, I'll take in some sights. I've also heard there's a great yoga teacher around these parts." He winks and takes another sip of coffee. "Maybe I'll check out one of her classes."

"Well, that might be tricky because she's very popular and her classes get booked up in advance. Did you consider that?"

"Hmm, I've an in with the instructor so I reckon I'll be all right. Besides, a few months back I wanted to do yoga with her in Bannock but Ally wouldn't let me."

That is true. One day when I was up visiting Emily, Ally was stressed out so I put on an informal class. Aidan had asked to join but Ally refused on account of his broken wrist, so it ended up just being me, Ally, and Emily—and the two of them couldn't keep their eyes off each other the entire time.

"I suppose I'll also have to hunt for somewhere to stay," Aidan adds. "It's such a shame, though. I mean, with a baby on the way, I should be saving up but hotels in London are so expensive . . ."

"Aidan!" I warn.

A sly smile tugs at the corners of his mouth. "Was sharing your bed with me really so bad?"

It wasn't, actually, but I don't tell him that. Despite the constant teasing and at times minimal clothing, Aidan proved he can, in fact, be trusted not to make a move. It's my own traitorous body I'm worried about. If I spend any more time around him when he's in nothing but underwear or a towel, I may succumb to temptation.

"Look, how about instead of giving money to a hotel, I give it to you?" Aidan suggests. "You could use the cash to buy stuff for the baby."

"Aidan, I was clear it was for one night only."

"You were." He nods. "But . . . let's be honest, I'm down here to get to know you. If you're working during the day then chilling in the flat at night, too tired to go out, it'll be hard for me to do that. Unless . . . I chill here with you."

The infuriating thing is, he's got a point. And a bit of extra money would be handy.

I drum my fingers on the table, thinking. "I may live to regret this but . . . if you're going to be staying, we need some ground rules."

Aidan perks up. "I'm all ears."

"Rule one: no wandering about in your underwear. While I'm at work, go out and buy yourself a nice pyjama set."

Aidan raises a brow and lets out a soft chuckle. "Fine. If that's what I have to do, that's what I'll do. What else?"

"No waking me up with grunting, even for workouts. I'm a pregnant woman and I need my sleep. That was rule two, and you already know rule three but I'll repeat it: no making a move. This"—I point between him and me—"is platonic. Got it?"

"Got it." He throws his arms wide. "Let's platonically hug on it."

"No. The phrase is 'let's shake on it'." I hold out my hand.

Smirking, he grasps it in agreement.

CHAPTER SIXTEEN

GRACE

I climb the stairs to my flat, fuming with Aidan. I'll have to have a word with him.

He came along to my early-afternoon yoga class. It turns out when you're a tall handsome Highlander in his prime, surrounded by twenty-eight women in a studio—and a couple of middle-aged men—it's impossible to go unnoticed. In his form-fitting navy sports top and black shorts, he'd been a distraction. Rather than focusing on my instructions, several of my clients had kept stealing glances at him. And to make matters worse, he'd lapped up the attention, grinning and winking whenever he caught one of them looking.

What annoys me even more—although this annoyance is focused inwards—is I also found it difficult to keep my eyes off him. Each time he pulled a pose, even if his form wasn't quite right, he exuded this aura of strength and power. Normally, yoga is a source of peace for me, but not only did Aidan's presence disrupt the flow of that class, it threw me off my game for the rest of the day.

Reaching my door, I have to knock since Aidan has my

keys. Footsteps pad my way, then the door opens and there he stands, his tall and broad figure filling the doorway.

"There you are! Just in time."

Oh, that bloody Highland accent, thick as honey and just as sweet to my ears. I was all set to give him what for. How come my resolve is already fading?

"Just in time for what?"

Before he answers, a rich, savoury smell hits me: the comforting scent of simmering soup, combined with smoked fish and the decadent aroma of heated butter and milk.

"Cullen skink!" he announces proudly.

"Cullen what?"

"Cullen skink. It's a Scottish dish and is just what you need when the days draw in and it's getting colder. Smoked haddock, potatoes, onion, butter, milk—boom! It's so good. Come in! Get your slippers on. I'll serve up."

He hurries back to the tiny portable stove and stirs a pot. I'm too thrown to object so I do as he says, putting my slippers on and closing the door behind me. I quickly pop to the loo and am checking my reflection while washing my hands when I catch myself. What am I doing? I'm not trying to impress him.

Back out in the main room, I sit at the table, which Aidan has set. There's a hunk of crusty bread on my side plate.

"All right, here you go." Aidan places a steaming bowl in front of me.

The thick broth is light cream in colour. Large pieces of flaky white smoked haddock are mixed with chunks of potatoes, and it's topped with parsley.

I'm not normally a fan of fish soup and it seems a bold choice for Aidan to have made. I've got to admit, though, it looks and smells really appetising.

Aidan picks up his spoon. "Go on, tuck in!"

I do, and as soon as the soup hits my tongue, flavours explode in my mouth—the creamy richness of the broth, the buttery haddock, the earthy potatoes, and a burst of freshness from the parsley.

"This is *really* good," I admit. "I didn't know you could cook."

"Well, my maw is a chef. I've learnt a thing or two. Some days I don't have the patience to make something from scratch, but for a special occasion, always."

"Oh? And what's the special occasion this evening?"

A smile creeps onto his lips. "You're letting me stay in your flat? We're having a wee girl? It turns out I'm brilliant at yoga? Take your pick."

"Not the last one anyway. That was the worst class I've conducted in a long time. You were a distraction!"

"In what way?"

"You know exactly in what way. The flirting and the winking."

"Hey! It's not my fault I'm irresistible."

I glower at him. Yes, I don't want Aidan to make a move on me, but I also don't want to see him getting on so well with other women. I'm carrying his child, after all.

"On the topic of my irresistibility," Aidan continues, ignoring the daggers I'm shooting his way, "I bought myself some PJs, just like you asked."

"Good." I should be happy I won't be seeing him in his boxers anymore, so why this pang of disappointment? To take my mind off it, I have some more of the hearty, filling soup.

"So, now we know it's a wee lass, are there any names you like?"

This is something I've been mulling over today. Every time I greeted a female student, I found myself assessing her name to see if it'd be a good fit.

"Hmm, there are names I like but I want to find one that really resonates with me."

"We should go for something Scottish. There are some beautiful Gaelic names."

I purse my lips. "And what makes you think you get a say?"

"Er . . . because I'm her da?"

"Right, and you're her dad because we had sex—a short and pleasurable experience for you. As for me, I've had to deal with morning sickness, I'm tired all the time, I'm getting fat, and after carrying her for nine months, I'll have to push her out of me. Don't get me wrong, it's admirable you've come down here and are trying to get to know me—it's more than I expected—but don't go overstepping the mark. I will be making the decisions about my child. Understood?"

Maybe it's the pregnancy hormones, or maybe it's because I'm tired and out of sorts, but it's quite the put-down. I'm likely being too harsh, given Aidan has just made a lovely meal for me, but before I can apologise, his lips curl up.

"A protective mother already. I like that."

Ugh, I've just criticised him, and he likes that? This man is infuriating. It'd make things so much easier if he had a few really unattractive qualities. Apart from the whole addicted-to-sex-but-not-commitment thing, he's kind of perfect.

"Where did the name Grace come from?" he asks.

"Mum already had the name David picked out, but she wasn't sure about a girl's name. I suppose you could say she had a favourite before we were even born." I offer a wry smile. "Anyway, on the way to the hospital, the Judy Collins version of 'Amazing Grace' played on the radio so I became Grace."

"Nice, a great song, and you know what? I think you win over David there—your name has more of a story to it."

I finish my bowl and Aidan collects it, immediately starting on the dishes. He's not even a slob—that would have been something. But no, he knows how to keep a clean house.

"I spoke to Maw and Iona, by the way. They were excited to hear it's a girl. Maw actually got pretty teary."

"Your mother is sweet. I called Emily and David and filled them in. Emily's scan is in a week so she'll find out what she's having soon. And David was over the moon but . . . yet again, he begged me to tell Mum."

Aidan lifts his soap-sud-covered hands in a gesture of impartiality. "I'm saying nothing! You've already warned me not to overstep the mark so I'll keep my thoughts on that matter to myself."

"Probably wise but . . . you think I should tell her, right?"

"Oh, absolutely I do."

"Humph! So much for keeping your thoughts to yourself."

For a moment he goes wide-eyed, like he's worried I'm about to rip him a new one.

I smirk. "I can tease too, you know."

"Oh . . . aye, you can. Kind of." He gives me an amused sidelong glance. "With a bit of practice, you'll get there."

◆ ◆ ◆

"Well, what do you think?" Aidan emerges from the bathroom and models his charcoal-grey pyjama trousers with a matching long-sleeved top. He even does a spin.

To be fair to him, the set leaves very little skin on display and yet . . . he still looks good in it. He'd look good in anything.

"Hmm." I turn back to my book.

"Ouch! And here was me thinking this was my colour." He climbs into bed beside me and gets comfortable under the duvet, lacing his fingers behind his head and staring at the ceiling with a contented smile.

Ugh! If you compliment him, he smiles. If you criticise him, he smiles. If you ignore him, he smiles. It's maddening.

I can't cope with the sight of his perpetual grin so I close my book mid-chapter, which is a rare thing for me. "All right, lights out." I flick the switch and his features disappear, replaced only by a silhouette.

"Night!" he says cheerily.

I hold back a sigh. "Night."

He shifts onto his side, facing me. For a moment I wonder if something more is coming, if he might challenge rule three—not to make a move—but . . . no. He's just a side sleeper, like me.

I roll onto my side too, my back to him. Aidan has done a good job of obeying the rules I set, so . . . why am I disappointed?

Could it be it's not a case of chivalry or respecting my wishes? What if the plain and simple fact is he no longer finds me attractive? My body has changed these last few weeks, and yes, my boobs have got bigger—something he's definitely noticed—but so has the rest of me. And I'm only going to keep growing, unlike him, who'll remain flawless, as always.

Then again, there *have* been times I've caught his eyes roving over me when he thinks I'm not paying attention. Occasionally, even when I'm looking right at him, there's something in his blue-eyed gaze . . .

But he's a player. He knows how to make a woman feel "bonny". He'd probably stare at anyone like that.

The fact is, around me, he's not living up to his reputation. Apparently, it's the easiest thing in the world for him to lie next to me in a bed. Yesterday, when he climbed in, he was asleep within minutes. Chances are, he'll nod off again just as quickly tonight.

I set the rules because they're what's best for the child we're having together. It's not as if I'm not tempted by Aidan. I am! So how come he's not tempted by me? How come it's so damn easy for him to fall asleep while lying next to me?

An idea comes to me, and although it's probably the stupidest idea I've ever had, in a fit of pique I decide to act on it before I can talk myself out of it.

"I'm cold," I whisper. "This doesn't mean anything, okay? It's just for warmth."

I scoot backwards a little, fitting the shape of my body into his.

"Mm-hmm," he murmurs, his breath tickling the nape of my neck, his breathing slow and even, suggesting he's already drifting towards sleep.

That won't do. Quite deliberately I move my bum from side to side, as though trying to get comfortable, rubbing it across Aidan's crotch in the process.

Maybe it's shock but Aidan doesn't say anything, so again I adjust my position, once more shimmying my arse against him.

His breath hitches. Awake now, he says, "Er, Grace—"

"Shh! No more talking. It's time to sleep."

He falls quiet, but his entire body is stiff and something is growing against me.

"Hmm, still not comfortable." This time I really grind my arse cheeks back and forth over his hardening length.

"Fuck!" he gasps under his breath.

I hear it but don't acknowledge it. Instead, satisfied with this response, and still with his erection nestled against my backside, I settle down to sleep.

Two can play at this game. If he's going to mess with me with his semi-nakedness and his flirting with my yoga students, I'll mess with him too. Let's see how he sleeps now.

CHAPTER SEVENTEEN

AIDAN

Grace's alarm blares, jolting me awake. Far from feeling refreshed, I'm absolutely knackered. I groan and rub my eyes. Grace, meanwhile, nimbly climbs over me and hops out of bed.

"Morning!" She draws back the curtains with a flourish.

"Morning," I grumble, giving my eyes another rub, though it doesn't help me feel any more alive.

"Ready for another action-packed day of exploring London while I work? How did you sleep?"

"Not great." I sit up and stretch.

Grace fills the kettle and takes down a couple of mugs. A few wayward curls have escaped the confines of her headscarf, and in the light that streams in through the window, her smooth skin is radiant. God, even in fluffy pyjamas, she really is something.

She catches me watching her and smiles. Her sparkling dark-brown eyes and full lips are enough to perk me up even before my morning coffee. I swing my legs over the side of the bed and manage a groggy smile of my own.

"If you didn't have a good night, why don't you go back to sleep?"

"Nah. Once I'm up, I'm up."

"That's a shame." She pops a teabag in one mug and some coffee granules in the other. "What was it that kept you awake?"

"Oh . . . nothing." Avoiding her eye, I stand and have another quick stretch, accompanied by a yawn.

She raises an eyebrow but lets it go. "Are you for toast again? Or there's muesli?"

"Toast would be great, but you sit down—I should be making breakfast. You're the one who's working today."

"Don't be silly." She waves to the table. "Sit!"

Too tired to argue, I do, scratching my arm. "Maybe when I'm out today, I'll pick up a blow-up mattress. That way, I can go back to the floor, where you originally wanted me."

She halts the breakfast preparations and turns to me, her brows drawing together, her lips pressing into a thin line. "Why? Are you saying I'm getting so fat there's not enough room in the bed for both of us?"

"*What?* No! Nothing like that. I just . . ." I trail off, no idea how to explain.

Grace holds my gaze for a few seconds more then bursts into a fit of laughter.

"Er . . . did I miss something?"

"I know why you didn't sleep, Aidan."

I chuckle nervously. "You do?"

She smirks and crosses her arms. "Yep. I felt you getting hard."

"Shit! I'm really sorry, I just—"

"You're sorry? There's no need to apologise. I *was* rubbing against you quite vigorously. It was a pretty natural reaction."

"Right . . ." Frowning, I scratch my head. "Sorry, but I don't know what's going on here. I thought we were keeping this platonic?"

"We are. That wasn't sexual. That was just . . . a prank. You did say I needed to practise my teasing."

I nod slowly. "Okay. Er . . . it's just . . . it was an odd kind of prank."

There's a click and Grace, fighting to keep a straight face, points. "Look, the toast has popped up—just like your willy did last night!"

My cheeks flush. I'm not used to this sort of dynamic. I can't remember a woman ever having made me feel embarrassed about sex before. "I . . . honestly don't know what's going on. And what adult says 'willy'?"

She giggles as she plates the toast then brings it over to the table. "Well, you kept on laughing the other day when I said 'penis', so I thought I'd try a different word."

I'm lost, with no road map for navigating this situation, and yet Grace's cheeky smile is infectious. Despite my confusion, I can't help but grin too. This is a brand-new side to her, and while it's taken me by surprise, I quite like it.

"Why not 'dick' or 'cock'?" I question.

She frowns and shakes her head. "No, those are way too vulgar." The kettle clicks off so she fills the two mugs with boiling water.

"Okay," I say, still puzzled but trying my best to play along with whatever is going on here. "Except . . . I don't know if I can think of it as my 'willy'. That's pretty emasculating."

This earns me a pitying look. "Oh dear, Aidan. It's an insecure man who's emasculated by a word."

"Wow! You really aren't pulling your punches this morning. You know, some people might say it was a pretty mean prank. I'm normally very sexually active, but it's been a long time since I had sex—I don't think I've ever gone this long, in fact—so someone rubbing up against me as a 'prank' . . . no wonder I hardly slept."

Putting down the mugs and joining me at the table, she glances at me curiously. "Why haven't you been having sex?"

I scoff. "Are you being serious? You dropped a pretty big bombshell on me six weeks ago. Did you really think I'd be going around having casual hook-ups after that? I've not exactly been in the mood. I've been trying to get my head around the news and figure out how this is all going to work."

"Oh." She sips her tea. "Well, I'm sorry if my prank upset you. It always hurts when you finally get a taste of your own medicine."

I shake my head, chuckling. "Are you really comparing my teasing to yours? They're on completely different levels."

We catch eyes, and man, even if I don't know what's going on, my heart does this odd wee jump. But . . . we have to be careful. Grace may be the one who set the rules but she had good reasons for them. We're having a kid together. We need to be responsible.

I grab a piece of toast and butter it. "So . . . there's this Benjamin Franklin quote the McIntyre brothers are fond of. It goes: *Guests, like fish, begin to smell after three days.*"

"Wow! Did Ally tell Emily that one when she booked into the hotel for a month?"

I grin. "My point is, I've already stayed at yours for two nights. Why don't I stay one final night then head home to Bannock tomorrow? I'm sure you'd appreciate getting the place back to yourself."

Something flashes across Grace's face—disappointment? Whatever it is, she only lets it show for a moment.

"Anyway," I continue, "I made you dinner yesterday, but if you'll let me stay one more night, I'd like to go one better. May I take you out for a meal, somewhere fancy?"

"Like . . . a date?"

"What? No! Don't go getting the wrong idea. Our relationship is entirely platonic, remember? I want to platonically take you to a restaurant the same way you platonically rubbed your arse against my 'willy'."

Grace's eyes crinkle. "Wow! So, do you feel emasculated having used that word or are you still as much of a man as you were before?"

I give her a sly wink. "Whatever. Anyway, I should warn you, my conversation may not be the best. For some reason I didn't sleep very well."

This gets a laugh from her. "Okay. Yes, Aidan, you may take me to a restaurant."

CHAPTER EIGHTEEN

GRACE

Taking advantage of a short break between classes, I close the door of my yoga studio and try calling Emily.

After two rings, her smiling face pops up on my phone's screen. "Hi, hun! What's up?"

"I was hoping for some advice, if you've got a few minutes?"

"Fire away! We're so lucky to be going through this at the same time."

"Oh, it's not actually a pregnancy question. It's . . . an Aidan question."

She wiggles her eyebrows. "Even better! Tell me more."

"Well . . . the thing is, Aidan's done what I've asked him to. He hasn't tried to make a move or anything like that."

"And they said he couldn't be trained. What a good boy!" Emily jokingly adopts a tone you might use for a dog.

"Right, except . . . I don't know if I want things to stay that way."

Emily's mouth forms a surprised "O" then breaks into a triumphant grin. "I knew it! This is brilliant."

"Excuse me?"

"You're falling for him, aren't you? Is he falling for you too? Please say he is!" The speed of her speech increases as more and more words tumble out. "I know he's slept with a lot of women, but I was sure you'd be the one to work your way into his heart. Ally didn't believe me—he thought I was off the mark and claimed he knew Aidan a lot better than me—but I was right, wasn't I? After all, who wouldn't love you? You're perfect! And oh God, we're having kids at the same time, and you and I are best friends and Ally and Aidan are best friends, and you'll have to move up to Bannock, of course, and—"

"Whoa! Emily, slow down!"

"Sorry!" She winces. "Too much?"

"Way too much. What's going on? You're normally calm and collected. Is this a pregnancy thing?"

She bites her lip. "I think it might be. But just imagine how amazing it'd be if you did move up here and—"

"Stop!" I hold up a hand. "You're going off the rails again and getting ahead of yourself. We've not even been on a date yet, although Aidan is taking me out for dinner tonight—to somewhere fancy, he said. My mind is all over the place, though, and I thought you might be able to help me out. But if you're going to blab away and put other thoughts in my head, confusing me even more, maybe I'll hang up and call David in—"

"Don't you dare! I *need* to hear this, Grace. Tell me the gossip! I promise to calm down, listen, and only offer the very best advice." She closes her eyes, breathes in deeply through her nose, and breathes out through her mouth. "All right, I'm ready. Tell me everything that's on your mind, and together, we will sort this matter out."

She holds her tongue, giving me a chance to talk, but she's now gazing at me with such intensity it's kind of unnerving.

"Er . . . just chill, Emily. Be your usual self, please. You look like you're trying to see into my soul."

"Sorry." Again, she closes her eyes, grounding herself. "Okay, shoot!"

"Right, issue one: I'm definitely attracted to Aidan, but could that be the pregnancy hormones? I mean, it does affect your libido, doesn't it?"

"Absolutely! I can't get enough of Ally at the moment. Just last night—"

"Thanks, but I don't need the details. If we could focus on me, that'd be great."

Emily offers a sheepish grin. "Sorry . . . again. But hormones or not, Aidan is a handsome man, and what's wrong with being attracted to the father of the little life growing inside you? Nothing, as far as I'm concerned. What's next?"

I blow out. "Okay. Well, after Mark, I swore off men and promised myself I'd focus on my own happiness, and—"

"Mark caused you enough problems when you were with him—don't let him dictate your future too. Sure, you were right to take time away from the dating scene after that relationship ended, but you don't have to swear off men for life. Next!"

I smile. Emily is fairly rattling through my points, and it is making me feel better.

"The next one is the big one. Even if I decide I'd like to give things a go with Aidan, it's not as if it's just my decision to make, and he has his stupid 'one-and-done policy'. Yes, he's been obeying my wishes to keep things platonic, but . . . well, I did think maybe he'd find me so irresistible he wouldn't be able to help himself. But no! Last night I even—wait, no, that's a story for another time.

"Anyway, the point is, this is probably all theoretical. We've already had sex, so according to the way Aidan lives his life, that's it—he no longer has any interest in me as a prospective partner. And yet, every so often, I catch him looking at me in this way that makes me think maybe he does feel something for me. Then this morning, just when I thought we were actually getting somewhere, he suddenly announces he's going back up to Bannock tomorrow, like he can't get away from me fast enough. I don't know what to think."

Emily nods. "Except . . . he's not going away today. He's going away tomorrow. Tonight he's taking you to a fancy restaurant."

"Well, yes, there is that."

"So, here's what you're going to do. Tonight you're going to make yourself irresistible and test how rigid Aidan's one-and-done policy really is. I wish I was down there in London with you to help you get ready, but it's okay, we can do this over video call. When you're done with your classes, we will transform you from pleasant yoga teacher into seductive sex goddess. Dress, shoes, make-up, hair, perfume—we'll get everything just right.

"If Aidan still resists, then you've got your answer, but I'm confident that won't happen. No, you are going to show him how ridiculous his silly little policy is. By the end of the night, he'll be begging you to give him a chance, and all the power will be in your hands. Understood?"

Goosebumps ripple across my skin. "Yes. Let's do it!"

CHAPTER NINETEEN

AIDAN

I arrive at the restaurant first. I've been sitting for a few minutes when Grace is shown to our table by the maître d'. He, like me, does a double take when she removes her coat because . . . wow.

Her silky forest-green dress clings to the contours of her body and emphasises, rather than hides, her neat pregnancy bump. The neckline is distractingly low, while heels give her a few extra inches, showing off her shapely calves and adding an air of confidence. Her hair is elegantly styled in an updo, with a few tendrils framing her glowing face, and a careful touch of make-up enhances her natural beauty.

Without even realising I'm doing it, I rise from my seat to greet Grace, as though pulled by invisible strings. Wrapping my arms around her, I draw her in for a hug and inhale her scent of vanilla and honey.

"Hello to you too, Aidan."

It's only when she speaks I realise I've not yet said a thing. I embraced her without even saying hi.

"Grace, you look . . ." My sentence goes unfinished because I don't know how to put it into words.

She doesn't seem to notice—she's paying more attention to the floor-to-ceiling window. "Wow, what a view!" she comments as she takes her seat. "If this is the sort of place you choose for dates, it's no wonder you've taken so many women to your bed."

Shaking myself out of my daze, I glance outside. We're up high, on the eighth floor of a building on the bank of the Thames, and have a stunning panoramic view of London's night-time skyline, with the iconic St Paul's Cathedral taking centre stage across the river. As beautiful as the sight is, all I want to gaze at is Grace.

"This is a wee bit fancier than my norm," I admit. "But you're carrying our baby and have put up with me the last few days, so I thought you deserved a treat."

Her lips, coated in a matte brown lipstick, curve upwards.

"You look incredible, by the way," I add.

"Do I?" Casually she glances down at herself. "It was between this and those fluffy pink jammies you like so much. Did I choose well?"

I grin and scratch behind my ear. "Aye."

"You don't look too bad yourself. I notice you've been growing stubble since you got here. I like it."

"Really?" I rub a hand over my cheeks and chin. "Honestly, I just forgot to pack my razor, but if you approve, I'll keep it."

"Ah, so my opinion is important to you? Interesting." Her eyes twinkle then drift down. "And what about your outfit? Was that rolled up in the bag you took with you from Bannock?"

I'm in a light-blue shirt with navy-blue chinos. "No, I picked up this ensemble today. I didn't think this was the place for jeans and a T-shirt."

"You picked well: the colour brings out your eyes. Of course, being a player, you *would* know how to dress nicely."

I raise an eyebrow. "I wouldn't call myself a player."

She cocks her head to the side and studies me with an amused expression. "I can't wait to hear this. Why not?"

"That word has negative connotations. I don't 'play' with women's emotions. I've been honest with every person I've ever hooked up with that it'll be a one-time thing. I've never deceived anyone or promised them something more."

"Hmm," is her only reply to this. Maybe she plans to say something further, but she's interrupted by a server coming over to take our drink order. Grace asks for a sparkling water.

"I'll take one too, please," I say.

The server goes away again and Grace turns her attention back to me.

"You're not drinking?"

"Nah. You can't drink so I won't either. I suppose I'm just a nice guy like that." I wink. "But nine months without alcohol, eh? You'll be desperate for some booze when the bairn is born."

Grace's eyes narrow disapprovingly. "How much do you know about babies, Aidan? Once she's born, I'll be breastfeeding and I still won't be able to drink."

"Oh."

It's ridiculous and incredibly immature, but after hearing the word "breast", I automatically glance down at her cleavage. I can't help it and I'm obviously not subtle enough because Grace notices. But instead of looking annoyed, she seems . . . amused.

I shoot her a sheepish grin then pick up my menu. "So . . . food. What are you thinking?"

137

"I don't know if I could do three courses. How about a main and a dessert?"

"Aren't you supposed to be eating for two?" I counter. "You're not trying to save my wallet, are you? Because please, go wild! Get what you want."

"Thanks. If I can get what I want, then we'll have a main and a dessert then go back to the flat and get into bed together." She pauses then adds, "To watch TV, of course."

I chuckle. "Of course! You don't have a sofa, after all."

The server returns with our drinks then takes our food order. I go for the beef fillet, while Grace opts for the duck. With a nod, the server glides away to pass this on to the kitchen.

Grace has a sip of her water then leans forward, closing the distance between us. "Tell me a secret about you, Aidan."

I shift forward too, happy for any excuse to move closer to her. "Now, why would I do that?"

"We're having a kid together. I want to know something about you not every woman gets to hear."

"That seems fair." My gaze flicks down to her lips, and I imagine how easy it'd be to move just a little further forward and press mine against hers. But I'm getting distracted. For now, her question.

"All right, here's something I rarely talk about. The other day, I told you about my da's double life. I left out one fact, though. When Maw and Iona found out the truth about my da, I'd already known for two years."

"What?" A subtle raise of her eyebrows conveys her surprise.

"Aye. I was eighteen when everything blew up, but back when I was sixteen, Da took me into Inverness to see a Caley Thistle game. Er, that's Inverness Caledonian Thistle, a football team, but that isn't important. What is important is we made a day of it, and before the game, Da gave me a few hours to wander the shops on my own—he didn't want to cramp my style, he claimed.

"So I go around the shops, spend my money, get bored, then decide to explore further afield. I'm going through a residential part of the city when, at a children's play park, I spot Da with another woman and a wee boy. He's holding both their hands."

"Shit!" Grace says.

"Da and I never did see the game that day. Instead he spent the rest of the afternoon begging me—really pleading with me—not to say anything to anyone about his lover, Kirsty, or my surprise half-brother, Archie. He told me it'd ruin everything if I did. So, even though I hated it and it kind of messed me up, I did as he asked and I kept the secret from Maw, from Iona, from everyone—even Ally—for two years."

"That can't have been easy."

I take a sip of water. As I put the glass down, Grace reaches out and brushes my hand, just for a moment.

"Your dad's affair would have been hard enough for you to get your head around. But by begging you to keep it a secret, it's almost like he made you complicit in the betrayal."

"Aye, well, it all ended up coming out anyway, and when it did, I admitted to Maw and Iona I'd known for a while. To be fair, neither of them ever blamed me for anything, although that didn't stop me feeling guilty, especially considering the toll it took on Maw. She was really devastated."

I give a small shrug. "Anyway, it's all ancient history now. But there it is, that's my secret. Well, I suppose technically it was only a secret at the time, but it's still not something I talk about much so I hope that counts."

"Hmm, one sec, I'll check the guidelines." Grace takes out her phone and pretends to look up something. "Yep! I can officially accept that as an answer."

I grin.

"And do you know what I find really interesting about that story?" she asks.

"What?"

"It's your origin story, Aidan. It explains why you don't do relationships."

I blink. "Huh?"

"Oh, come on! When your dad pulled you into his secret, you were at a formative age, a stage when most teenagers are beginning to explore relationships and sex. Then, when everything came out and you saw the effect it had on your mum, you probably told yourself you'd never hurt a woman like your dad did. Maybe it was a conscious decision, maybe it was an unconscious one, but either way, the result was you've kept women at a distance ever since, except to sleep with them. That way, you can't hurt them, right?"

I laugh and clap my hands together. "Wow, I didn't realise I was sitting opposite Sigmund Freud! Thanks for the psychoanalysis. Oh, and I appreciate you giving me such a noble motive. I'm just a kind guy who doesn't want to hurt anyone—that makes me sound so sweet. But I'm afraid you've got the wrong end of the stick. I just like sex. That's all there is to it." Cockily I lace my hands behind my head.

"Hmm." Grace isn't convinced.

I point a warning finger at her. "Hey, I worked hard to cultivate my image around the young men of Bannock as an

140

absolute legend. Please don't go spoiling that and turning me into some tragic lad with issues."

Grace laughs then we put a pin in the conversation because our food arrives. My beef is served with a red-wine sauce, artichokes, and oyster mushrooms, while Grace's duck comes with Madeira sauce, Savoy cabbage, and mashed potato.

I cut into the beef, my knife gliding through the tender meat effortlessly. I pop a piece in my mouth and let out a contented sigh. It's rich and slightly smoky, with a hint of saltiness, and the sauce perfectly complements it.

"This is incredible," I say. "You have to try some." I slice a bit, spear it with my fork, and hold it out to her.

Grace hasn't even tasted her duck yet—maybe I'm being overly keen to share. She tilts her head, considering, then leans forward to accept the offered morsel. The way she slides it off the fork and chews on it, her eyes closing to further appreciate the taste, gets me hot and bothered. Fuck!

When her eyes reopen, her mouth forms a sly smile. I think she knows exactly what sort of effect that had on me.

"Delicious," she says.

Her tongue flicks out, licking her luscious lips, and I give an involuntary shiver.

She tries her duck next but I can't watch. Instead I glance out the window, giving myself a few moments to cool down. These last few days with Grace have been a new experience for me. Normally, when it comes to a woman I'm interested in, there's a quick resolution. Either she's up for a casual hook-up, in which case my urges are satisfied, or she's not, in which case I move on.

But sharing a room with Grace—sharing a bed with her— while keeping my hands to myself has been quite the challenge.

The more time I spend around this tantalising woman, the more my desire for her grows. Aye, we've already slept together, but with her, I want more.

"Aidan, you can look at me, you know."

"Aye, sorry." I meet her gaze again, forcing my emotions down.

We're in a fancy restaurant. I have to behave. I take a sip of water.

Her playful expression becomes a wee bit more serious and she says, "You told me something you don't normally tell people so I think it's only fair that I open up too. This maybe isn't the done thing on a date—even a platonic one—but can I tell you about my last relationship?"

"You can talk to me about anything you want."

Grace gives a small smile then takes some more of her duck, chewing it slowly, perhaps mentally preparing herself to begin the story. "It was with a man called Mark, a banker, very career-driven. I was with him for two and a half years, which is embarrassing because I should have realised much earlier it wasn't a good match.

"Looking back, I'm not sure why I always tried so hard to please him when he never prioritised me. I suppose, when we went out together, it was amazing. He had money to splash on posh restaurants and great seats at shows and incredible experiences. But . . . he worked long hours, and as time went on, date nights became fewer and fewer, although he never missed a lads' night out.

"He had this brilliant flat, which he invited me to move into. With the crazy hours he worked, I ended up cooking most of our meals . . . and cleaning up the place . . . and ironing his shirts.

142

To be fair, yoga instruction left me with more free time than his job, and he did earn a lot more than me. It seemed a reasonable distribution of responsibilities. But then . . ." She trails off.

"Oh, shit. Did he cheat on you?"

She shakes her head. "No, I suppose I should be grateful for that. What he did instead was suggest making our relationship open. He wanted to be free to see other people, with my agreement. Now, I know that works for some couples and that's fine. The last thing I want to do is judge anyone else's setup. But towards the end, I was getting so little from Mark, other than his promise of monogamy, and then he wanted to take that away too.

"It hurts that he didn't respect me enough just to end the relationship outright. Essentially, it felt like he wanted to keep me on as a maid to help around his flat. I'm not even sure how he envisioned it working. Would he have taken the other women to a hotel? I'll never know because I didn't listen that far. The offer left me feeling utterly worthless."

"Fuck! What an arsehole. I'm so sorry."

Another small smile. "Thanks. It's nice to hear that. Every so often, Mum still likes to tell me I made a mistake in leaving him."

I almost choke on a bit of beef. "What? No way! She wanted you to stay with him?"

"Well . . . okay, maybe I didn't tell her the whole story. Some people can talk about anything with their mother, but that's not me and Mum. Besides, I was too ashamed and she's so judgemental—I can't think of anything more embarrassing than explaining to her how an open relationship works. Plus, knowing Mum, she'd have marched around to his place and given him what for, and I didn't want any more drama. So . . . I just told her I'd left him.

"Anyway, they say every cloud has a silver lining. After things ended with Mark, I realised how much I'd sacrificed my own needs and desires in favour of his. I didn't want to get into that trap again so I swore to focus on *me* and only me. And that's what I've done. I've taken a leaf out of your book: I'm not interested in relationships anymore. I mean . . ." She nods at me. "I'll share my bed with a man, of course, but only platonically."

I smirk. "Of course."

Leaning closer, she adds, "I'll even wiggle my bum against his crotch but . . . only platonically."

"Aye, that makes sense." Just as I did earlier on in the dinner, I glance down at her breasts, although this time I don't attempt to hide it. Meeting her gaze again, I say, "Do you know what surprises me about platonic relationships? It's how very . . . *sexual* they can be."

CHAPTER TWENTY

GRACE

Back at the flat, I kick off my heels.

"That was a fun night, wasn't it?" Aidan says.

"Yeah. The food was amazing and the view was incredible. With better company, it would have been perfect."

"Oi!" He points a stern finger at me, his eyes glittering with amusement. "I should really swat your arse for that comment. I'm only letting you off because you're carrying my baby."

A thrill runs down my spine. I wouldn't mind a playful pat on the backside.

I unbutton my coat, watching Aidan as he slips off his own jacket and hangs it by the door. The last few days, I've enjoyed his laid-back style—the casual jeans and T-shirt—but tonight I can't help but admire the way his fitted shirt hugs his athletic frame. And although his normally clean-shaven face accentuates his strong jawline, a bit of stubble is damn sexy on him.

Of course, I'm not so superficial as to only be attracted to him based on his looks. His other qualities are growing on me too, and I saw a new side to him tonight when he opened up about his past. It helped me understand him a little more.

Hanging my coat beside his, I say, "I'm desperate to get my jammies on. Would you mind unzipping me? It's hard to reach." I present my back to him.

"Er, aye." He moves closer, the floor creaking beneath him. "This is the kind of thing platonic friends do for each other, right?"

"Oh, absolutely."

Aidan's fingers gently brush a stray curl from my neck, sending shivers along my skin. Slowly he lowers the zip and the back of my dress falls open. He doesn't step away but lingers, and I can practically feel his gaze on my exposed flesh. I treat his pause as an invitation and move back, pressing my body against his, then I sway my hips from side to side, just like I did last night.

"Fuck!" he groans, his voice dropping an octave. Catching himself, he manages an unconvincing chuckle. "Another prank?"

"No."

I continue the back-and-forth movement, and he grows hard, his breathing—which fans the nape of my neck with warm air—becoming more ragged. With both hands, he grazes the bare skin of my arms, then he lowers his head, his lips brushing my neck. His touch sends ripples of pleasure through me, but suddenly he withdraws.

"Grace, I'm . . . not sure we should do this." His voice is low and gravelly. There's even a slight tremor to it, like he's struggling to control himself.

I turn and he attempts a weak smile, running a hand through his hair. His face is flushed, his expression a mix of desire and uncertainty. The usual teasing glint in his eyes is gone.

I've had enough of this game. It shouldn't be so hard to get Aidan Stewart, of all people, to lay his hands on me. Grabbing his shirt, I yank him down and press my lips to his.

For a single moment he stiffens. Then his arms envelop me, drawing me closer to him. I open my mouth to let him in and his tongue dances with mine, every nerve in my body sizzling to life. The taste of him intoxicates me.

I run my fingers over his chest, exploring the contours of his muscles through the thin fabric of his shirt, while one of his hands drifts down the small of my back and over the curve of my backside. He squeezes and pulls me closer still, and I let out a soft murmur of satisfaction as his erection presses against me.

I don't know how long we kiss for—I lose all sense of time. When our lips finally part, we're both panting heavily.

"You were saying?" I prompt once I catch my breath.

"I . . . was saying . . ." Aidan is dazed, his eyes wide. He shakes his head. "Never mind."

He slides down the straps of my dress and it drops to my waist, exposing my black lace bra.

The sexy lingerie was Emily's suggestion, and judging from the carnal hunger in Aidan's gaze, it's having the intended effect.

Feeling bold, I shimmy out of the dress, letting it fall to the floor.

Aidan takes in the matching underwear and scrubs a hand over his face. "Lass! I'm only a man. How am I supposed to resist?"

He moves closer again, kissing me softly then stroking the bump he helped create. Taking my hand, he guides me to the bed and lowers me onto my back. He climbs on top of me and, still fully clothed, stares down at me. Even now it's clear he's struggling. A part of him wants to do this but something is holding him back.

"Aidan, I—"

His lust wins over and he takes my breasts in his hands. My words die on my lips, his touch setting me alight. He's tender, almost reverent, in his caresses, his thumbs eventually grazing over my sensitive peaks through the lace. Then his fingers sneak around me and unbuckle the bra, and it's tossed aside.

He kisses the area between my breasts, his stubble tickling me, although not unpleasantly. Planting kisses across my skin, he moves to my left nipple, which he teases with his tongue before latching on and sucking gently.

I reach for his hair, running my hands through it and messing it up as he shifts to my right breast, giving it equal attention. Then his kisses drift lower, leaving a trail of fire down my body until he reaches my underwear, which he snags with his teeth and tugs down my legs. He casts my knickers onto the floor then turns his gaze to my centre.

I thwart his intentions, though, pushing him off me and sitting up. "Uh-uh. My turn."

Slowly I unbutton his shirt and slide it off his shoulders, revealing his chiselled torso in all its glory. After seeing him topless that first morning, when he was doing his press-ups, it's freeing to be able to touch and explore him as I wish. Heat radiates from his skin as I trail my fingers through the hairs of his chest and along the grooves of his abs.

I guide my hand lower and slide it over the bulge in his trousers. He groans, a sound I silence by pressing my lips back against his. We lose ourselves in the kiss and I close my fingers around him, gripping him through his chinos and stroking his length.

It's a blessing Aidan wore smart clothes tonight—I'd never have been able to feel him this well through denim. But I'm hungrier for more, keen to grasp him without any barrier between us, desperate to strip him just as bare as me. The night of the engagement party, everything was so fast and frantic, I never got to see him properly. Now it's time to fix that.

I break apart from his lips and reach for his belt, but he places a hand over mine, stopping me.

"What's wrong?" I ask.

His eyes are clouded with desire but there's something else there too—that hesitation again. "Grace, I can't let you do that."

"What?" I laugh, sure he's joking. "I'm completely naked. It'd hardly be fair if you kept your clothes on."

He offers me a grin, although it's not as easy-going as his usual one. "I . . . want this to be about you, lass."

"And I want it to be about us."

I reach for his belt again, but again, he stops me.

"Please, Grace. You're not making this any easier for me. Normally, with women, all I care about is the sex. But these last few days with you—and even before that, on the video calls—I've been . . . well, I've been developing feelings for you. This is all new for me, and I don't want to spoil what's growing between us by thinking with my cock rather than my heart. I want to focus on the emotional side of things and let that grow."

Aidan's words touch me, and yet in the midst of my passion, they're not what I wanted to hear. "But—"

"But *you*," he continues, speaking over me, "don't have the same problem I do. So . . ."

Guiding me down onto my back once more, he trails his

hand up my left leg, taking his time, his fingers dancing across my skin, teasing me with every inch. When he reaches my inner thigh, I lose any semblance of control I had. The anticipation is agonising.

He slides a finger into me and the world melts away, pleasure coursing through me. His other hand cups my right breast, massaging it gently.

"You feel so good, Grace." His voice is husky.

I don't have words. I just whimper, desperate for more, moving against him.

He adds another finger and my muscles instinctively tighten around him, but then his thumb finds that sensitive spot at the core of me and I surrender to the bliss. He studies my face, discovering exactly how I like to be touched, making me gasp and arch into him.

Then suddenly his fingers are gone and I'm aching, craving their return. But he settles between my legs, widens them further, then carefully parts my lips and plants a featherlight kiss against my clitoris. My breathing quickens and he laps at me slowly, tentatively, savouring each taste, his hands sliding to grip my thighs, keeping me open for him. I'm trembling, my body alight with need and the exquisite pleasure he's creating.

"Aidan . . . yes!" I'm already experiencing the familiar sensations that come before climax.

His eyes flash up to meet mine then he picks up the pace, alternating between sucking and licking. Suddenly an intense orgasm rips through me and Aidan sucks harder, at my clit, absorbing the tension with his skilled lips while I grip the duvet beneath me. Once the last of the waves have dissipated, my body turns to jelly, the aftereffects relaxing and exhausting me all at once.

I let out a loud, long, satisfied groan.

Aidan props himself up on one elbow and watches me, his expression still full of heat.

"That was . . . incredible," I moan.

"It was? Er, this is a bit embarrassing but that wasn't . . . sexual. It was just a prank."

I glare at him and his eyes shimmer with mischief. Then my gaze drifts down to the erection that's still clearly showing through his chinos.

"You're still hard."

"Aye."

"Aidan, you didn't sleep well last night because you were frustrated. Why don't you just lie back and let me—"

"No!" He stands and steps away from the bed, out of my reach. "I meant what I said, Grace. I feel for you and I think you feel for me too. Isn't that a good thing?"

"Of course it is. But . . . won't you get blue balls? And a follow-up question, is that even a thing?"

He combs his fingers through his dishevelled hair and manages a half-grin. "Aye, it is but . . . I'm going to go have a cold shower. As for you, you've had a busy day and you're carrying our child. Get ready for bed. You need your sleep."

I want to protest some more—it seems almost cruel to leave him with that big bulge in his trousers—but I *am* tired and the thought of closing my eyes is a pleasant one.

"Fine. I just hope your balls are okay."

CHAPTER TWENTY-ONE

AIDAN

When I wake, some dawn light is filtering through the curtains but not much. It's still early.

Grace, fast asleep, is cuddled up beside me. Her features are soft and relaxed, her lips parted. I can't resist raising my head from the pillow and planting a gentle kiss on her cheek. She stirs, snuggling closer and wrapping one of her legs around mine.

At the contact memories of last night flood my mind, and in my PJ trousers, my cock twitches. Damn! I close my eyes and try to calm myself but it's no use. Soon I'm sporting a full-blown hard-on.

Shit. There's no way I'm getting back to sleep now—that's me up for the day. Time for another cold shower.

I manage to get out of bed without waking Grace then wash and dress. I'm in the midst of collecting my stuff together when she finally stirs.

She yawns, gently stretching. "Oh! I can't remember the last time I slept so well."

I chuckle. "I'm glad I was able to help relax you."

She sits up and rubs at her eyes then takes in the scene. "Why are you packing up your things?"

"You know why. I'm going today."

"But after last night, I thought . . ." She trails off.

"Remember that quote about guests, like fish, becoming smelly after three days?" I lift my armpit and sniff. "I've just had a shower so I *think* I'm all right, but I don't want to risk it."

She gives a half-hearted laugh. "Seriously, Aidan . . ."

I perch on the bed and take her hands in mine. "Look, this thing that's developing between you and me? I like it but we have to nurture it. I'm new to this and I'd be devastated if I messed this up. There's a lot at stake.

"You're carrying our baby, Grace. If this works out between us, it could be something really special. I don't want to rush this, and if I stay here, I won't be able to go on resisting you. Last night, when you tried to undo my belt and I stopped you? That took heroic self-restraint."

Grace scoffs. "Heroic?"

"Oh, aye. It's the kind of thing legends are told of. If people saw you, they'd understand."

She giggles.

"Anyway, if I don't go, I'll be on ten cold showers a day, and even then, I may still cave. For us, as well as for your water meter, this is what's best. But we can start up the video calls again. We could maybe even speak more than once a week."

"How about every day?"

I grin and nod. "Aye, I'd like that."

"And . . . you'll be sending me dick pics, right?"

I laugh. "No, Grace. I want to focus on the emotional side of things. Those belong to a different category."

Her eyes sparkle with mischief. "Just joking! I get it and it's sweet. I'm impressed, but to be clear, the next time we meet up, your clothes are coming off and I'm going to do what I want to you."

"Fuck, I'm going to get hard again. See? This is why I need to go."

She wraps her arms around me and lays her head on my shoulder. "Well, when will we next see each other in person?"

"It's just under a month until Christmas. Why don't you come up to Bannock for it? I mean, you'll want to celebrate it with your brother, won't you?"

She squeezes me. "And you."

"Great, then it's settled. Oh, and you'll need to take your mum up too: she'll want to spend the festive period with her children. Which means . . ." I draw back from Grace and give her a stern look. "You're going to have to tell her."

"Yes, yes! I get the message. Tell Mum I'm pregnant . . . no problem. And . . . what about us? Are we telling people we're a thing?"

"Oh, we're a thing, are we?" I tease.

"Well . . ." she says shyly.

"Honestly, you know what Bannock is like. Gossip spreads so fast and I don't want us to be influenced by wagging tongues. Then again, you tell Emily and David absolutely everything, don't you?"

She nods. "Yep, pretty much."

"All right, well, you can tell them but maybe ask them to keep it to themselves? If you're saying to Emily, I'll mention to Ally, but how about we leave it at that? For now I don't think anyone else needs to know."

She smiles, and man, she really is beautiful, even first thing in the morning in her pyjamas. "Agreed."

"Great. Well, let's have a last breakfast together then I'll next see you on video."

"Tonight! As soon as you get back to Bannock, call me. And if you want to fire me the odd message during the journey up, feel free."

"Perfect." I place a soft kiss on her forehead. "I'll do that."

CHAPTER TWENTY-TWO

GRACE

The terminal at Inverness Airport is small, a stark contrast to the hustle and bustle of London's major airports, but because it's Christmas Eve, there's a buzz of excitement as travellers head home for the holidays.

I've only just collected my case when I'm pounced on by my brother and Johnny, who are here to drive me to Bannock.

"Grace! My baby sister! It's been too long." David wraps his arms around me in an almighty hug.

"Baby sister?" I laugh. "You're only twenty minutes older than me. Has being apart from me for a couple of months made you sentimental? Wait, what am I saying? You've always been sentimental. Anyway, mind the bump!"

He springs back. "Of course. Sorry." His gaze drifts downwards. My coat is open, my jumper stretched over my not insignificant belly. "You're huge!"

"Thanks, David. Just what every woman wants to hear. I'm only twenty-three weeks. I've still got a long way to go."

"Sorry about him!" Johnny shoots me a bright smile then draws me into a much gentler embrace. "He's been looking forward to this reunion and he loses his filter when he's excited."

"Oh, I know. If ever you need to blow off steam about some of his more irritating quirks, call me, anytime. We can vent together."

Johnny winks then takes my case from me, putting down the retractable handle and lifting it instead.

"Such a gentleman!" I give David a playful nudge. "I notice you didn't offer to carry it."

David dismisses the criticism with a wave of his hand. "Grace, a while ago I mentioned I like muscles, and the next thing I know, Johnny's hitting the weights to impress me. I've got him wrapped around my little finger already. He can use his new strength to carry your case. You and I have to catch up."

The slight blush that colours Johnny's cheeks confirms this story is true.

David squeezes my arm. "Before we head outside, how was Mum this morning? I'm devastated she couldn't come. We've never done Christmas without her."

Mum had been planning to come up on the same flight as me, but a friend of hers recently received some troubling health news, and since this friend is divorced and childless, Mum didn't want her to be alone on Christmas Day. She's going to come up a few days later instead.

"She's fine," I say. "She seemed okay about it."

"And . . . you told her, right? Please tell me you did. Whenever I speak to her on the phone, I dread I'm going to put my foot in it and accidentally mention the pregnancy."

"Er . . ." I smile sheepishly.

"Grace! You can't put it off forever. You said you'd do it before Christmas. This morning was your last chance."

Earlier I caught up with Mum at a café, since I won't be seeing her tomorrow. I *was* planning to tell her but I bottled it and kept on my big winter coat the entire time, disguising my bump.

"I'll tell her when she comes up to Bannock. It's only a few more days. This way, I can enjoy tomorrow without the inevitable drama that sharing the news would have caused."

"Sis, I'm so happy to see you but I'm so annoyed with you too! I arranged a surprise for you—an early Christmas present—but I'm no longer sure you deserve it. On second thoughts, you do. Follow me!"

The three of us head out of the terminal, the cold winter air nipping at my cheeks. I don't mind, though, because—with a contented sigh—I admire the delicate snowflakes drifting down from the inky sky, creating a dusting of white on the ground.

"Snow on Christmas Eve! That's a lovely surprise, David, although to be completely honest, I did notice it when getting off the plane. I'm also not sure you can take credit for organising it." I give him a sly smile.

David smirks. "That's not the surprise. He is."

I turn and my pulse quickens at the sight of the tall figure approaching, his blond hair peeping out from beneath a woolly hat, his stubbled cheeks flushed from the cold, his breath misting in front of him. Aidan!

With two long strides, he closes the distance between us and wraps me in his arms. He kisses me, his lips cool but delicious and leaving me craving more.

David claps and cheers, and Johnny joins in, although in a more restrained manner than my brother. Aidan grins at me, and despite the chill in the air, it warms my heart that he didn't hold back but kissed me in front of these two. Aidan Stewart, the man who was once so opposed to relationships, has changed and he's not afraid of people knowing.

I place my palm against his face and rub his stubble, drinking him in. We've spoken every day by video call but seeing him in person and being able to touch him, to kiss him . . . it just doesn't compare.

"We'll give you two lovebirds a minute," David says. "See you in the car."

He and Johnny set off and Aidan presses his lips back to mine.

When he withdraws, he gazes down at me affectionately, his arms still wrapped around me. "I've been looking forward to doing that. You're not annoyed with me, are you?"

"Annoyed? Why on earth would I be annoyed?"

Aidan glances in the direction of my brother then whispers, "David's great, he really is, but I'd have been happy just to tell you I'd see you at the airport. Instead he came up with this elaborate ploy and made me an unwilling accomplice to it. I felt terrible messaging you that I had to help Maw with Christmas preparations and wouldn't see you until tomorrow. You're really not upset?"

Smiling, I brush some snow from Aidan's shoulders. "Trust me, I understand. It's usually easiest just to go along with David's ideas."

"Thank God. Anyway, as if that wasn't bad enough, he then made me hang about out here in the cold. Tell me honestly, if you'd arrived and seen me waiting for you with David and Johnny, inside where it's warm and bright, would that have been any less surprising? How much did it add to the stunt that I was instead standing out here freezing my balls off?"

I can't help but giggle at this little tirade, unused to his faux anger. The sound sends Aidan's mouth back into a wide grin, and he squeezes me closer to him.

"My brother takes a bit of getting used to but he's got a good heart," I say.

"Aye, he does. He was really excited about seeing you again, although not quite as excited as me. I've missed you, lass."

Lass. My knees weaken at the word.

"And I've missed you, Aidan. But . . . it *is* really cold out here. Can we go to the car now, before I lose all feeling in my fingers and before you literally get blue balls and they fall off? After all, I'd been hoping to have a play with them later."

He chuckles. "Aye, it'd be terrible timing if I lost them now, after saving myself for you. Let's go!"

◆ ◆ ◆

The snow gets heavier during the drive, and by the time we reach Bannock, the town is a pretty winter wonderland. Bright Christmas lights hang across Main Street, fending off the darkness of a December night in the Highlands. Ornament-covered trees twinkle in windows we pass, and smoke spirals out of chimneys.

Johnny turns the car off the main road and onto the charming little lane he and David live on. I crane my neck to get my first glimpse of their cottage, and when I do, a gasp of horror escapes my lips.

"David! What have you done? Every other house has beautiful, classy decorations, but your place . . . it's so . . . *garish*!"

The normally adorable cottage is festooned with lights that flash erratically in a dizzying array of colours, while the path to the door is lined with illuminated candy canes. An assortment of characters adorn the front garden, including skiing reindeer, sledging penguins, and an oversized inflatable snowman.

In the passenger seat, David twists to look at me. "Why are you so sure I did the display? Maybe these are Johnny's decorations he puts up every year and you're hurting his feelings right now. Did you consider that?"

As Johnny steers into the driveway, I catch his eye in the rear-view mirror. Grinning, he shakes his head.

David notices. "Okay, yes, I bought them, but you know what? They brighten the place up and we've actually received some lovely compliments."

"Aye, from the kids around town." Johnny pulls up the handbrake. "I'm not sure what people over the age of twelve think."

"Well, I'm thirty and I reckon they're fun." Aidan pats David's shoulder then opens his door, climbs out, and jogs around the car to open mine.

David meets my eye and raises his brows. "Getting your door for you? And I thought I had Johnny wrapped around my finger. Obviously, I'll have to take some tips from you."

Ignoring him, I gladly accept the hand Aidan proffers and step out of the car with his support.

"Careful! There's snow everywhere and you're carrying precious cargo. Hold on to me so you don't slip."

Johnny closes the driver's door and heads for the boot. "You two head on in. I'll get the case. Oh, and Aidan, I'll get the other thing too."

While David gets out his keys and opens the front door, I whisper to Aidan, "*Other thing?* That wouldn't by any chance be a present for me, would it?"

"Nah, it's a dancing Santa for the garden. I thought it'd go well with the other decorations." He winks.

Inside, the open-plan living room and kitchen has been decked out with festive knick-knacks and a Christmas tree. It's sweet and much classier than the riot of colour outside.

"*These* are the decorations Johnny puts up every year, aren't they?" I say.

"Yes, yes," David mutters, kneeling to turn on the tree lights. "I get it: you prefer Johnny's style to mine. But Aidan got you pregnant and he likes my garden display, so there!"

Johnny comes in and stamps the snow off his shoes on the doormat. As well as my case, he's carrying a shiny red gift bag.

"Dancing Santa for the garden, my arse," I murmur to Aidan.

"Och, it's just a wee one."

Johnny puts down the items. "The spare room is set up for you, Grace. You know where it is and I'm sure Aidan can carry your things through. I'll pop some wood in the stove then David and I will nip out to the Pheasant for a drink or two. Won't we, David?"

"What?" David, who's in the process of removing his coat, firmly shakes his head. "Nope! We're only just back from Inverness and it's freezing outside. I'm thinking warmed mince pies, mulled wine, a soft drink for Grace, a Christmas film . . ."

"Aye, that sounds great." Johnny opens the door of the wood-burning stove and tosses in some logs. "Let's do that after the pub. I know you're desperate to catch up with your twin, but I've got a funny feeling Aidan might like to catch up with Grace too. Maybe we shouldn't hang about and cramp their style?"

"Oh," David says. Then, more emphatically, "*Oh!*" He

buttons his coat back up. "Yeah, on second thoughts, a drink at the Pheasant would be nice. You two have an hour, okay? That's it. I've already shortlisted a selection of feel-good movies. If we're going to finish one before bed, we can't wait too much longer before starting."

Johnny ushers David out and, with an apologetic smile, closes the door behind them.

"Well, I wonder why they were so keen to hurry off." Aidan shrugs off his jacket and hangs it up. "I mean, what do they think you and I are going to be getting up to?"

"Hmm, I have an idea." I step closer to him, place a finger on his chest, and slowly trail it down his body. "They probably don't want to be around when we're . . . exchanging presents!" I point to the gift bag. "Can I open it now?"

Aidan, whose cheeks are slightly more flushed than they were a few moments ago, scratches the back of his head. "Er . . . aye, I suppose. Let's use the limited time we've got alone together to . . . exchange presents. We wouldn't want to do *that* in front of David and Johnny. It's not exactly what I've been desperately anticipating this last month, but all right."

"Did it occur to you I may have got you something a little . . . kinky? Besides, it might be tricky to swap gifts tomorrow, what with the big McIntyre and Stewart family dinner. If you and I slink off, it might arouse suspicion."

Other than David and Johnny, Emily and Ally remain the only people in Bannock who know things are no longer platonic between us.

Aidan's expression brightens at the mention of a kinky gift. "Aye, let's do presents!"

I have to stifle a giggle. I didn't, in fact, get him anything sexy so he's going to be disappointed. But I was for ripping his trousers off him that night in my flat—he's the one who stopped me. Since he made me wait, I'll make him wait, just for a little while.

I remove my coat and Aidan's gaze drifts to my bump with something close to adoration. It's enough to make me feel better about my growing size, but before he can comment on my appearance, I instruct him to carry my case through to the spare room. I then fetch my gifts for him from it, and back in the main living area, we settle on the rug in front of the stove, which is now crackling with life and radiating heat.

"I can't wait to see what you got me," I say.

Aidan drums his fingers on his leg. "I took you at your word when you made me swear to save up for the bairn and not get you anything big. I hope I've not failed some test and I was actually meant to get you something expensive."

"As long as there are diamonds in it somewhere, I'll be happy."

He smirks. "Prepare to be disappointed, then."

"I'm just kidding. We came up with rules and you were supposed to stick to them. Two *small* presents. That's all I got you, and I hope that's all you got me."

He passes me the red gift bag. I take out the first present and tear open the wrapping. It's . . . a cuddly toy of the Loch Ness Monster.

Laughing, I hold it up. "Aw, it's cute!"

"Aye? Shops around the Highlands are full of them, but I reckon I may be the first ever local to buy one. They're there for the tourists. Anyway, your present is more than just the toy—there's a promise that goes along with it. Remember, back in the spring, you and David were going to go on a boat tour of

Loch Ness but then there was a bit of drama with Ally and Emily?"

Of course I remember. David and I were about to board when we got a call from Emily. She'd had a falling-out with Ally and, sure things were over between them, wanted us to take her home to London. We collected her and set off, although thankfully, Ally caught up with us on the drive south and won Emily back.

"Since you never did get to explore Loch Ness, I'd love to show you around it one day. And actually, there are a lot of places I'd like to show you. Do you remember the video call we did about travel?"

"Back when you still came up with a topic for every conversation because otherwise you thought we'd run out of things to talk about? Yes, I've not forgotten."

"Aye, well, I told you the most beautiful place I've ever been is the Highlands, which you said was cheesy. But it's true! So here's the real present: whenever you come up to Bannock, I'd like to take you somewhere bonny and help you get to know the area as well as I do. When our wee lass comes along, she'll accompany us on our trips too."

"Ah, sneaky! An ongoing present—a clever way of getting around the spending restriction we agreed on. But yes, I'd love to visit some 'bonny' places with you. Thanks, Aidan."

He grins, pleased with himself.

"And since you mentioned our 'wee lass', here's your first present." I hand him a flat rectangular-shaped gift.

"Wow, is it a football?" No sooner does he say this than his face falls. "God, I'm not even a dad yet and already I've started on the dad jokes. Sorry!"

He tears off the wrapping paper. "Ha! Perfect. *A Bear*

Called Paddington. I'll read this to the bairn." He flicks through some pages. "Thank you."

"Can I open my second present now?"

"Fire away."

Like the cuddly toy, the second parcel feels soft. Opening it, I discover . . . Christmas jammies.

I can't hold back a laugh.

Aidan raises an eyebrow. "Are they okay? Since we both liked your fluffy pink ones, I thought you might appreciate some Christmas PJs. I'm sorry if it's a rubbish present. See, I'm new to relationships, so—"

"Whoa! Calm down, Aidan! You're taking this whole present-exchange thing way too seriously. It's just a bit of fun, and anyway, I love them. If you open your gift, you'll see why I found it funny."

I hand him it. He tears it open and . . .

"Ha! Christmas PJs. Great minds think alike, eh? These are brilliant." He holds them up. They're red and white with a Fair Isle pattern. "So . . . no kinky gifts, then?"

"Nope, sorry. I was just teasing. Anyway, get sex off your brain for a moment. I know I set a two-present limit but . . . I have actually got you a third gift."

"You're showing me up! I only got you two—as we agreed."

"Well, this is a different kind of present."

Taking Aidan's hand, I place it at the side of my bump. We wait then . . .

"I felt her!" Aidan meets my gaze, his eyes filling with wonder. "I felt our wee girl."

I first experienced her fluttery movements a couple of weeks ago. Although it's a slightly surreal sensation, whenever it occurs, I'm reassured she's growing strong.

He keeps his hand in place and laughs when she kicks again. "Wow! Does she do that a lot?"

"Yes, usually when I'm trying to sleep."

Chuckling, Aidan leaves his hand on me, marvelling at this first contact with his child, acting like he could do this all night. I'm touched and yet . . . David did impose a time limit.

"I may not have got you a kinky gift but why don't you try your new jammies on?"

He glances up, his lips curling into a playful smile. "Oh, you'd like to see me in them, would you?"

"Mm-hmm. I would."

CHAPTER TWENTY-THREE

AIDAN

I emerge from the spare room. "Well? Do you approve?" I hold out my arms, showing off my new Christmas pyjamas.

Grace has been waiting for me by the crackling stove. "Hmm . . . I need to take a closer look. Come over here."

I walk over and stand before her. Her skin is dewy and fresh, the dancing flames of the fire catching it beautifully. I swear she's even more attractive now than when I was with her in London. Am I just imagining it or is this the "pregnancy glow" I've heard about?

Grace rises and wordlessly circles me, scrutinising me from head to toe. She takes her time, going around twice.

"Well, they *look* fine but how do they feel?" She catches her lower lip between her teeth, deep in thought.

"They feel—"

"Shh! It was a rhetorical question. I'm the one doing the inspection."

I bite my tongue.

She adjusts my collar then lightly trails her fingers down my left arm, sending tingles of excitement through me. She traces my biceps then glides her hand lower, to my forearm. I can't help but shiver. A mischievous smile tugs at the corners of her mouth, and in the firelight, her dark-brown eyes glimmer with undisguised heat.

"They feel very soft." She presses both her hands to my chest then rubs them down my torso and over my abs. With a devilish smirk, she steps closer and reaches around me, taking a hold of my arse cheeks. "And the fit is"—she squeezes them—"good."

She lets go and her gaze drops to my crotch, where the fabric is already tenting. I can't help it. I've refrained from sex for way too long and this is too fucking hot.

"What's going on here?" she questions with feigned innocence. "We have a problem: your trousers aren't sitting right. Let me see what's wrong."

Slowly she grazes a single nail along the underside of my shaft, from my balls all the way to the very tip. I hiss, bending forward, scarcely believing the intensity of the sensation, the soft fabric of the pyjamas doing nothing to mute it. My cock reacts, swelling and pointing higher.

"Oh dear, that didn't help. Something just isn't right with these trousers. Let me investigate further." Brazenly she wraps a hand around me. "Ah, this seems to be the source of the problem."

She squeezes and a low growl escapes my throat.

"Grace," I warn, trying my best to keep my voice steady.

"I thought I told you to be quiet?" With her other hand, she puts a finger to my lips. "Shh! These trousers will have to come off so I can see what's causing *this*." Another squeeze.

My muscles tense, my skin prickles. What's happening to me? I'm experienced in the bedroom so how come my heart is already beating so fast? It must be the months of abstinence. It's the only explanation.

She sinks to her knees.

Despite her commands to stay quiet, I croak, "Grace? What are y—"

She yanks my trousers down, and like a coiled spring suddenly released, my cock leaps free, bobbing in front of her eyes for a moment before standing tall and proud.

She stares at it and licks her lips. "Take your top off. I want to see all of you."

I don't hesitate. I yank the pyjama top over my head and toss it to the side, then I step out of my trousers and kick them away. In the middle of the living room, I stand in front of her, completely naked.

"You're shivering," she observes. "Are you cold?"

I glance down and see she's right. My whole body is shaking, but not with cold—with need.

"It's just . . ." I begin.

But she's not interested in my answer. She wraps a hand around my length, her grip somehow both gentle and firm at the same time. My words die in my throat.

Tenderly she kisses the tip. I groan but it's only the start. Next she teases me with her tongue, licking around the entire circumference.

"Fuck!"

Chuckling softly, she gazes up at me and, maintaining eye contact, takes me into her mouth.

"*Fuck!*"

Her free hand rises and gently cups my balls, rolling them lightly in her palm.

Oh God. One hand cradling my balls, the other stroking the

base of my cock, her mouth and tongue stimulating the head . . .

It's too much. After just a few minutes, I realise I'm going to come. No, no, no—not this fast.

I reach out and grip her shoulder, trying to gently push her away. Instead her grasp on me tightens and her movements intensify, all of them working in concert to bring me to the edge of ecstasy.

"Grace! I—"

I can't hold it back—I surrender to the waves of euphoria. It's a struggle even to remain upright but Grace stays with me, riding it out. Only once it's over and I'm left panting heavily, the pleasure slowly ebbing away, does she remove her lips from around me.

She rises from her knees, wipes a hand across her mouth, and smiles smugly. "That was very . . . quick. Haven't you slept with hundreds of women? No offence, but I thought you'd have lasted a little longer."

I'm all for a bit of light-hearted teasing—I'm usually the one dishing it out—but in the vulnerable moments following orgasm, I'd rather not be the butt of the joke.

Trying to catch my breath, I say, "Jesus, lass! I've been denying myself for weeks, and besides, it's *you* and I've wanted you so badly. Take it as a compliment."

"I'm flattered." Grace's lips twitch with amusement. "Oh dear, Aidan. I fear this will change your reputation around Bannock."

"Oh, aye? And who's going to hear about it?"

"Well, I tell Emily *everything* and she'll definitely tell Ally, who'll almost certainly tell his brothers, and then before you know it, half the town will have heard."

She's enjoying this way too much.

Rubbing the back of my neck, I grin. "All right, how about a deal? If I can turn things around, you keep what happened to yourself."

"And how do you plan to turn things around?"

Smirking, I take her hand and lead her into the spare room then draw her to me and press my mouth to hers. Our kiss is deep and intoxicating, our lips moving together in a passionate rhythm. I can taste myself on her, a slight salty tang, but it's not a turn-off. Our tongues dance freely and without inhibition.

I slide my hands over Grace's warm winter clothes then stop. Clothes? No, that's not right. I'm still stark-bollock naked, while she's fully dressed. I'll have to fix that.

I tug up the hem of her sweater, and we pause our kiss to get it up and over her head before pressing our lips back together. I remove Grace's clothing in stages, our lips finding each other again after each item is discarded. By the time she's down to her bra and underwear, my cock is back at full mast.

"Just two more things to come off," I say huskily.

Our mouths rejoin and I reach around her, unclasping her bra and releasing her wonderful tits. As my tongue continues to play with hers, I shimmy her knickers over her arse and let them drop down her legs.

I break away from her and step back, admiring her openly. Despite the clear desire in her gaze, there's self-consciousness too.

I let out a soft chuckle. "Why are you pretending to be shy? I've already explored you with my fingers and my mouth, or have you forgotten?"

"I've not forgotten and I'm not *pretending* to be shy. But you're looking at me so . . . hungrily."

"Aye, well, I am hungry for you." I reach out and trail a finger along her slit.

She gasps.

"And you're wet for me, Grace."

Gently I lay her on the bed and take another opportunity to drink in her beauty. In the soft lighting of the bedroom, her skin is lustrous and her full breasts are mouthwatering.

I guide her onto her side then settle myself behind her. "For the record I'm clean, but if you want me to use a condom then—"

"Why? You can hardly get me pregnant again." She wiggles her arse against me. "Just get on with it!"

Laughing, I nibble at her earlobe, then I lift one of her legs, line up my shaft, and enter her. We both groan at the same time. She feels incredible, like heated silk wrapping itself around me. I move slowly, savouring every inch of her, as well as each shudder that goes through her. My hips find a gentle rhythm.

"Oh!" Grace moans. "It was good at the engagement party, but was it this good?"

"We were rushing then. Now we're taking our time."

"Mmm . . . we are."

I reach around and cup one of her voluptuous breasts, stroking the nipple with my thumb, drawing small gasps from her. Our pace gradually increasing, I slide my hand to rest on her raised hip, and I pull her closer with every thrust, her pleas spurring me on.

Leaning forward, I plant a kiss on the back of her neck, then I move my fingers yet again, trailing them down to where we're joined. I explore the delicious wetness of her around my shaft then delicately brush her clit.

She gasps louder, tightening around me at the added stimulation. The tension in her builds with every thrust of my hips, every flick of my fingers against her most sensitive spot. She's getting close but . . . so am I. This was supposed to be for her— I wasn't expecting to blow my load again so quickly. And yet . . .

Everything about this is perfect. It's more than just the physical sensations. These last few months, between the video calls, the messages, and the time I spent with her in London, I've formed a strong bond with Grace. Expressing our deep emotional connection by coming together physically feels so . . . right.

I drive into her with greater urgency. The pace picks up, our breaths escaping in shallow puffs and gasps. There's a frenzy now—a desperate need.

A loud moan tears from her lips. "Aidan!" There's desperation in her voice. She's on the brink and just the knowledge of that sends a wave of exhilaration through me.

We don't stop, our bodies moving together, perfectly synchronised in their rhythm, until she shudders and cries out. Even then I keep going as she trembles around me. The sensations and her groans push me over the edge. With a final deep thrust, I empty myself into her.

We pant, still connected, both of us trembling from our climaxes. With the last of my strength, I withdraw from her and collapse onto my back.

I lie on the bed, eyes closed, basking in serenity. The sheets rustle then Grace rests her head on my chest. Her fingers trace lazy circles on my skin, sending little shivers of pleasure through me.

"I think that was the best sex I've ever had," she murmurs. "No, I *know* it was. Wasn't it great?"

I wrap my arms around her protectively. "Mmm, don't take

this the wrong way but . . . could we not talk? You've just made me come twice in what could be a world-record time. I'm knackered. I need to sleep."

"You're joking, right? It's not even that late."

"Not joking."

"But you're supposed to be some Casanova!" She reaches down and gives my still-tingling cock a playful flick.

"Oh, Grace, that was the old me—a carefree twenty-something with energy and vitality. Now I'm a thirty-something dad who wants nothing more than to nap."

"You only turned thirty a couple of months ago, and I don't think you can call yourself a dad until the baby has been born."

"Shh . . . I said no talking. Not until tomorrow." I stroke my hand up and down her back, hoping the touch might satisfy her because I'm way too tired for words.

"You can't stay the night! Your mum is expecting you at hers. You can't worry her on Christmas Eve."

I groan. "I'm too old to go around having sex in secret. It'd be so much easier if we told everyone we're giving things a go. Then I could just say to Mum I'm crashing here."

"Well, maybe we *could* tell people—tomorrow. But you're not breaking the news to your mum by firing off a message because you're too tired to walk home after sex."

"Och, you've got a point but I'm not sure I can move."

"Look, you can't sleep here overnight but you can have a nap. I'm enjoying snuggling with you. If you want to sleep, sleep. I'll wake you when you have to go. I won't even comment on the fact you're being a big baby because you're not the one who's pregnant and you don't know what it means to be tired."

"Except . . . you just did comment on that. But thanks anyway."

I settle down for some shuteye, but a few moments later, she lifts away from me and gets to her feet.

"I thought we were going to snuggle?"

"We will. I just remembered your pyjamas are strewn across the living room. I'll tidy them up before David and Johnny get back."

"Ah . . . cheers." Chuckling, I close my eyes again.

CHAPTER TWENTY-FOUR

GRACE

It's a white Christmas, and in the light of morning, Bannock looks even more magical, the fallen snow sparkling under the cool winter sun. David and I, wrapped up against the cold, are heading across the old stone bridge, following the peals of the church bell.

Elspeth invited us to attend the Christmas service with her, Aidan, and Iona. I'll be seeing the three of them later as well, for Christmas dinner. I reckon Elspeth is keen to spend as much time as possible with the woman carrying her granddaughter.

Johnny was invited along to the service too, but he declined, saying church isn't really his scene. It's not really my scene either, or David's, but we're both curious to see a Highland service, especially on Christmas Day.

As we draw nearer, we encounter families, couples, and individuals coming from other directions. Like us, they crunch through the snow towards the church, whose spire stands taller than all the other buildings in Bannock. Cheery greetings of "Merry Christmas!" are directed our way, which David and I enthusiastically return.

The churchyard and its gravestones are blanketed under a layer of white, but the path through to the charming stone building has been cleared and gritted. A warm and inviting glow emanates from its stained-glass windows, and outside the entrance, clusters of people are engaged in conversation.

I spot Elspeth chatting away to a similar-aged woman whom I recognise as Morag, who runs the town's bakery and makes the most incredible cakes. Emily introduced me to them on my first visit to Bannock. As the pair laugh, their breaths turn into small clouds in the crisp morning air.

Iona stands near her mother and is talking with a teal-haired young woman—Maisie from the Pheasant. With a flutter in my heart, I catch sight of Aidan too. He's exchanging words with the kindly widower Tom, who owns the Coffee Bothy.

When Aidan notices me, a smile sneaks across his lips and mischief sparkles in his eyes. It seems he's back to his usual self after he was utterly spent last night. He excuses himself from Tom and approaches us.

"Here he comes," David murmurs.

But before he can reach us, Elspeth does with Morag in tow.

"Merry Christmas, Grace!" Her eyes crinkling at the edges, Elspeth pulls me into a warm hug. "And to you too, of course, David. And there's another person I mustn't forget." Bending her knees, she waves to my coat-covered belly. "Merry Christmas, wee one!"

"Maw, you're embarrassing Grace." Shaking his head, Aidan joins our group. "I don't think you're meant to do that to a pregnant woman's bump."

"Well, at least I'm saying something! You've not even said hello to Grace yet. *Please* try to make an effort, Aidan. She is carrying your child, after all." Elspeth squeezes my arm. "I'm so sorry about him, I really am. I tried my best to instil manners in him but there's only so much a woman can do."

"I'd say hello if I could get a word in edgeways," Aidan grumbles. Meeting my eye, he grins then reaches an arm around me and draws me into a very respectable hug. "Grace, it's . . . good to see you again." The way he says it, you'd think we hadn't seen each other for a month, which I suppose is the idea.

Morag—who Emily has informed me is not only the town's baker but also chief gossip and rumour-monger—nudges Aidan with an elbow. "In my day, if a man got a lass pregnant, he'd make an honest woman of her and put a ring on her finger. Didn't that occur to you?"

I half wonder if Aidan might pick this opportunity to spill the beans and admit we are actually seeing each other. Elspeth, however, steps in before he can speak.

"Oh, don't go stirring things, Morag! Not today, on Jesus's birthday. Times have changed and for the better. Although . . . Grace *is* a lovely woman and it's just a shame they live so far apart. If only they were able to spend a bit more time together . . . I can't help but imagine what might happen!"

"You two are as bad as each other," Iona says, coming over, having finished up her conversation with Maisie. She gives David and me a hug. "Merry Christmas! I'm so sorry about this pair of meddling old women."

"*Old?*" Morag gasps with mock outrage. "I'm not old. I'm still of working age, young lady!"

"Just!" Elspeth comments.

Morag laughs loudly at this. "Well, it's clear where your daughter gets her impudence from. Anyway, I'm going to head on in. If I don't see you again, have a lovely Christmas, all."

After Morag leaves, Elspeth says, "We should probably go in too. Shall we?"

The five of us make our way towards the entrance.

As we approach the door, my brother leans close to me and whispers, "What are the chances you and I burst into flames the moment we cross the threshold?"

I chuckle. I see what he's getting at. He's a gay man and I'm carrying a baby out of wedlock. Not so very many years ago, attitudes were quite different.

"Not high," I murmur, "but not negligible either."

He raises his brows then takes a deep breath. We enter and after a few seconds, when there are no signs of immediate divine retribution, he lets out a mock sigh of relief.

A magnificent Christmas tree stands at the far end of the church, decked in white lights that twinkle like distant stars. In front of that, the wooden pews on either side of the aisle are filling up, the congregation chattering amongst themselves in hushed voices. While hats, gloves, and scarves are removed, jackets remain on. There's some heating in the old building but it's not exactly toasty.

Aidan, who's leading the way, reaches an empty pew. He's about to enter it, followed by his sister, when Elspeth objects.

"No, no, we can't have you and Iona sitting together, and Grace and David sitting together. We should mix things up. David, why don't you go next to Iona?" She basically shoves her daughter down the pew first then encourages David to follow her. "And Grace, you can go beside Aidan. There! That's better."

There's no subtlety whatsoever to Elspeth's matchmaking attempts—she clearly wants Aidan and me to spend time in each other's company. Little does she know we already did a good bit of that last night.

Aidan fires me a quick wink then we sit, ready for the service, him on one side of me and Elspeth on the other. She beams at me encouragingly while, unbeknown to her, one of Aidan's fingers reaches out and gently tickles my thigh.

◆　◆　◆

I savour my last mouthful of roast turkey then let out a contented sigh. That was delicious but I'm completely stuffed. The satisfied expressions on the eight other faces around the table suggest they all feel similarly.

We're in the Bannock Hotel's restaurant, which under Emily's careful eye has been beautifully and stylishly decorated for Christmas. The brightly coloured paper hats perched on each head, pulled earlier from crackers, don't quite match the classy theme, but then neither do the assortment of garish Christmas jumpers on display.

Everyone's cheeks are rosy from alcohol, except for Emily's and my own. The three McIntyre brothers have really indulged, celebrating that for once they can relax in their home without having to wait on guests, the hotel being closed today.

"Now, there's more!" Elspeth's voice is louder than usual. She, too, has been marking the absence of patrons by refilling her glass at regular intervals. "Who's for seconds?"

There is a chorus of protests.

Aidan pats his stomach. "Maw and Lewis, that was incredible but I couldn't eat another thing. I don't think any of us could."

He's sitting beside me—Elspeth made sure of that—and is

wearing his Christmas present from his sister: a jumper featuring a cartoon sheep in a Santa hat and the words FLEECE NAVIDAD. Somehow, even in this goofy outfit, he's attractive. I don't know how he does it.

Elspeth isn't convinced by her son's claim. She gazes around the rest of us: the four McIntyre siblings, Iona, Emily, and me. David isn't here—he's eating with Johnny's family.

"There are two pregnant women in our midst," Elspeth says. "Your bairns need to grow big and strong so surely you'll both go for seconds?"

"Thanks, Elspeth, but no." My stomach aches pleasantly. There's no way I could put anything else in. "It was delicious but I need some time to digest."

"Me too," Emily agrees.

While Aidan is to my left, she's to my right. A vegetarian, she had a nut roast. I had a taste, and just like the turkey, it was really good.

She undoes the top button of her jeans. "Ah! That's better."

I glance down at her jeans and frown. "Wait, didn't you wear them before you got pregnant?"

"Yep. I've bought maternity clothes but I don't need them yet."

"*What?* You're only a week behind me!"

"I know. I'm so jealous." She eyes my belly. "I'd love a proper bump. No one realises I'm pregnant unless I tell them."

I chuckle and shake my head, scarcely believing her. "Oh no! You're managing to retain your figure while a child is growing inside you? That must be so difficult for you."

"If no one is for seconds, then it's on to dessert," Elspeth says, gracefully moving things along without acknowledging my playful remark. "Lewis has made a trifle and a Yule log.

There's a different compartment for sweet food, you know, so I'm sure you'll all manage something."

Lewis groans. "They both taste great, if I do say so myself, but . . . could anyone actually stomach them yet? Normally, I track everything I eat but Christmas is the one day I give myself off. I'm not used to feeling this bloated."

Jamie pats his brother's shoulder. "How about, as a last-minute Christmas present for us all, you don't mention your nutrition-tracking app or your gym routine for the rest of the day? None of us care."

Cat snorts. "So true!"

"Aye, although I am with you on the bloated thing." Ally rubs his stomach and winces. "Anyone up for a pre-dessert walk? It won't be light for much longer, so if we're going to do it, we should go soon."

It gets dark early in winter in the Highlands. Right now it's three o'clock. Christmas "dinner" was really more of a lunch.

"I'd be up for a walk," Iona says, "but . . . I can't move anywhere for at least five minutes."

"In that case let's have a five-minute break, then a walk, then dessert," Elspeth suggests. "Any objections?"

There are none.

Elspeth turns to me and Emily hopefully. "Perhaps, during our wee break, you two ladies could show me the scan pictures again?"

Emily went for her scan a week after Aidan and I went for mine. She and Ally are having a little boy.

"Maw, you get teary looking at them when you're sober," Aidan points out. "You've had a few wines—you'll be a mess. None of us want you blubbering on Christmas Day."

"Well, excuse me if it's a lovely thing that the first of the new generation are on their way," Elspeth says, her eyes already shimmering. "And you two wonderful ladies are having children at the same time, just as Mairi and I had these two at the same time." She indicates Ally and Aidan then, sniffing, adds, "Your mother and father would be so proud, Ally. I'm just sorry they're not here to see it."

"Nope!" Cat objects. "No, no, no. You're going to set us all off. I miss Maw and Da too but Aidan's right: no blubbering on Christmas Day."

Jamie gives a firm nod of agreement. "Anyway, how much more time can you spend staring at those pictures, Elspeth? Let's be honest, right now both babies look like aliens. All we can do is pray that, when they come out, they resemble humans."

"Don't listen to Uncle Jamie!" Emily gazes downwards and rests a hand on her neat, almost nonexistent, bump. "You're perfect."

"As is the wee one Grace is carrying," Elspeth adds. "The bonniest lass I've ever seen."

"Thanks, Maw," Iona mutters. "Not me, then? Your own daughter?"

"At least Richard thinks you're the bonniest lass he's ever seen," Jamie offers. He scans the faces around the table and frowns. "Wait, where is Richard? Why isn't he spending Christmas with his bonny lass?"

Iona shoots daggers at him. "You know fine well why. He's spending Christmas with his family and I'm spending it with mine. We'll be seeing each other for Hogmanay, though."

"Right." Jamie nods thoughtfully. "Well, Lewis is here and I'm pretty sure he thinks you're the bonniest lass he's ever seen, so that's something, right?"

Lewis, who's normally the most mild-mannered of the three brothers, glowers at Jamie. I remember what Aidan mentioned in London, that Lewis and Iona used to be best friends until something happened between them.

It's meant to be the season of cheer and goodwill, but in many families it can spiral into a period of disagreement and conflict. I don't want that to happen here so I try to change the subject.

Turning to Cat, I say, "How are you getting on down in Glasgow with your teacher-training course?"

She curls a lock of auburn hair around her finger. "Hmm . . ."

"The answer better be that everything is going perfectly," Ally warns.

Wow, now *he* is on edge. Maybe this wasn't the best direction in which to move the conversation.

"If you drop out, you're on your own," Ally adds. "This is your fifth year as a student, Cat. I can't go on supporting you indefinitely. Aidan and I have a fledgling business, I've got a bairn coming—"

"Don't get your knickers in a twist! I'm not going to drop out. I think I'd make a good English teacher. It's just . . . it's been four and a half years since I left this tiny town and escaped my three overbearing older brothers." She grins at Ally, Lewis, and Jamie. "I didn't think I'd ever look back but I've finally found something about Glasgow I don't like."

She pulls a face. "The teenagers! I shouldn't generalise but . . . Highland teenagers are *so* much nicer than Glasgow teenagers. I mean, when we were young, we fooled about and gave our teachers the odd bit of grief, but on the whole we were all right. In Glasgow classrooms, though, it's completely different. Some of these kids are wild! Was it the same in London?" She glances at me and Emily.

"Er . . ." I try to think.

Cat doesn't wait for an answer but pushes on. "Anyway, I'm having to consider which local authority to request for my probationary year. A few months ago I'd have put down Glasgow, no hesitation, but now I'm wondering if the Highlands aren't so bad after all. So . . . exciting news, bros: I may be coming back!"

"God help us," Jamie mutters.

"Jamie!" Elspeth reprimands. "It's Christmas. I normally let these things go but don't take the Lord's name in vain today."

"Oh, you pick him up on *that*," Lewis grumbles.

Elspeth ignores this comment. "Anyway, Cat, it'd be wonderful to have you back. Would you teach at Bannock High School?"

"It depends. You don't actually get to pick your school, only the local authority. They send you wherever needs a teacher, and because the Highland Council is *huge*, even if a lot of it is just empty land, they could send me miles and miles away. Still, no matter where I end up, I'll be closer than I am now so I'll be able to drive back at the weekend and visit my wee nephew."

"Hmm." Jamie takes out his phone and taps at it.

"What are you looking up?" Cat questions.

"Just checking which high school is furthest from Bannock. I'll put in a good word for you."

Cat rolls her eyes. "You act like I'm the problem but I'm not. It's you, Jamie. If we could just send you away somewhere, the rest of us might actually have nice, pleasant family meals."

There are general murmurs of agreement. Even Elspeth nods.

"Aye, but they wouldn't be as fun." Jamie winks.

As the McIntyre siblings continue their bickering, Aidan turns to me and flashes a grin, shaking his head at their antics. I return the smile. His gaze drifts down and he reaches out and tenderly picks something off my shoulder. He lifts it—just a piece of tinsel. He puts it on his plate then goes back for another piece. I hadn't realised my top was a tinsel magnet.

"Wait, is something going on between you two?" Iona whispers from across the table.

It's not a great whisper because all other conversation stops and every head in the room turns to us. Most faces display a mix of confusion and curiosity. Only Emily and Ally aren't surprised because they of course already know.

"What did I miss?" Cat asks eagerly. "Are you two seeing each other?"

Elspeth leans in, her eyes widening with equal interest.

Aidan and I exchange a glance and I raise my brows questioningly. Emily and I are the newcomers here. He's known everyone else around this table his entire life. It should be up to him what he tells them.

He rubs the back of his neck and chuckles. "Er, please don't get overexcited but . . . aye, Grace and I are giving things a go."

Elspeth clasps her hands together in teary-eyed delight, and there are grins and exclamations of approval from the rest of the group.

Jamie leaps from his seat and runs off, returning with mistletoe. "Thanks for getting this, Emily. Who knew it'd come in handy?" He comes up behind me and Aidan and holds it over our heads. "Well, go on!"

For a moment I wonder if Aidan might refuse. After all, having spurned romance his entire life, he's only just getting used to the small acts of affection couples share. Maybe it'd be too much for him to kiss me in front of his family and the McIntyres, who are as good as family.

But he barely even hesitates. He leans close and presses his lips to mine, while everyone else around the table erupts into applause.

CHAPTER TWENTY-FIVE

AIDAN

We go through Bannock Woods for our pre-dessert walk, all nine of us bundled up in our winter gear. Most of the trees are bare and have been for weeks, but the Scots pines retain their evergreen needles and look bonny covered in glistening snow. The crisp forest air is pure and clean, each breath I inhale as refreshing as a gulp of icy water—the perfect remedy after indulging in a heavy meal.

Our group has split off into three pairs and a trio. Lewis and Jamie are up front, Ally and Emily following behind, then it's Cat, Iona, and Maw. Grace and I bring up the rear, maintaining a comfortable distance from the others and walking with our gloved hands linked.

For many people, holding hands with another in public is an everyday occurrence, but for me, it's a novelty. It feels good.

Grace points to the icicles hanging from branches and the tracks of wildlife in the snow and says how lucky I am to have these woods on my doorstep. She's right—the forest is pretty, especially today—but I'm more interested in the sharp slope of her high cheekbones, the spiral curls spilling from under her woollen hat, and the way her full lips part slightly as she takes in her surroundings.

I draw her towards me and press my lips to her luscious ones. She tastes cold, as I'm sure I do too, our faces the only parts of our bodies not protected from the chilly air. But she opens up to let me in and our tongues meet, the kiss becoming warm and sweet.

"Oi, lovebirds, stop canoodling!" Ally calls from up ahead.

The rest of the group have stopped and are watching us with amusement. Maw is positively beaming.

Breaking apart, Grace and I exchange a smile. She squeezes my hand and we crunch on through the snow, catching up with the others. Together, we follow a trail that winds its way to the edge of the woods, arriving at the adventure playground. The climbing frames, swings, slide, and other equipment poke out from under the blanket of white and are covered in sparkling frost.

"Do you all remember the long summer days we spent here?" I ask, directing my question to Iona and the McIntyre siblings.

"Aye, we'd play for hours and hours," Ally reminisces. "When we got hungry, we'd run home for food, wolf it down, then come straight back."

"No parents to supervise us, no mobile phones," Iona adds. "Just freedom."

"Those days really did seem to last forever," Lewis says.

"All right, Bryan Adams, calm down!" Jamie retorts.

Lewis shakes his head.

"Sometimes we all played big games together," Cat remembers, "but other times, Ally and Aidan, you did your own thing, while Lewis and Iona did their own thing, and I was stuck with you, Jamie. Which was horrible." She lets out a deep sigh, her breath misting in the cold air. "I wish I could go back and tell my younger self things get better."

"Aw, c'mon, you love me really. We all know that spiel about Glasgow teenagers was just an excuse. You're returning to the Highlands for one reason only and that's to see more of your favourite brother. This lot are all older but you and me, Cat? There's only a year between us. Sure, it's not quite Grace and David, but it's still a special connection."

Cat raises an eyebrow then turns to Grace. "How come you won the lottery? I've got three brothers and they're all rubbish, but you've just got one and he's a gem. And Emily"—she shifts her attention to her—"an only child? What I wouldn't have given to switch places with you some days. At times all I wanted was a bit of peace and quiet."

"Charming!" Lewis grumbles. "And here was me thinking I was a pretty good big brother."

"You must have had plenty of peace and quiet around Bannock, no?" Emily says. "I think it'd be a magical place to grow up as a kid and I'm excited about raising our boy here." Her gloved hand goes to her belly, almost like it's an instinctive reaction to the mere mention of her baby. "It'll be a very different upbringing from my own."

"Bannock is a wonderful place to raise a family," Maw agrees, her expression growing nostalgic. "Your wee one will be very happy here, Emily. And Grace, your wee one will love visiting. I'm going to spoil her rotten every time she comes up so she'll always look forward to coming back."

It's a sweet sentiment but it reminds me that Grace lives six hundred miles away in London, as will our wee girl when she's born. As much as I'd like to move closer to them, I've just started a business with Ally, and even if I were to chuck that in, I'm an outdoor instructor. London is a bustling metropolis with endless employment options, but when your job is literally working in the great outdoors, it's not the best place to be.

Would Grace ever consider moving here? I've no idea.

We continue on, choosing a path that will take us on a circular tour back through the woods. We've been going for a while when Grace suddenly stops.

"Wait, it looks different in the snow but . . . isn't this where I fell?"

This question brings the rest of our group to a halt.

I chuckle. "Aye, you're right. It was there I picked you up." I point with my free hand, my other still intertwined with Grace's.

"You carried Grace all the way to the hotel from here?" Iona blinks. "That's quite a distance."

"It is!" Cat chimes. "That's so sweet, Aidan."

"And romantic," Emily adds.

I shrug like it was nothing.

"Still, you'll be glad it happened when it did," Jamie comments. "You wouldn't want to be carrying Grace now, not with that big bump. No offence, Grace."

She offers an unconvincing laugh but I grit my teeth.

"Jamie, you can't say whatever you like then add 'no offence' after it, as though that somehow makes it okay. That was out of order."

He raises two gloved hands in surrender. "All right, jeez, sorry! I take it back."

He turns and walks on but I'm not done with him yet. I bend, scoop up some snow, press it into a snowball, then hurl a belter that gets him right on the back of the head. He staggers in surprise, and for once it's Jamie who's the butt of the joke. Even Maw can't resist a wee giggle.

He spins around, and far from being annoyed, his expression is one of delight. "This is war!" he proclaims.

"Aye, it is." Lewis tosses a snowball of his own and gets Jamie square in the face.

This is met with even louder laughs, and the next second, all the men—and Cat too—are scrambling to make snowballs. They're chucked left, right, and centre.

"I'm waving a white flag and so are the pregnant ladies. Over here, girls!" Maw leads an amused Grace and Emily to a safe distance.

Dodging a snowball meant for me, Iona frowns. "Aren't we too old for this?"

"Nope." I hurl one back. "When else will you get to hit Jamie without consequence?"

"Good point!" She kneels, gathers together her first snowball, and—like most of the rest of us—aims for the youngest McIntyre brother.

From the sidelines, Maw says to Grace and Emily, "Just a few minutes ago, they were reminiscing about being children. I'm not entirely sure they've grown up! Would you guess by looking at them we have here a vet, a hotel manager, a teacher in training, and two dads-to-be?"

Scoring a good hit on Jamie, Iona makes me her new target. I see it coming, though, and get her first. This only spurs her on, and Ally joins sides with her, going for me too.

Jamie, whose gaze is darting left and right as he watches out for incoming snowballs, calls to Maw, "You only mentioned five people. You left off me!"

"No, I didn't," she retorts. "You, Jamie, are acting exactly as I would expect you to."

"Fighting talk! Emily and Grace have an excuse but I reckon it'd be ageist of me not to go for you. This one is coming your way, Elspeth."

"Don't you dare! Jamie McIntyre, I am warning y—"

Jamie swings his arm and Maw throws up her own two to protect herself. But Jamie doesn't actually let go of the snowball. He winks.

"Just kidding! Thanks for making us an amazing Christmas dinner."

It may only have been a prank, but the next second, he's pelted from all angles.

"That's my maw you're bothering!" Iona bellows.

"All right, all right, that's enough!" Jamie laughs. "I surrender."

The snowballs stop flying and there are chuckles as we brush ourselves down. Then, out of nowhere, a final ball sails through the air and strikes an unsuspecting Jamie in the mouth. He has to spit out snow.

We all turn to see who threw it.

"Sorry!" Grace grins bashfully. "If I'd known it was going to be over so quickly, I'd have thrown one earlier. I didn't want to miss my chance to get Jamie, though—not after that comment about the size of my bump."

I let out a deep belly laugh. Grace really is incredible. Taking out Jamie after truce had been declared? That was magnificent.

"Well, after running around like bairns, have you all now found some space for dessert?" Maw asks.

There is a resounding "Yes!" from everyone.

"And a hot drink as well, please." Emily shivers. "Oh, and

afterwards, Ally was telling me it's tradition for you to play board games?"

"Aye." Lewis nods solemnly. "If you thought the snowball fight was ruthless, wait till we whip out Trivial Pursuit—then you'll see us get competitive. It can be an emotional roller coaster."

"Er . . ." Grace says. "Shouldn't it just be a bit of fun?"

"*No!*" Maw, Iona, Ally, Lewis, Jamie, Cat, and I all let out the same exclamation at once.

Grace's eyes widen with surprise.

"Sorry," I murmur, "but it *is* about the winning, obviously."

We head back to the hotel, the sun sinking out of sight, leaving a twilight gloom. Grace and I once again take up the rear.

"Seeing as everyone knows about us now," she says softly, "you don't have to sleep at your mum's tonight. You can stay at David and Johnny's with me. We can snuggle up together against the cold."

"Just snuggle?" I wiggle my eyebrows. "There's another way a man and a woman can warm up, and it's pretty great."

"Sounds . . . interesting. By any chance, would this way also help us relax after a stressful board game?"

I laugh. "You shouldn't worry about that—a bit of competition makes things more fun. But aye, the thing I have in mind has a reputation for relieving stress."

The corners of her lips turn up playfully. "Good. Well, we should give it a shot, then. Maybe you'll even last a little longer than you did yesterday."

"Oh, low blow!" I squeeze her hand. "Last night was different. I'd been saving myself for you for so long. Tonight,

195

though? You better prepare yourself. I've one more Christmas present for you and it'll have you screaming out my name."

"I'm sure David and Johnny will love that."

"Aye, well, if you'd planned ahead, you'd have got them earplugs for Christmas. Plus a pair for me too—I've not forgotten you're quite the snorer."

"And with that comment, sex is off the cards."

"No!" I chuckle. "It was just a joke. I take it back. Please!"

"Hmm . . . how about a foot massage when we get to the cottage? Maybe then I'll reconsider."

"Deal."

CHAPTER TWENTY-SIX

GRACE

It's Boxing Day and I'm in the living room of Elspeth's house. Aidan isn't here—he's gone out and has been a bit vague as to what he's up to. Elspeth and Iona, meanwhile, are in the loft, searching for old baby things, in case there's anything that might be of use. I'd offered to go up with them but they wouldn't hear of me crawling about in the dust.

So . . . it's just me, on the sofa, nursing a peppermint tea. I help myself to another Abernethy biscuit from a plate on the coffee table. They're pretty good.

Elspeth invited me here for some "girl chat", and it's been fun, but right now I feel like a spare part. I wish Emily had come along too, but the hotel has reopened today and she's expecting guests.

Putting down my drink, I get up and examine some ornaments Elspeth has dotted around the room. I like the wooden carvings of animals best—a Highland cow, squirrel, otter, and stag.

I go over to a shelf in the corner on which a number of photo albums are neatly organised. Taking down the first one, I open it and smile when I see Aidan as a newborn, swaddled in a blanket and sleeping soundly. He's in the arms of a younger Elspeth, who gazes at him lovingly.

On the next page, Aidan is being doted on by a man who has brown hair but otherwise shares many of Aidan's features—the same jawline, strong forehead, and playful smile. There can be no doubt this is Aidan's dad.

I flick through, Aidan growing older with each turn of the page. Sporting golden curls and a gummy grin, he lies on a mat beside another, grumpier, baby, who must be Ally. Aidan sits in a seat, supporting his own head. He crawls through this very living room, although the decor has since changed. He stares in wonder at his first birthday cake; he wobbles on his feet; he pats a dog; he takes a bath with Ally. I remember this last pic from the thirtieth party. They're both adorably cute in it.

Reaching the end, I put back the album and take out another. Aidan, as a three-year-old, gazes into a Moses basket at his baby sister, Iona. Over the page, he cuddles Iona on a sofa while, beside them, Ally hugs Lewis.

I skim through then reach for the next album. Aidan and Ally, in their uniforms, hold hands and beam at the camera, ready for their first day of primary school. Iona and Lewis, also holding hands, feed ducks at a pond.

Elspeth has lovingly captured every stage of her children's lives. Because there's so much to go through, I decide to check out just a few pages of each album before moving on. Aidan quickly grows into a tween and then a teenager, and soon it's his last day of high school and he's again posing with Ally, their white shirts scrawled with messages from their classmates.

The next album is different. It hasn't been created by Elspeth but by Aidan himself, and it showcases his travels around the world. A slightly younger Aidan, wearing only a pair of shorts, stands on a beach, perhaps in Australia. With sand in his hair and squinting against the sun, he grins at the camera. I can't help but smile: he really is an incredibly good-looking man.

As I flick through his visual journal of his years away, my smile falters. On every other page, he's posing next to a woman—a different one each time. What exactly is he recording here? The places he visited or his conquests?

I should close the album and put it back—I know I should—but for some reason I can't stop myself from going through more and more of it, seeing more and more women.

Did he sleep with all of them or are some of them just people he met and chatted with on his travels? Does it make a difference? Even if he only slept with half of them, it's still a lot.

I'm aware I don't have any right to get upset. It's not like I didn't know about Aidan's reputation or that he tried to keep it a secret. But *seeing* these women with my own eyes makes it real. It doesn't matter how much I attempt to rationalise it in my head, I can't stop my body from having a physical reaction to the pictures. My grip on the album tightens, my hands shake, my palms grow clammy.

Is it even possible for a man like Aidan to settle down? This last month, I'd come to think he and I could have a future together, but have I been deluding myself? Isn't it inevitable he'll get bored at some point and move on? Isn't that what his dad did?

The only reason Aidan is giving me a shot is because of the baby. Is that a solid basis for a relationship?

No. Of course it isn't.

I snap the album closed and put it away. What am I doing?

Why am I trying to convince myself we can't make this work? We've been sensible and Aidan especially wanted to take things slowly at first. Why can't I just see how it goes? Why do I have to assume the worst?

Then again, isn't it important to have realistic expectations?

Footsteps on the stairs indicate Elspeth and Iona are on their way down. I return to my seat, lift my cup of tea, and plaster a smile onto my face.

"I didn't realise Maw was such a hoarder." Iona lugs a carrycot and folded pram chassis into the living room then tries to figure out how to fit them together. "There's enough stuff up there for her to open her own nursery!"

"And Grace is free to pick what she wants and reject what she doesn't." Elspeth comes in with a couple of vacuum storage bags filled with baby clothes. "Anything you don't take with you to London could be useful for when you visit. Babies may be small but they need a lot of things. If the bairn has some supplies here, it'll make it easier for you when you're packing."

She pops down the bags, which are both labelled O TO 3 MONTHS. "There are plenty more in the loft for when the wee one is older. I've got a few more big items too, such as a walker, but she won't be using that until she's six months or so."

"Oh, wow," I say. "This is great. Thank you."

In my head, though, I'm thinking the pram alone will cut into the limited floor space in my flat. I'll need to put in a cot too, of course, and apparently she'll need some room for a walker and what else? A high chair? How will it all fit?

And . . . what about all those women in that bloody photo album?

Elspeth opens the first vacuum bag and takes out items one at a time, holding them up. She and Iona coo over the cutest little dresses Iona wore when she was a newborn. I compliment them too but my heart isn't really in this today. It's not that the clothes aren't nice. I'm just distracted.

Folding an adorable pink coat, Elspeth lets out a contented sigh. "I'm so looking forward to becoming a grandmother. Now, the last thing I want to do is stick my nose in someone else's business, Grace, but even if the baby wasn't planned, I'm sure your mother will be pleased too. I hope you don't wait too much longer before telling her."

"Oh, I won't. Mum said she'd come up to Bannock sometime between Christmas and New Year, although she's still to confirm when. Anyway, I'll tell her when I see her."

"Wonderful!" Elspeth beams, satisfied.

The front door opens and a moment later Aidan strolls into the living room. He shoots me the same charming grin I saw in the photos of him with all those other women. I have to suppress a shudder.

"Wow, baby stuff! I didn't know you kept all this, Maw. I don't want to interrupt the party, but Grace, there's something I'd like to show you. Can I steal you away for a wee while?"

"Er, sure." I put down my tea. "If that's okay with you, Elspeth?"

"Of course. We can go through the rest of this another time. She's all yours, Aidan."

◆ ◆ ◆

Aidan drives me out of Bannock and through white-blanketed countryside. The roads have been cleared but snow remains everywhere else. It's late in the afternoon and darkness is already drawing in.

"Do you remember, at the airport, you moaned about my brother and his love of surprises?" I ask.

Aidan chuckles, briefly glancing my way before returning his attention to the road ahead. "Aye."

"Well, why are you now doing the same thing to me? Why can't you just tell me where we're going?"

"I thought a bit of mystery would be fun, no?"

"I've had my fill of surprises this year."

"Fair enough. The thing is, there's something I'd like to discuss with you and it'll be easier if we do it in the place I want to show you. It'll make sense when we get there, I promise."

"Can you at least tell me how far away it is?"

"Not far. It's only ten minutes from Bannock and we've been driving for a few minutes already."

"Okay, I suppose I can wait that long."

A short while later, Aidan slows the car as we approach a turn-off. "Ah, now that is a slight problem."

Unlike the main road, the track Aidan wants to take is covered in untouched snow. He pulls over, lifts the handbrake, and kills the engine.

"We'll just have to continue on foot. We're close."

I narrow my eyes. "This better be worth it. I'm a pregnant woman—I'd have put on warmer clothes if I'd known we were going for a winter walk."

"I think you'll like it. C'mon!" He winks then gets out, goes around the car, opens my door, and offers me a hand, my less-than-enthusiastic attitude not dampening his mood in the slightest.

Accepting his help, I step out and we set off up the track, crunching through the deep snow. An unpleasant wetness seeps into the bottom of my jeggings and slowly rises up the fabric, which grows cold and clings to my skin. Ugh!

"As you know, I've not wanted to rush things between us," Aidan says, oblivious to my discomfort. "But these last few days, I've been thinking a lot and I don't like how difficult it's going to be for us when the baby comes.

"I live in the very north of this island, and you live in the very south. When our lass arrives, you'll have your hands full, and I'll want to help but it won't be easy. Bannock Adventures is quiet right now, but Ally and I will get busy again in the spring, and in the summer, all going well, we'll be working seven days a week.

"It's not like I'll be able to take a break when I feel like it and nip to London to see you both. Ally and I make our money when the weather is good, and we can't turn down work then. It's not a 'Monday to Friday, nine to five' kind of job. It's a 'long hours in the summer, lots of free time in the winter' job."

He's right, of course. It's going to be tough.

"So . . . where is this conversation going?"

"I've been planning to move out for a while. I even went to see a place on my thirtieth birthday, right before you dropped a certain bombshell. After learning you were pregnant, I put the idea on hold but maybe that was stupid. The property I was looking at is easily big enough for me, you, and the bairn. Maybe it'd be perfect for us?"

"Aidan, I—"

"I know it's a lot. We can still be sensible and go slowly—I'm not suggesting we force this thing between us. But we are having a baby together and I can't see how else this is going to work, so maybe we should give things a proper shot? You don't have to say anything just yet. Take some time to let the idea sink in. We'll have a look around the place, then we can chat."

My heart rate has picked up. I wasn't expecting this. Yes, we've been talking every day for a while now, but these last few months, I can count on my fingers the number of days we've spent in each other's company and still have a few fingers left over. To go from that to moving in together is crazy, isn't it?

But I don't immediately shoot the idea down. Aidan asked me to think over it before replying so that's what I'll do.

"The place you saw on your birthday is still available?" I say instead.

"Aye, it is, and I know the estate agent, Finlay Cochrane, pretty well. Earlier, when I left you with Maw and Iona, I went to see him and convinced him to let me give you a private tour." Aidan pulls out a set of keys and jangles them. "I've got these for an hour, even though Cochrane and Munro Estate Agents is technically closed today. Finlay did mention there'd been some interest from another party recently, so no pressure, but if you like it, we may have to move quickly."

"Great," I murmur. "So I can take time to think this over, but just not too long?"

Aidan chuckles and kicks some snow. "Aye, but we're getting ahead of ourselves. As I said, let's start with a tour, then we can chat."

The snowy track broadens out into a clearing and I get my first glimpse of the house. Still, gloomy, and nestled against a backdrop of snow-dusted trees, it's hauntingly isolated. There are no streetlights nearby, and with day now turning to night, the entire landscape will soon be shrouded in darkness. Why on earth would Aidan want to move here?

He leads me to the front door, fiddles with the keys, then

opens up and searches for a light switch. Finding it, he grins and beckons me in. "A quick warning: you will have to use your imagination. A lot of the decoration has to be modernised, and a good deal of the furniture will need to be changed too, but there's so much potential. This could be a really amazing home."

Maybe I also have to use my imagination to picture some neighbours or the house being in a completely different location, but I keep that thought to myself.

Aidan takes me through the cold, quiet property, showing me the living room and large kitchen then ushering me upstairs to see the three bedrooms and bathroom. He talks me through his vision—he's already decided which room will be ours and which the nursery, and he's got some ideas for the last room, although he's not yet certain what to do with it. He suggests we could come up with a plan together.

I listen but say nothing. I don't understand why he's so enthusiastic about this place. It's all wrong.

Tour completed, he takes us back to the kitchen and plonks himself on a sofa that supposedly looks out to the garden and the forest beyond, except it's even darker outside now, and with the light on in here, it's hard to make out much at all. If there were someone out there in the trees, peering in at us, they'd be able to see everything, while we wouldn't even know they were there. My skin crawls with the thought.

Aidan pats a spot beside him on the sofa and I reluctantly sit.

"Well, what do you think? Isn't it crazy that you rent a wee box down in London and yet we could own all of this?"

"Hmm."

"There's a public footpath that runs from Bannock to

Duntreath, and it goes right past the house. It'd take close to an hour to walk to Maw's from here, but . . ."

He trails off. Maybe he can see in my expression that I'm not impressed. He bites his lip.

"I don't think this place is at its best in the winter. When I saw it in the autumn, it was stunning. There was an amazing view of the trees from here, their leaves turning golden. And, oh, just imagine it in the spring or the summer. It'd be perfect!"

I scoff. "Perfect?"

"Crap. You really don't like it, do you?"

I shake my head. He grimaces.

"But if we did it up, made it our own, and—"

"I'm sorry, but there's no way I'd ever live somewhere like this."

After Mark, I swore I wouldn't fall back into the trap of giving up my own needs and wants for someone else's. On this issue I'm putting my foot down.

"Hypothetically, were I to move up north, it'd be to stay in Bannock, not a place as remote as this. I love that Emily and David are just a few minutes' walk from each other. It'd be nice to be able to pop out my front door and visit them or nip into the bakery or the pub or Bannock Stores. There's also the sense of community: the church on Christmas Day, the lights brightening the town, the fact everyone knows each other . . . that all has a certain appeal.

"But you're instead suggesting we live apart from all that and by ourselves. Like you said earlier, you'll be working seven days a week throughout the summer, so . . . what? I'd be stuck here, alone, with a baby? Why would I want that? Yes, I stay in a box in London, but I'd rather be in a tiny flat somewhere that has a bit of life to it than in a big house in the middle of nowhere."

Aidan wrings his hands. "Fuck, this wasn't how I was expecting this to go."

He falls quiet and I wonder if he's angry, although maybe he's just taking this in. I've already made my point, so rather than jumping in to say even more, I give him some time. Eventually he takes a deep breath.

"I'm sorry, I've messed up—and everything was going so well yesterday! Can we rewind, please? I'm rushing things, which is something I said I didn't want to do. This was a stupid idea. Can you forget I took you here?"

Normally, Aidan looks so confident, so cocky. Now, though, he's faltering and I'm not used to seeing him like this. Any annoyance I felt about being brought to this creepy house evaporates, and instead my heart aches at this display of vulnerability.

I realise too I've maybe been a bit blunt with my opinions. I stand by them but I could probably have found a more diplomatic way of expressing them. Perhaps I'm still a little annoyed about the photo album I saw earlier, but it's not fair to get upset with Aidan about that. That chronicled a time in his life before we met, and it showed a side of him he's never attempted to hide.

I place a hand on his knee and squeeze it. "Here's the thing: you and I are unique individuals and that's okay. In any relationship, there are shared qualities and there are differences. You're an outdoorsman and I understand why this property would appeal to you. But . . . imagine a Venn diagram."

On his leg I draw a circle with my finger. "This is you." I draw a second circle. "And this is me. See this area where the two circles overlap? That's the sweet spot. Honestly, I'm still not sure we're ready to move in together, but if we did, it'd need to be somewhere in here—a place that appeals to both of us. Right now you've instead taken me to a house that's all the way over here." I move my finger down his leg towards the far end of the zone I said represented him.

He smirks. "I may be new to relationships but I get the concept that this property is more me than you. I could probably even have grasped it without a diagram."

I slap his thigh. "Hey! I'm not trying to belittle your intelligence. I'm trying to help."

"I know, and actually, it felt kind of nice when you were drawing on my leg. You got pretty high when you were doing your circle. I'm frantically thinking up other things I could ask you to explain to me. If you could go just a wee bit higher and a little to the side, that'd be perfect."

I let out a sigh and shake my head. "A minute ago, when your eyes went wide and you realised you'd messed up, I felt bad for you. That didn't last long."

"I'm only kidding! Well . . . okay, if you did want to draw circles on my crotch, I wouldn't stop you, but—"

"Aidan! You've just shown me around a freezing house that could be the setting for a horror film, and my jeggings are wet and cold from walking through the snow. Why are you under the impression you've earned some kind of sexual reward?"

He considers. "All right, maybe I picked the wrong place, but suggesting we move in together is quite romantic, isn't it?" He squeezes my thigh and, in a low voice, adds, "We do have this house to ourselves for a while longer. Would it be crazy to have sex in a home that doesn't belong to us and which is up for sale?"

"Yes, Aidan, that would be crazy. Even if I wasn't shivering, there's no way I'd do that. Unlike you, I have some self-respect."

"Noted. Kind of a boring answer but I see where you're coming from. I suppose we're still getting to know each other. Today I've learnt that, while you're happy to suck me off in your brother's living room, getting up to mischief in a house that's for sale is a step too far."

"*That's* what you've learnt? Not that showing me a cold, lonely building in the middle of nowhere, and suggesting I move into it, was a terrible idea?"

"Oh, aye, I suppose I learnt that too. Wow, two things in one day—before you know it, we'll be like those couples who finish each other's sentences."

That mischievous glint in his eye. That cheeky grin. Aidan wasn't knocked down for long. He's taking this in his stride, as he does most things. He's not going to get upset over the minor fact I detest a property he'd set his heart on.

I sit up straighter. "Let's see if you can finish this sentence. I want to go back to your mum's and have a . . ."

"Shag in my bedroom?"

With a sigh, I slouch back into the sofa.

He winks and instead offers, "Cup of tea?"

"Bingo! And we can look through the rest of the baby things your mum wanted to show me."

"All right, but before we go, can I just say . . . I really am sorry, you know, for bringing you here. Everyone thinks I'm this smooth guy who always knows what to say and do around women, and to be fair, I am great on a first date." He grins cockily. "But this stuff? It's all new to me. So, aye, maybe I've been a little overeager, like some lovestruck teenager."

"Lovestruck?" I repeat in a teasing tone. "Have you fallen in love with me, Aidan?"

He shrugs. "Well, I did just ask you to move in with me, so . . ."

"Wait, what?" I jerk up. "I was only kidding. It's too early to talk about love—way too early."

He winces. "Crap, have I messed up again? I really am bad at this. Maybe this isn't love—I don't know. What I do know is the way I feel about you is unlike anything I've experienced before, and it's a nice feeling, one I'm keen to explore more. And it does seem a lot like the kind of thing soppy love songs go on about, so . . ."

He drums his fingers on his leg. "I like being around you, I want to spend as much time with you as possible, and the thought of you going back to London hurts. Does that mean I love you or do I just really like you? Maybe it's the latter but I wouldn't be surprised if that grows into love."

This is too much to take in.

"You can't throw all these words about! Remember at the restaurant? You told me you didn't like being called a player because it suggests you play with women's emotions, and that's something you deny."

"I do deny that. I'm not trying to play with your emotions, Grace. I'm literally being as honest with you as I can. I'm telling you exactly what's going on in my mind."

"Shit. Well . . . I really like you too." I lean over and peck his cheek. "Now that's out in the open, why don't we go get that tea?"

CHAPTER TWENTY-SEVEN

GRACE

Emily and I are at a table in the snug of the Bannock Hotel. It's just the two of us. We're catching up over hot chocolates and going over plans for motherhood.

Even though it's only an informal chat between friends, when I arrived, Emily produced an A4 binder, as though this were in fact a business meeting. The folder covers everything from cots and prams to maternity bras and baby-led weaning. Handwritten notes are mixed in with clippings from magazines and printouts from websites. There's even a mood board for transforming one of the hotel's rooms into a nursery. It shows off a soft neutral colour palette and various pieces of stylish oak furniture.

I shouldn't be surprised by how organised Emily is. She was, after all, a successful wedding planner back in London, while she's now employing her skills to put on events in the new function room. Even so, I can't help but compare us and feel a twinge of inadequacy. I've saved a few bookmarks on my phone's browser but that's about it.

It's not just Emily's organisational ability that has me

feeling inferior. As she turns the pages of the binder, her engagement ring sparkles in the light of a lamp—a reminder that our situations are very different.

Luckily, before my comparisonitis can spoil our catch-up, Lewis arrives carrying two plates. "Sorry to interrupt but I made some scones earlier. I thought you ladies might fancy a snack?"

"Yes, please!" Emily says.

"That'd be lovely," I agree. "Thanks, Lewis."

Grinning, he places down the plates. On each is a fruit scone, a small jar of jam, a pot of clotted cream, a napkin, and a knife. "Enjoy! I'll leave you to it." He departs as quickly as he arrived.

Emily lets out a contented sigh. "I swear living here is dangerous for my figure."

"Hmm."

She remains nearly as petite as she was before she fell pregnant.

"I'm being serious! Having Morag's Bakery just down the road is both a blessing and a curse. Normally, I find it too hard to resist temptation, but Morag has closed up shop between Christmas and New Year. I thought this would be the perfect time for a no-cake diet, but it's not working out very well because Lewis is into baking too."

I halve my scone, slather on the cream, then top it with jam. "Planning a diet for Christmastime was a mistake—that was never going to happen. Anyway, if we'll be gaining weight no matter what, I say we might as well enjoy it."

With that comment, I take my first bite, closing my eyes and savouring it. Ah! Crispy on the outside, velvety soft on the inside, punctuated by the sweetness of the jam and the richness of the cream. Bliss!

"You're right." Emily bites into her scone too then groans with satisfaction. "Oh, this is incredible. I don't know how Lewis keeps his gym-honed figure when he can bake like this."

So as not to get crumbs on the binder, we don't touch it while we're eating. It remains open at some clippings of items Emily has identified as being essential from birth: her preferred sling, bouncer, bath, and breast pump.

"When you add up everything a baby needs, it gets so expensive, doesn't it?" I say. "And some things, they'll only use for a few months or maybe even just a few weeks."

Emily considers this. "True, but then again, their little brothers and sisters will get use of them, right?"

I giggle. "Little brothers and sisters? How many are you and Ally planning to have?"

"Good question! Even though Ally is the eldest of four, he says he'd happily stop after one, but since I didn't have siblings, I really want our child to have at least one but ideally a few. I expect I'll get my own way in the end."

We share a smile. Ally may moan at times but he dotes on Emily and would do anything for her. Chances are he'll come around to her way of thinking.

"Anyway, how are things going between you and Aidan?"

"Fine, I think, although yesterday he did something a bit weird." I briefly explain about the visit to that awful house.

"Typical man! He doesn't understand what it'll be like for you when the baby comes. Of course you wouldn't want to live somewhere like that. Although . . . he may have picked the wrong house, but what about the idea of you moving up here?

I'm biased but I think having you in Bannock would be the best thing ever."

I take another sip of my hot chocolate while I mull this over. "I can't deny it has a certain appeal but how would I earn money? My business is down in London and I refuse to be a kept woman—I need my independence. To be honest, I doubt Aidan earns enough for that to be a possibility anyway."

"Why do you think you'd have to come up with a completely new business? You could teach yoga here too."

"Oh, yeah? And where would I do that?"

"Have you forgotten about the function room I basically bullied Ally into finishing? That would be the perfect spot."

I tap a finger on the table, considering this. "True, but would anyone actually come along?"

"Yes! Trust me, the people of this town love any sort of social event. I guarantee if you put on classes, they'll be filled. Sure, some folk will mainly show up for a chat and to get out of the house, but they'll still take part."

I laugh. "Do you really think so?"

"I do. Things are different here to how they are down south. In London there's so much competition that at times it can feel like everyone is constantly vying against each other. Here, though? People want local businesses to succeed. No one is going to see you as their enemy, only as someone to support.

"There's also the Glen Garve Resort. Ally and Aidan are working with them—you could work with them too. I bet they have guests who'd love nothing more than to attend a yoga class while their other halves are out doing a round of golf. Then there'd be couples who'd want to participate together, plus the resort gets some solo travellers, and it's also a popular spot for corporate retreats. All of them would be potential clients for you.

"I'm sure it's an idea the Glen Garve would be interested in. If only you had an in with them. Oh, wait a minute! Your twin brother is dating *and lives with* Johnny MacDonald, whose dad is the manager there—and Johnny works at the resort as well. You're also currently staying in Johnny's cottage. I reckon you could easily wangle your way into the Glen Garve's leisure schedule."

Smirking, I polish off the last of the scone. "You may be right, but would there be enough work around for me to make a living?"

"I think so. There'd be other opportunities to explore too. Bannock is the biggest town in the area, but there are little villages dotted all about, and pretty much all of them have a church hall that can be hired out for classes.

"If necessary, there's also Inverness—it's forty minutes away. You could do a day or two there every week to top up your income, but that might not even be needed. I wouldn't be surprised if you were able to drum up a decent amount of business locally. In fact, it could be a really flexible lifestyle that'd work well around having a baby."

The thought is tempting. I've been worrying recently that, thanks to my ever-increasing overheads, my rates are pushing away clients who just can't justify the expense. Up here, though, my costs would be a lot less than in London and that'd allow me to price my classes at a level that should be more affordable. I like the sound of that.

Emily's voice rises in pitch as she excitedly adds, "And we could help each other out! If you're doing a class in the function room, I could look after the babies, then when I'm putting on an event, you could return the favour. Oh, please, Grace! It'd be so great to have you here. Bannock is almost perfect but the one thing it's missing is you. Please, please, *please* say you'll at least consider it."

"You're doing a very good job of selling the idea to me," I admit, chuckling. "Let me have a chat with Aidan. And, oh yeah, there's something else I've not mentioned yet. After showing me the house, he told me he thinks he might love me. He then clarified that maybe he just really likes me—he wasn't sure. It caught me off-guard anyway. I didn't know what to say."

A sly smile forms on Emily's lips. "I was so right about you and Aidan. I knew you'd win him over."

"But isn't it too soon for him to be talking like that? We've not spent that much time together yet."

"Hmm, well, I've got a really good feeling about you two—always have—but to play devil's advocate, let's say it doesn't work out. I'm not saying that's what's going to happen; I'm just saying let's consider all possibilities. In that scenario I reckon you'd both be mature enough to stay friends and raise your girl amicably.

"It's not as though, if you give things a shot and they don't go as hoped, that's it, everything is over and you'll be passing her between you without so much as exchanging a word. In a way, you've got nothing to lose. If it works out, great, and if not, well, you're still getting a wonderful baby out of this whom you'll love and cherish."

I nod, absent-mindedly tracing patterns on the tabletop. "You make it sound so easy. I do like Aidan and maybe we could have a future together, but I'm bothered by his reputation. Given how he was, has he really got it in him to be a loving boyfriend and father?"

Emily squeezes my arm. "I think so, but as I say, what have you got to lose? There might be a house in the town itself you and him could move into, and you could see how things go? Ideally, it'd be somewhere you could rent—buying a property together is a strain you could do without, for now at least. I can picture you being happy here, though, Grace. Bannock is very you."

"It is, isn't it? All right, I'll have a conversation with Aidan and we'll take it from there."

Her eyes sparkle with glee and she comes around the table and wraps me in a hug. Just then my phone goes. Breaking apart from Emily, I check the name on the screen.

"It's Mum," I say, then I tap to answer it. "Hi, everything okay?"

There's a pause on the other end. "Hello, Grace. And . . . no, everything is not okay."

CHAPTER TWENTY-EIGHT

AIDAN

At an ad break in our Christmas TV viewing, Maw mutes the sound then stands. "Well, I'll pop the kettle on and make us all some more tea."

"No, Maw," I say. "You sit. I'll do that."

"I could do with stretching my legs," she insists. "All this sitting in a chair relaxing . . . my body is going to seize up!"

She sets off for the kitchen, leaving just me and Iona in the living room. Grace is away catching up with Emily.

Soon the hum of a warming kettle reaches us.

Iona leans closer to me and murmurs, "So, I was speaking to Da earlier."

Maw has never banned us from talking about Da around her. It's simply an unspoken agreement between me and Iona that we don't bring him up while she's within earshot.

"What does he want? I already sent him a message saying Merry Christmas."

"He'd like to meet up with you in person, Aidan, and he's keen to meet Grace too. He thought, with a baby on the way, this could be an opportunity for a fresh start. He wants to be a part of his granddaughter's life."

I let out a sigh. "Of course he does."

"Give him a call and get something arranged. And also, don't shoot the messenger."

"Fair point—sorry. Okay, I'll speak to Da. Anyway, when is it you're heading off to see Richard?"

Iona's lips curl into a smirk. "Oh, trying to get rid of me, are you? And here was me thinking we were spending quality family time together."

"Not trying to get rid of you! Just making conversation."

"When have you and I ever talked to one another about our relationships?"

"We haven't but Grace and I are having a baby, and you and Richard have been together for quite a while now, right? As Bob Dylan would say, *the times they are a-changin'*."

Iona smiles at this but then the front door creaks open and slams shut again.

"Aidan?" It's Grace. Her voice is shaky and high-pitched. Something isn't right.

I jump to my feet and stride into the hall. She stands there, eyes wide, a nervous tremble to her lips.

"What's wrong?" My first thought is it's connected to the baby and my chest tightens.

"It's . . . Mum."

"What's happened? Is she okay?"

Grace's breathing is shallow and punctuated by slight gasps. I wrap her in a hug and hold her close.

"You . . . you know how she's been supporting a friend?" Grace says. "A friend who received some bad news about her health?

Well, it turns out that was a lie. Mum's the one who received the bad news: she was diagnosed with thyroid cancer a week ago. She's been in London on her own while David and I have been here having fun. She didn't come to Bannock for Christmas because she 'didn't want to bring down the mood'. I feel so guilty!"

Sniffing, Grace pulls back and gazes up at me. She bites her lip, her eyes glistening. "Why didn't she tell us what was going on?"

My heart aches at seeing her upset like this. "Oh, Grace. I'm so sorry." I gently rub my hand up and down her arm. "What can I do?"

She shakes her head. "You don't have to do anything. David's outside in the car. There's a flight leaving soon and he was able to book us a couple of seats. We've already packed—I'm here to say a quick goodbye."

The suddenness of this catches me off-guard, but she's doing the right thing by going straight to see her maw.

"I'd like to come too, if you'll have me?"

Grace takes my hand and squeezes it. "Given Mum doesn't even know I'm pregnant yet, I don't think that's a good idea. We'll keep in touch, though, yeah?"

"Aye, of course."

She offers a brave smile. "I'm sorry to cut my trip short but I really better go now—we can't miss the flight. Please say goodbye to your mother and sister for me."

"I will, and pass on our love to your maw. We'll be thinking of her."

I give Grace one more quick hug then she opens the door and hurries to the car. All I can do is stand and watch as David pulls out then drives off.

CHAPTER TWENTY-NINE

AIDAN

"Will you stop moaning and pass me another pin so I can hang this up?" Ally is up a ladder in the Bannock Hotel's function room, clutching a banner that says HAPPY NEW YEAR.

"Sorry. Here you go." I hand him a drawing pin.

It's Hogmanay, and for the very first time, the hotel is putting on an event to celebrate the end of one year and the start of another. It's been organised by Emily, of course, and she's roped in Ally and me to help with the decorations.

To be honest, I'm not really in the mood to toast the bells with a dram of whisky or to belt out "Auld Lang Syne", but even so, I can't deny that Emily is doing a great job in her role here. She's breathing life into the hotel. It takes me back to my childhood, when Ally's maw and da were still alive and they ran the place.

But despite the festive atmosphere, all I can really think about is Grace and how I won't be spending today with her. I've barely heard from her since she left four days ago, except for one message to let me know she'd arrived safely at her maw's and another yesterday to confirm she's still doing okay. Otherwise, my phone calls and messages have gone unanswered.

"Does it look straight to you?" Ally asks.

"Aye, it's fine."

"*Fine* isn't good enough. Emily will have my balls if it isn't perfect."

There was a time I'd have joked that Emily already has Ally by the balls—he does everything she tells him to—but I keep my mouth shut. Not long ago, I was a free man who didn't have to answer to anybody and didn't understand the appeal of relationships. Now? I'd much rather Grace were here bossing me around too. If anything, I'm envious of Ally.

"It's perfect," I assure him.

He pushes in the last drawing pin then comes down the ladder and gazes up at the banner. "Aye, it's not bad."

"Right. So . . . in your opinion, I should just give Grace some space and stop trying to contact her?"

Ally throws his head back and groans. "Mate! When you started seeing her, I thought it was a good thing, a sign you were finally growing up. I didn't realise how bloody boring and needy you were going to become. I've got a theory about this, actually. Want to hear it?" He doesn't give me a chance to say no.

"Because you've always avoided relationships, you've been left emotionally stunted and now you're playing catch-up. I mean, Jesus, you've never even had a proper break-up before, have you?"

"Shit, is that what you think this is? A break-up?"

He wipes a hand across his face. "*No!* She's gone down for her maw, you know that. I was just meaning . . ." He waves his hands vaguely. "Everyone thinks you're this stud who's been

222

with countless women, but right now you're more like a nervy teenage boy who has no idea how to cope with all these new emotions he's experiencing. You're definitely not something for men to aspire to. You're . . . tragic."

"Thanks." I thump Ally's arm. "Well, at least I know my best mate has my back."

He grins.

Scratching my head, I add, "It doesn't help that I've got time on my hands. We don't have any bookings and there's only so much Christmas TV I can watch. I need a distraction to stop me obsessing over why she won't call me and tell me what's going on down there."

"Mate, that's literally why Emily and I asked you over here. You're meant to be helping me get this place ready for tonight—that's your distraction."

"Crap, good point. All right, what next?"

"Balloons, and the great thing about them is you can't talk while we're blowing them up."

I smirk. "Am I really that bad?"

"Aye." He sets off to fetch the balloons but stops after a few steps. Sighing, he turns back around. "I get you're feeling rough at the moment but that's just a sign you like her. Emily and I had our share of ups and downs at the start but look at us now."

His gaze becomes dreamy. "It must be the pregnancy hormones but Emily's wanting to do it all the time. My life consists of eating Christmas food, watching TV specials, then having fun with her in the bedroom. It's a bloody good existence. Next Christmas won't be like this, with the babies here, so I'm enjoying it while I can."

I shake my head. "Cheers. I really appreciate hearing how

well everything is going for you and how perfect your sex life is."

"Thanks, mate." Ally nods seriously. "There have been times in the past I've been jealous of you so it's nice knowing that, for once, I'm winning at this stuff."

I sigh but then my phone rings. I eagerly pull it out, hoping to see Grace's name, but it's an unknown number.

"Give me a minute," I say to Ally, then I slip away in search of a quiet spot. There's no one in the snug so I take a seat there and answer the call. "Hello?"

"Aidan? This is Viola Adefope."

Grace's maw—I'd never have guessed it'd be her. Why is she calling me?

"Oh. Er, how are you doing? I mean, if that's not insensitive to ask. Grace mentioned about the diagnosis. I'm so sorry."

My mind is racing. Has something happened and Grace isn't able to get to the phone herself? Is that why Viola has called me?

"There are still more tests to do but I'm hopeful they've found it at an early stage. If so, the prognosis is good."

"That's encouraging. I mean, obviously it's awful you were diagnosed with it in the first place, but—"

"I'm not calling to talk about me, Aidan. I'm calling to talk about Grace."

"Is she all right?"

"She's fine. She's gone out to pick up a few things from the shop. As for David, he's upstairs, doing a bit of graphic design work."

"Oh, I see."

"I've been waiting for an opportunity to speak to you."

A knot of unease forms in my stomach. I can already tell whatever is coming will not be good.

"Grace has told me everything. I know she's carrying my granddaughter and that you're the father. I know, too, about your reputation as a 'player'—and I thought you such a well-mannered young man when I met you. I've also heard about what your father did to your family, and as the saying goes, the apple doesn't fall far from the tree."

This hits me like a punch to the gut.

"Despite all this, Grace seems besotted with you, but I'm familiar with your type. You're not in this for the long haul. I'm not having you uproot her and take her and my unborn grand-daughter up to the Highlands, only for your eyes to then drift to other women. You probably think you're 'doing the right thing', but trust me, it'd be far, far better to wrap things up now than break her heart when the baby comes.

"Grace has a life here in London—don't drag her away from that. You're not cut out to be her boyfriend, and you're certainly not cut out to be a father. End this charade before you do any more damage. Do you hear me?"

I'm so taken aback I don't know what to say.

"I said, do you hear me, Aidan Stewart?" Her tone is sharp.

"Aye, Viola, I hear you but—"

"Good. That's settled, then. Goodbye."

Before I can get another word out, she hangs up. I lower my phone and stare at it, shock ricocheting through me. I can't believe that just happened.

CHAPTER THIRTY

GRACE

With a bag of supplies in each hand, and shivering against the cold, I make my way to Mum's mid-terrace house in Haringey, North London. When I get there, I let myself in, put down the bags, and take a moment to relish how pleasantly toasty it is inside.

"I'm back!"

The last few days, David and I have been staying here in our old teenage bedrooms. Mum bought this place when we were thirteen and was rightly very proud of the achievement. Before that, my brother and I shared a room in a small flat—although it wasn't nearly as small as the one I'm now in.

"Come through and get warm!" Mum calls from the living room.

I take off my shoes and coat then leave the shopping by the door and go to say a quick hello. "How are you doing, Mum? Are you okay?"

From her armchair, she tuts. "Of course I'm okay. You were barely gone for any time at all. You and David must stop fretting—I'm not about to fall apart."

"Right, sorry."

There must be something in my tone she doesn't like because she lets out an exasperated sigh.

"For goodness' sake! We've caught it and we're taking action. Besides, thyroid cancer has one of the highest survival rates of all the cancers, so if anything, I should be thankful."

I shake my head. That comment is so Mum. Even in this challenging situation, her strength and resilience shine through. And yet I swear she seems . . . smaller somehow, more fragile. There are lines around her eyes and mouth I don't remember, but then I suppose I've been studying her more closely than usual. Maybe I'm projecting frailty onto her because I know what she's going through. In any case I'd never tell her she looks different—she'd hate that.

"David was upstairs if I needed him," Mum adds. "But really, it's you we should all be focused on." She gestures towards my bump.

Of course, Mum was surprised when I told her I'm twenty-four weeks pregnant, but she accepted it more readily than I was expecting. In fact, it's given her something to concentrate on—a distraction from her own news—and it's made her even more determined to get through this and be around for a long time for her granddaughter.

Her acceptance, while wonderful, has only worsened the guilt gnawing at me for not telling her sooner. Then again, Mum also kept a secret from me and David. Yes, she's only known about the cancer for a week, but before that, there were tests and appointments. She went through the whole process by herself, which breaks my heart. We're a family, and in times such as this, we need to support one another.

Everything that's happened has made me realise my relationship with Mum isn't as I'd like it to be. I don't want to hide things from her anymore, and I hope she's learnt she doesn't have to keep things from me and David.

"I got us some goodies for tonight," I say. "I'll go pop them away. Do you fancy a tea?"

"That'd be lovely. Thank you, Grace."

I shoot her a smile then collect the bags and take them through to the kitchen. It'll be a quiet New Year's celebration for us, just me, Mum, and David in front of the TV. But given my pregnancy and Mum's diagnosis, that's what we all need.

As the kettle boils, I put away the crackers, cheese, chocolates, and posh soft drinks I picked up while I was out. When I close the fridge door, my gaze falls on an old picture that's stuck to it. It shows Mum holding David and me, one of us in each arm. We can't be older than a few weeks and Mum, although thirty years younger and sporting a smile, is clearly tired.

My pregnancy has prompted Mum to open up about what it was like to raise twins and I've been learning about a different side to her. To me, she's always been strong and almost invulnerable, someone who knows her rights and how to demand what she deserves. But she's admitted that, raising me and David as a single parent, she often felt anxious and uncertain.

Back then, things weren't like they are now, with everyone carrying around a smartphone that can answer any question. When we were babies, she didn't have access to the internet at all—it was beginning to take off but wasn't yet mainstream. There were times she didn't know what she was doing and felt overwhelmed and lost, unsure how she was going to cope.

The revelation that there are chinks in her armour—a vulnerability beneath her tough exterior—has brought us closer. It's also led me to confide in her in a way I never did in the past. I've told her, for example, about the photo album I found of Aidan's travels, showing all the women I suspect were his conquests. I half expected Mum to tell me I'd be better off on my own, but to her credit, she bit her tongue. She simply listened without, for once, passing judgement.

Growing in confidence, I voiced other concerns too. I told her what Aidan's dad did to Elspeth, and saying it out loud felt good. At the back of my mind, there had been a silly, nagging worry that one day Aidan might betray me in the same way. By facing my doubt rather than burying it, I was able to remind myself Aidan is his own person and there's no reason to suspect he'll repeat the mistakes of his father. Again, Mum listened to me without making a single critical comment.

The kettle clicks and I prepare the hot drinks, a breakfast tea for Mum and a camomile for me. I pop a few biscuits on a plate too, put everything on a tray, then head through to the living room. I'm just placing the tray down when my phone buzzes.

"Who's that?" Mum asks.

We may be growing closer but her nosiness remains a source of irritation.

I take out my phone and check. "It's Aidan. He's asking if he can call me."

Since coming back to London, I've focused all my attention on Mum. Because I didn't want her to know about the pregnancy, I avoided her at a time when she needed me. If I'd seen more of her, maybe she'd have opened up to me sooner and wouldn't have had to spend Christmas by herself. To make up for that, she's now my top priority and that means putting Aidan on the back burner, at least for a little while. If he's as good a man as I think he is, he'll understand.

I put my phone down. "I'll speak to him another time. Here's your tea, and take a biscuit too. Can I hear a few more stories about when David and I were little?" I settle on the sofa.

"Give Aidan a call. We can reminisce later."

"I've just made us teas, Mum. I want to chat with you while we're drinking them."

"Don't be silly! Go up to your room and give the man a call. I'll be fine here."

My phone pings as another message comes through: *Please, I really need to talk to you.*

"Aidan again. All right, if you're sure, I'll quickly catch up with him."

I head upstairs, taking my tea with me, then tap to call Aidan.

He answers after a single ring. "Grace?"

"Hi, sorry I've been elusive—I've been trying to spend as much time as possible with Mum. I feel so guilty about everything. How are you?"

"Er, okay, I suppose. About your maw—"

"She's doing all right at the moment. She's been telling me some stories I've never heard before and it's been really nice, actually."

Briefly I fill him in on the last few days and what we know so far about Mum. I explain she'll need further tests before the doctors can devise a treatment plan. Aidan thanks me for the update but there's this strange hesitancy in his voice.

"Is everything okay? You sound a bit off."

"I just . . ." He takes a deep breath. "I miss you, Grace. Can I travel down to see you?"

"It's not the best time—I want to give Mum all of my attention for a while. You get that, right? You'd do the same if it were your mum."

"Aye. I get it."

There's something in his tone I can't quite pinpoint, but I don't have the energy to drill down into it. Aidan will just have to wait until I'm ready for him. As he's been single for his entire adult life, except for the last few weeks, I'm sure he can cope for a couple more days.

"Anyway, I best get back to Mum. Happy New Year for when it comes."

"Oh, right. Happy New Year to you too. And . . . it's good to hear you again, Grace."

"You too, Aidan. Bye!"

I hang up, pick up my tea, then step out onto the landing. I stick my head around David's door, but he's at his laptop with his headphones on so I decide not to disturb him. Earlier he mentioned he was trying to finish a project so he could relax tonight then take a few days off.

I go downstairs to the living room and make myself comfortable on the sofa.

"Well? What was Aidan saying?" Mum wants to know.

"He seemed a bit down but I think he just misses me. That's nice, isn't it?"

"Hmm." Mum frowns. "He didn't have any news?"

"No, it was only a short call. Anyway, have you checked what's on TV tonight? There's normally some good stuff on New Year's Eve." I reach for the remote and open the guide.

CHAPTER THIRTY-ONE

AIDAN

The crisp air of Bannock Woods clears my head of the lingering grogginess from last night's celebrations. It helps that I went easier on the booze than I normally would on Hogmanay. It was a great party—Emily did a brilliant job—and I joined in with the laughter and the ceilidh dancing since no one would have appreciated me sitting around moping. But I couldn't shake Grace from my mind.

Now, as I follow the quiet path from Bannock to Duntreath, I attempt to sort out my thoughts. Today marks the start of a new year, and an incredibly important one. Grace and I are due to become parents in April. Suddenly the birth doesn't seem far away at all.

What I'd like more than anything is to speak with Grace about what her maw did. I'm still thrown that she phoned me and told me to end things. I was close to raising it on the call yesterday, but then Grace mentioned how Viola is doing and the further tests she'll need. After that, I couldn't bring myself to get the words out.

It'd be easier to discuss it with Grace in person, but she

doesn't want me going down at the moment so I'm at a loss what to do.

I crunch on through undisturbed snow. More fell last night but the skies are clear now, weak sunlight filtering through the bare branches. With most Bannock residents at home nursing hangovers, the only footprints to be seen are my own and those of wildlife.

What I'm wrestling with most is whether there might be something in what Viola said. Is it possible the best thing I can do for Grace is let her go?

The idea is painful and my immediate reaction is no way in hell, but am I being selfish? I tried selling Grace on the idea of moving up north, and aye, I picked the wrong house, but would it work for Grace with a different house? Or is she better off where she is, in London with her maw nearby and with her yoga business? Because if so, I should end things. If Grace is where she needs to be, and I'm where I need to be, then she and I should be friends, nothing more.

But . . . the thought tears me up.

A robin flutters onto an oak branch. Against the backdrop of snowy woodland, it could be a scene from a Christmas card. I take out my phone and capture the shot. For half a moment, I consider messaging it to Grace, but no, she's asked for space and I need to respect that, don't I?

I walk on.

The other thing that's eating me up is whether Viola might have been right when she said "the apple doesn't fall far from the tree". Another equally damning phrase is "like father, like son". I understand it'd be stupid to pay too much attention to such sayings, but then again, don't they exist because there's some truth in them?

Da really hurt Maw, and if there's a chance I'd ever do that to Grace, it'd be better to let her go now. But would I do that? Da's sneaking around, the double life . . . that's not my style at all. Aye, until Grace, I'd never committed myself to a woman, but I'd also never messed one around or pulled the wool over her eyes.

Betraying Grace is something I just can't imagine doing. My instinct is to protect her from harm, and more than anything, I want her to be happy.

Shit, what to do?

I'm so wrapped up in my head it's a while before I realise I'm close to the house I was considering buying and which I disastrously showed to Grace. From here, it's off the path and through the trees. I didn't set off with a particular goal in mind, but since it's so near, I decide to take one last look.

I reach the edge of the clearing, approaching the property at an angle that grants me a view of the back, side, and some of the driveway. The house stands as lonely and isolated as ever—wait, no, scrap that. Why is there a motorcycle parked out front?

I round the house. When I brought Grace here, we left my car at the main road, but someone has cleared a narrow path along the drive, just wide enough for a motorcycle. I only have to study the bike for a moment to recognise it. What the hell?

I rap on the front door. Footsteps sound then the door swings open. Robbie MacDonald—older brother of Johnny—stands on the other side. I'm a tall guy and it's not often I find myself looking up at someone, but Robbie has a few inches even on me. He has dark hair, almost black, with icy-blue eyes and a piercing in his left brow. Clad in his signature leather jacket, he takes me in then smirks.

"Well, if it isn't Aidan Stewart. I heard you're going to be a da. Rather you than me, mate."

His tone is antagonistic, as always, but I don't rise to the bait. Robbie's father is the general manager of the Glen Garve Resort, and since Ally and I started working with them, we've run into Robbie here and there. I've learnt to keep it civil despite his best efforts to push my buttons. Even Ally's been doing an okay job of checking his temper, and it's him and Robbie who were really at each other's throats when we were lads.

In a level voice, I say, "Aye, well, I'm excited about meeting my wee lass."

Robbie shakes his head. "Don't give me that. Everyone knows you like to sleep around. You're not cut out for settling down."

His words sting because he's hit on the exact issue I've been mulling over myself, with my worries I may be more similar to my da than I care to admit. Robbie is managing to get a rise out of me, but I take a breath and stay calm.

"People change."

"Pfft." He crosses his arms, unconvinced.

There's no point arguing the matter so I say, "Anyway, what are you doing here?"

"I'm planning to buy this place."

Well, that's a kick in the teeth. I try my best to keep my expression neutral.

"I'm just taking one last walk around to decide what I should offer. Why are you here?" His cold eyes narrow. "Wait, you're not interested in this house too, are you?"

On Boxing Day, Finlay said there'd been some recent interest from another party. I'd never have guessed it was

Robbie. Finlay probably lent him the keys for an hour or so, just like he did for me.

Given I had more than my fair share of scraps with Robbie when we were boys and teenagers, I should really be annoyed he intends to buy the property I'd dreamed about living in. But, strangely, as the idea sinks in, I realise I'm okay with it.

Grace is right: this isn't where we should raise our baby. When I was young, my best mate lived just across the road from me. So long as I didn't have to wait for traffic to pass, I could run from my bedroom to Ally's in nineteen seconds flat—I timed it. Whether our lass grows up in London or here, I'd like her to have friends nearby, as I did.

"Nah," I say, "I was passing and saw your bike and wondered what you were up to. It's a nice property—I hope you're happy in it. Oh, and Robbie? Happy New Year."

With a smile, I hold out my hand. Robbie glances down at it in surprise. As lads, after a playground scuffle, our teachers would force us to shake and make up. This is different—I'm suggesting we do it voluntarily.

He hesitates for a moment then grasps my hand. "Cheers, and the same to you."

With a nod, I turn and set off. That felt . . . good. It was an opportunity to let go, not only of the house but also of old grievances. I'll soon be a father and I don't want to bring negativity into my lass's life. It's time to put the past behind me and focus on the future.

On that note, there's another person I owe a Happy New Year to.

CHAPTER THIRTY-TWO

AIDAN

I approach the door of my da's semidetached house in Inverness then pause. Is this a mistake? There's still time to back out, but no, I've driven all this way.

I reach for the doorbell then hesitate again. I've never actually been here before. Da has invited me on multiple occasions but I've always preferred to meet him somewhere neutral, like a pub or café. Until now I haven't wanted to see the space he shares with his partner and other son.

I tell myself to grow some balls and stop being such a baby, then I ring the bell and take a few deep breaths. For a moment I wonder if Da might be out so I don't have to go through with this, but I'm being pathetic again. Besides, there are lights on and the car is in the drive, so someone is definitely home.

Through the frosted glass, I spy a figure approaching. The lock clicks, the door swings open, and . . . it's Da himself. At the sight of me, his thick grey eyebrows shoot up.

"Aidan! This is a surprise."

"Hi, Da. Happy New Year."

He breaks into a wide grin and claps a hand onto my shoulder. "It's great to see you, son. It really is. Come on in!"

"Er, as long as I'm not intruding? I'm sorry for showing up unannounced."

"Don't be silly. Make yourself at home!"

"Thanks." I step inside and pass him a bottle of whisky. "This is for you. I thought I might be the first-foot."

Tradition dictates the first visitor to a house on New Year's Day must bring a gift. Whisky represents good cheer for the year ahead.

"Thanks, son. You didn't have to do that but I appreciate it. I'll enjoy this."

He leads me into the living room, where his partner, Kirsty, sits in an armchair.

"Look who I've got here," Da says.

Kirsty rises to her feet, fidgets with her hands, and attempts a smile. "Hello, Aidan."

I'm not sure what the appropriate greeting is, but I doubt either of us is up for a hug so I simply incline my head. "Hi, Kirsty."

This is my first time meeting her, unless you count the occasion fourteen years ago when I spotted Da with her and Archie in a play park. But . . . that wasn't really a meet-and-greet kind of situation. I saw red that day and shouted at Da, demanding answers, not caring that there were children about. Kirsty hurried Archie away before I could say a single word to either of them, and I've not seen them again since.

Over the years Da has tried on several occasions to introduce me to them but I've always refused. Iona catches up with them every now and again, though—she's proved to be more forgiving than me. Maybe I can finally follow her example and let bygones be bygones.

Glancing around the plush room, I say a little stiffly, "This is a lovely place you've got."

A chandelier-style light hangs from the ceiling, a luxurious rug lies across the wooden floor, and high-end furniture adds to the air of elegance. My gaze settles on the mantelpiece, where several photos show Da and Kirsty with Archie, who has the same fiery-red hair as his maw. That day at the park, he was just a toddler. By the looks of it, he's now almost fully grown.

"Thank you, Aidan." Kirsty gestures towards the sofa. "Have a seat. Can I get you a tea or coffee?"

"I'll take a tea, please. Thanks."

With another smile, she leaves to go prepare that and I sit.

"Well . . ." Da settles into an armchair. "It really is fantastic news about the bairn. It can't be long now, eh?"

"She's due the twenty-second of April. It feels like no time at all since Grace told me so I bet the next few months go fast too."

"They probably will. It's exciting, though." Da pauses then adds, "Did Iona mention I'd spoken with her? I'm keen to be a part of your daughter's life, if you'll let me."

"Aye, that's why I'm here."

"Good. Well . . . I'm glad you're finally meeting Kirsty. Archie's over at a friend's but I could call him and ask him to come back, if you'd like to meet him too?"

"No, there's no need."

Da's expression falls. "Oh, right. Of course."

"What I mean is, let him hang out with his friend. I can meet him another time. Maybe sometime soon?"

Da's lips curl up again. "That'd be great. Iona and him get

on well. They don't see a lot of each other, with Iona living in Glasgow, but Archie appreciates having a half-sister. He asks about you too on occasion. He knows about the baby and was wondering if she'd be his half-niece. I'd never heard the term before, but we looked it up and it exists—as does half-uncle."

Even though this whole situation is so strange, I force a smile. "You can tell Archie I'll bring his half-niece to meet her half-uncle at some point. We can maybe even drop all the 'halves'. If he likes, he can just be Uncle Archie."

Da grins. "Aye, I'm sure he would like that."

I'm trying my best to act as if this is all perfectly ordinary— being here in Da's living room and casually chatting with him about Archie while Kirsty is through in the kitchen. If I pretend it's normal, maybe I'll eventually feel that way too. Sorting out my relationship with Da and his new family is my one New Year's resolution, but to be fair, it's a pretty big one. For it to happen, I'll need some answers and those are what I'm here for.

Kirsty comes back through carrying a tray on which there are three cups and saucers, a teapot, some shortbread, a wee jug of milk, a bowl of sugar, and some teaspoons. "Now, I wasn't sure whether to bring a cup for myself. I can always leave you two men to chat?"

Da glances my way questioningly.

"Er, Kirsty, I would like to get to know you better. I'm trying to turn over a new leaf before the baby is born. But . . . I have some questions for Da, and maybe it'd be easier if—"

"I'll pop upstairs and read my book. I'm at a good bit anyway."

"Thanks."

She leaves and Da checks the teapot.

"Hmm, I'll give it a few more minutes. Some shortbread, son?"

"Cheers." I take a piece, as well as a saucer to catch the crumbs. I'm not really hungry but chewing on a biscuit will buy me a few moments to formulate my thoughts. It's tasty—crumbly and buttery with just the right amount of sweetness.

"So . . ." I swallow. "I've been trying to figure out where I stand with Grace. I like her, but she's down in London and I'm up here, and I can't see how it'll work long-distance. That's the first problem, but if she and I chat about it some more, we might come up with a solution.

"The bigger problem is . . ." I hesitate. "Well, I keep on worrying that one day I'll do to her what you did to Maw, and that's holding me back. I need to understand why you did it, Da—why you led two separate lives and lied to everyone for years."

Da nods slowly then checks the teapot again. "You know what? I think the colour is all right now. I'm going to go ahead and pour. Is it still just milk you take?"

"Aye."

The tea comes out a bit pale but I get it. Da is using this as an opportunity to plan what to say, like I did with the shortbread.

He puts down the pot, tops both cups with milk, then stirs. It's not until he's passed me my tea and taken a sip of his own that he speaks again.

"I've wanted to talk to you about this for a long time, but you didn't want to listen before, which I completely understood. The first thing I need to make clear is it was, of course, wrong. If I had a time machine, I'd do everything differently. I

241

won't try to justify my behaviour to you because, quite frankly, I can't."

I don't say anything to this. I just wait for Da to continue.

"A little over thirty years ago, I found myself in the same situation you're in now. When your maw fell pregnant with you, we weren't married and you were . . . not planned. Back then, societal expectations were quite different, especially in a small town like Bannock. There was a certain pressure for us to become husband and wife, and so that's what we did.

"We were wed, and in time our family grew with the addition of Iona. I have many fond memories of that part of my life, as well as a lot of respect for Elspeth. We were . . . good friends. But here's the thing: did we love each other?" He shakes his head. "I don't believe we did, and I mean that both ways. I don't think your mother ever truly loved me—not the way a husband and wife are supposed to."

"You and Maw always seemed happy," I say, a little defensively. "That's why it was such a shock."

"I'm not saying we had big stormy rows or fiery arguments, but we married for the wrong reasons. We thought it was our duty. With Kirsty, though, it's different. I know it might upset you to hear this but she's the love of my life, son. The only love of my life."

I take a sip of tea. Da's right: that isn't easy to hear.

"Although I regret the way I handled everything, I don't regret meeting Kirsty—I won't ever regret that. What I should have done was end things with your maw first. Instead I was selfish and a coward, and Kirsty and I had an affair. When she fell pregnant, I kept up the secrecy and frankly that wasn't fair on anyone. I could go over my reasons for it, but at the end of the day, it was wrong—that's the long and short of it. What's more, begging you to stay quiet after you found out about Kirsty and Archie? That weighs heavily on me. I shouldn't have dragged you into my lies."

"Hmm. Right." I'm not sure what to say to this. His words aren't bringing me any closer to forgiveness, at least not yet.

"Please don't allow my mistakes to affect your life. When it comes to you and Grace, all that matters is how you feel about her and how she feels about you. So . . . how do you feel about her?"

I think about Grace and warmth blooms in my chest. "I . . . I like her, Da. I really like her. But . . . I don't want to mess this up. I don't want to hurt her the way you—"

"Stop. Just stop. You're worrying too much about what I did when you should be focusing on yourself. Here's the thing: I'm well aware of your reputation as a bit of a ladies' man, and trust me, you don't get that from me. I've only ever been with two women, son. That's it. And of them, I've only ever loved one—and that's the woman upstairs. Aye, I've made a lot of mistakes, but if you genuinely believe you're not suited to settling down, please don't point to me as proof of that.

"I'm not some serial philanderer. I'm a man who, when I was young, married a woman I didn't love because I thought that's what I was supposed to do. Now, though? I'm with Kirsty and I've no wish to ever be with anyone else. We'll be together for the rest of our days—I know we will. She makes my life complete, and I, hers.

"The world is a different place than it was when your maw fell pregnant with you. No one expects you to propose to Grace and so you don't have to put that kind of pressure on the relationship. You can just . . . see how things go. But she's obviously special—the way you're worrying proves that—so I reckon you'd be a fool not to give you and her a shot. If she's someone you can imagine yourself spending your life with, don't hold back because you think history is bound to repeat itself. It isn't. You get to make your own choices and create your own future, Aidan."

I take this in then offer a small smile, and this time I don't even have to force it. "That's really helpful. Thanks, Da."

◆ ◆ ◆

"Is that you, Aidan?" Maw calls from the living room.

"Aye." Closing the door behind me, I kick off my shoes then head through to see her.

Iona left a few days ago to spend Hogmanay with Richard, so Maw and I have the house to ourselves again.

Maw pauses her crime drama. "Are you hungry? I wasn't sure if you were planning to eat here or not, but I made enough for you. Shall I go heat it up?"

"Thanks, Maw, but I can do that. You sit."

On a whim I cross the room and peck her cheek.

She laughs. "What's this? I don't normally get a kiss when you see me, unless you've been away travelling or it's my birthday."

"I know, but you're a great maw and I don't always thank you for that."

"Ha! Well, I do try."

I collapse onto the sofa—the food can wait. "Can I ask something? Sorry to spring this on you, but did you ever . . . I mean, after Da, did you ever think of looking for someone else?"

She peers at me curiously. "What's brought this on?"

"Nothing. I've just been thinking, that's all. First, Da left you, then a few years later, Ally's parents died in the crash and Mairi was your best friend. Don't you get lonely sometimes?"

She scoffs. "In Bannock? Never. I can't leave the house without bumping into someone who'll stop me for a wee blether. Besides, not only have I got you and Iona to keep me busy, I've got those three lads in the hotel across the road, plus Cat in Glasgow—and now a granddaughter on the way, and then there's the boy Emily is expecting. I'm quite happy, Aidan. Trust me."

"I'm glad." I nod and then, even though it's not related, blurt out, "I'm going to go down to London. I need to see Grace."

"Good. You be there for her, all right? She's precious and it can't be easy for her at the moment with the news about her mother."

I haven't told Maw or anyone else what Viola said to me. I don't want to gossip with others before speaking about it with Grace herself.

"Oh, and another thing," I say, "if I were to move out, would you be okay with that?"

Maw chuckles. "Your head is all over the place today—I can barely keep up with these changes of topic. But yes, if you were to move out, I'd be absolutely fine. I really am happy, you know. Are you going to tell me what's prompted these concerns?"

"Like I say, I've been thinking. But also . . . I've just come back from Da's." I scratch my neck. "He wants to be a part of the bairn's life, and he and I have agreed to wipe the slate clean. I realise things are strained between you and him, but—"

"Oh, really!" Maw waves a dismissive hand. "You've not been worrying about this, have you?" She studies me and there's a warmth in her gaze. "You're doing the right thing, trying to make amends with him. I don't want my granddaughter being denied anything, and she should grow up knowing all her family. With any luck, she'll be blissfully ignorant of quarrels that happened long before she was born.

"Please don't go thinking you can only invite one or the other of us to birthday parties or other special occasions. It won't be easy being in the same room as your father, but I'm sure I'll manage, and Kirsty and their wee boy are welcome too. Although, come to think of it, I don't suppose he's very wee anymore, is he?"

I was spot-on earlier when I said what a great mother this woman is. She couldn't be taking this any better. She addressed all of my concerns before I even had a chance to voice them. No doubt it will be hard for her initially—no one could blame her if there's some lingering resentment there—but she's putting my daughter first and I love her for it.

"Archie wasn't there today but I saw photos, and aye, he's getting tall."

"They really do shoot up in their teens. Now, do you have any other big issues you want to talk about or is that everything?"

"Er . . . that's everything."

"Good. In that case I'll take one more peck on the cheek, please, then I'll go and heat up your dinner."

Grinning, I oblige.

CHAPTER THIRTY-THREE

GRACE

"Twist," I say.

David deals me another card: a jack.

"Ah. Bust, yet again." With a sigh I toss in my hand.

Mum, David, and I are seated around the dining table, playing pontoon with matchsticks rather than money. When the doorbell chimes, I get to my feet before either of them can.

"I'll get it."

I'm growing tired of the game—and I'm also losing—so I'm quite happy for a distraction.

As David is a serial online shopper, I'm expecting it to be a delivery. Instead I open the door to find Aidan standing there, in a kilt—the same one he wore the night of the engagement party. It sways in the breeze, red with lines of green, blue, and yellow.

His cheeks flushed from the cold, he flashes me a wide, charming grin. "Hi, Grace."

At first I'm too startled to say anything at all. Only after a few moments do I stammer, "A-Aidan? What are you doing here?"

His surprise visit shocks and thrills me in equal measure. I hadn't realised how much I'd missed him these last few days. And seeing him in his kilt, it strikes me what a crime it is he doesn't wear it more often. Damn, he looks good.

"I wanted to give you these." He passes me a bouquet of sunny yellow roses. Their sweet, citrusy scent teases my nostrils.

"You came all the way from Bannock to give me . . . flowers?"

"Aye. Well, okay, I was also hoping to chat with you. I even dressed up to impress you, in case you hadn't noticed." He glances down at himself. "It's not really the weather for it, though. I'm bloody freezing." He shifts his weight from foot to foot. A jacket keeps his top half warm but his knees are bare.

I can't help but giggle, and at the sound, Aidan's smile grows even wider.

"I know you told me not to come down, but I thought maybe you'd find me so irresistible you'd have no choice but to throw your arms around me and tell me how happy you are I came. That's not happened yet but you're still just getting over your initial shock, right?"

Trying to adopt a serious demeanour, I frown and put my hands on my hips. "Oh, that's how you saw this going, is it?"

He nods. "I've been turning heads all over London. Either I'm the most handsome man who's ever lived or people couldn't believe some nutter would dress this way in winter. Personally, I like to think it was the former but who knows? Anyway"—he stretches his arms wide—"hug?"

"Hmm . . . yeah."

I lay the roses on a cabinet then rest myself against Aidan. He gathers me up and holds me in a strong, comforting embrace.

I breathe in deeply, savouring his familiar and enticing masculine scent. "I missed you."

A wolf whistle marks the arrival of David, and I quickly withdraw from Aidan. My brother bounds along the hall, followed by Mum, who wears a more serious expression.

"Check you out, Aidan!" David's gaze runs up and down him. "Looking sharp. What are you doing here? Couldn't bear being apart from Grace?"

"Aye, pretty much."

David claps his hands together. "That's so romantic. I'm really missing my Scotsman. Can I ask you a favour? If you're back up in Bannock before I am, could you give Johnny a message from me?"

"Sure."

David beams, squeezes past me, then throws his arms around Aidan and holds him tight. "Love you, Johnny!"

I roll my eyes and grumble under my breath.

David retreats again and Aidan chuckles nervously, running a hand through his hair.

"I don't know that it'd mean quite the same coming from me. Maybe I can just tell him you miss him?"

"Hmm." David's brows knit together. "Okay, fine. Hug him and tell him I miss him."

"Oh. The hug is mandatory, is it?"

"Non-negotiable."

With a brave smile and a hint of resignation in his voice, Aidan says, "All right. I can do that for you."

David grins with delight. Mum, meanwhile, shuffles a little closer and Aidan shifts his focus to her. Something changes in him: his gaze loses some of its brightness and his shoulders tense. I get it—this is his first time seeing Mum since she learnt

249

about the pregnancy. It must be a pretty nerve-racking encounter for him. God knows I felt awkward when I finally showed her my bump.

"Viola." Aidan offers her a stiff nod. "How . . . are things going?"

"Fine, thank you. I'm lucky to have my children here with me, keeping me company. Grace didn't mention you were coming down."

"Aidan surprised me," I say. "He brought me flowers." I pick them up and show them off.

"Hmm." Mum briefly glances at them then turns her attention back to Aidan. "And where is it you're staying?"

"I booked into a hotel nearby, just for a night. I was hoping to steal Grace away and take her out for dinner."

"Well, that's a bit of a problem, actually, because Grace was going to cook a meal for me and David, so—"

"I'll make us something, Mum," David interrupts. To Aidan, he adds, "Yes! Grace will go for dinner with you. And yes! She'll pack a bag and stay the night too. Mum and I will hang out here and spend some quality mother-and-son time together. You two head off and have fun."

"Don't I get a say in this?" I ask.

David pulls a quizzical expression, leans close to me, and whispers, "How could you say no to him? He's in a kilt, Grace. A kilt!"

I glance at Mum. She purses her lips but says nothing. The last few days, she's been telling me and David to stop fussing over her. I've hardly wanted to leave her side because I feel so guilty about avoiding her when I could have been supporting her. But she's right: she doesn't need me and David worrying about her twenty-four hours a day. Truthfully, all we can do is offer our company anyway, and she'll be fine if David is here.

"Okay." I meet Aidan's gaze and break into a smile. "Come in out of the cold for a few minutes. I'll get changed and throw a few things in a bag."

◆ ◆ ◆

"It's not as upmarket as the last restaurant I took you to, but I hope it's okay," Aidan says.

We're at a quirky gastro-pub that isn't far from his hotel. Exposed brick walls are adorned with retro posters and black-and-white photographs.

"It's perfect," I insist.

Another thing that's perfect is my view. Aidan sits opposite me and he's taken off his jacket, revealing a white long-sleeved T-shirt that clings to his torso, showing off his strong frame. Its casual style is a sexy contrast to the kilt.

His outfit attracted a lot of attention on our journey here, and he's already drawn the stares of several female diners, but he pays them no notice. He only has eyes for me.

He reaches across the table and places his hand on mine. "I missed you."

"I missed you too. Thanks for coming down and for taking me out for dinner."

His mouth lifting at the corners, he sits back again. "Don't mention it. I'm happy I get to spend some more time with you. How are you doing anyway? The last few days can't have been easy."

"They've not. Mum's doing well, though. Nothing ever fazes her—not even this, it seems. She's always so strong and sensible and practical. Sometimes I wish she'd just let it all out. It's cancer, for God's sake! It's scary and everyone needs a cry now and again, but that's not Mum's style. When David and I first arrived, I swear she spent more time comforting us than we did her."

Aidan shifts in his seat and I wonder if maybe he isn't sure what to say. That's okay—it can be a difficult subject to discuss.

"I'm still annoyed she didn't tell me or David she was going for tests. She shouldn't have had to go to those alone."

"Hmm . . ." Aidan tilts his head to the side and a glimmer of mischief shines in his eyes. "Well, you didn't tell anyone about your pregnancy until it came out at my birthday lunch. You both kept secrets. Maybe you and your mum are more alike than you care to admit?"

"Absolutely not!" I stick my tongue out at him. "If you don't have anything sensible to say, we should decide what we're going to eat."

We study our menus and chat about what's on offer. When he handed me the flowers, Aidan mentioned he wants to talk with me about something, but whatever it is, he's not yet broached the subject. That's fine by me. While a part of me is curious, things have been pretty intense since I last saw him, so if it's anything heavy, I don't know that I'm ready for it. It might be better to keep the conversation light, if possible.

When our server comes over, I opt for the halloumi burger with sweet potato fries, while Aidan goes for the spicy chicken tacos. Order taken, she leaves again.

"So . . ." Aidan drums his fingers on the table. "I went to see my da."

"Oh?"

He nods. "We were overdue a catch-up, plus I needed some answers."

I'm pleased to hear Aidan has been putting some effort into his relationship with his dad. I'm not exactly in the right head-space for the full details, but Aidan tells the story and I try my best to concentrate.

"So . . . my maw and da gave things a shot because of me, but it didn't work out," he sums up after filling me in. "I realise our situation isn't a million miles away from theirs but it *is* different. I like you, Grace, and I want to be sure you know that. Aye, you're carrying our wee lass and I'm excited to meet her, but there's more to our relationship than the baby. I think . . . well, I think you and I could have a happy-ever-after together."

He swallows and there's a strange intensity to his gaze. My heart rate picks up.

"Once again, I'm sorry for taking you to visit that house. That was a mistake but maybe the idea of you moving up north wasn't so crazy. I was thinking—"

"Shh!" I lean forward and place a finger to his lips.

His eyebrows rise but he does stop talking.

"Aidan, I'm touched you came here to see me," I say, choosing my words carefully. "But . . . emotionally I'm at max capacity at the moment. I really like you too but it's still early days between us, and with what's going on with my mum, I can't even think about moving right now. I don't have the mental bandwidth."

Aidan grimaces and rubs the back of his neck. "Sorry, I just—"

"You don't have to apologise but let's talk about something else, okay? No big topics, please—something light."

Aidan nods. "Aye. Of course."

He offers a small smile but I can tell he's disappointed. I wonder if I'm being unfair—after all, he travelled six hundred miles and donned his kilt just to talk to me. Then again, I specifically asked him not to come to London and he came anyway. After I left Mark, I vowed to prioritise my own needs above all else, and I don't want to fall back into bad habits. To protect my wellbeing, I'm perfectly entitled to ask Aidan to park this conversation.

Thankfully, he recognises and respects this. Changing tack, he says, "So . . . have you watched any good Christmas TV since you got here?"

◆ ◆ ◆

Aidan holds the door open for me and I leave the pub, the chilly air hitting me.

"Ah, bracing!" With a grin, Aidan crosses his arms and stamps his feet. The temperature has dropped further while we've been eating.

My lips twitch. "You do have underwear on under there, right?" I nod at his kilt. "Please tell me you didn't go true Scotsman in this weather."

He chuckles. "I'm not that crazy, but it turns out a thin layer of cotton doesn't do a great deal to protect my most sensitive parts from the cold."

He grimaces, and while I do feel a wave of sympathy, I can't hold back a chuckle.

"Hey! It's no laughing matter."

"It kind of is, though." I nudge his shoulder with my own.

"Well, we better get to the hotel quickly, for the sake of your dangly bits."

He winks but then glances at my bag, which he's carrying for me. "About that . . . it was great having dinner with you, but I could tell your mind was elsewhere. If you'd prefer to go back to your maw's tonight, that's okay. I can see you to her door then head to the hotel myself."

My heart does a little flutter—it's sweet that Aidan cares. As we ate, we engaged in small talk, deliberately avoiding any important issues, just as I'd requested. I might not have been as present as I normally am, but it was exactly what I needed: a break from all the emotions I've been experiencing the last few days. Concern for Mum, guilt for having kept her in the dark for so long, regret that my relationship with her isn't as strong as it could be . . .

Talking about other things was a good escape, but there's another type of escape—one that's both physical and mental— that I could really do with right now.

"Aidan, I'm going to spend the night with you. But . . ." I grip his hand and squeeze it. "I don't have the energy for any more chat. I just want to walk with you by my side and enjoy your presence. Then, when we get to your room, maybe we can communicate with our bodies instead of words?"

He wraps an arm around me. "Aye, I'd like that, and that's the last thing I'll say to you for a wee while."

His lips find mine and we share a warm, tender kiss before setting off for the hotel together.

CHAPTER THIRTY-FOUR

GRACE

Our sex is hot, sweaty, and primal, made more passionate by my pent-up emotions, which find an outlet in this ancient act. We move all over the bed, trying every pregnancy-friendly position we can think of.

Now I clamber onto my hands and knees, and Aidan comes up behind me and carefully re-enters me. I gasp and work myself on his thick, hard length, but he lets out a low warning growl, the sound almost animalistic. Gripping my hips, he stills me. Then, very slowly, he draws me closer to him, burying himself even deeper.

I let out an involuntary moan. I want to tell him how good it feels to have him inside me, but so far I've honoured our vow of silence, as has he. We've not spoken at all, although I haven't been able to contain my wordless exclamations of pleasure.

Aidan moves his hips, tantalising me with measured thrusts. The sensations are exquisite but I want more, and faster. I try to quicken the pace but his grip on me tightens, a voiceless command to respect his authority, at least in this moment. He may be denying me what I desire but there's a primitive thrill in his exertion of dominance. I cave, letting him dictate the speed, which—to my delight—he gradually increases, sending shock waves of pleasure through my body.

He slides a hand around me to play with my clit, circling and teasing, while pushing himself faster and harder into me. The tempo continues to pick up until he's pounding me, my heavy breasts swaying back and forth. I realise I won't last much longer, but based on his ragged breathing, I doubt he will either. I want this to go on forever, but at the same time, the desire for release is overpowering.

Aidan's grunts are feral and untamed, but suddenly his breath catches, and with a final forceful thrust, he empties himself into me. That's what sends me over the edge. Squeezing my eyes shut and gripping the sheets tight, I cry out so loudly he has to clamp a hand over my mouth. Euphoria spreads through my entire body, and it takes me a few moments to remember I'm in a hotel and the walls are only so thick. I don't care, though. I groan with satisfaction.

Aidan pulls out and collapses onto his back, panting heavily. I slide onto my side and lay my head on his chest. His skin is slick with sweat, his heartbeat thunderous. With interest, I gaze down his body at his still-erect penis. From this angle, it's only the glistening red glans I can see.

He seems sated but I can't resist reaching out and taking a careful hold of him. Lying spread-eagle, collecting himself, he makes no attempt to stop me, so I loosely run my hand up and down his length. After a few strokes, a final bead of cum appears. I know how sensitive a man's penis can be post-sex, but even so, I graze my thumb over his tip, wiping it away.

Aidan emits a low groan, so just for fun, I rub his head some more, teasing him.

Still breathless, he manages a chuckle. "Lass, that's enough!" He guides my hand off of him then pulls my body closer to his, my bare breasts pressing against his skin. He kisses my hair then relaxes into his pillow, hugging me protectively.

"That sex was . . . amazing," he murmurs.

"Mmm," I agree. "But . . . no words, remember?"

"Aye, no words." Gently he squeezes me. "Just sex . . . and now sleep."

I hum contentedly then close my eyes and snuggle deeper into his comforting embrace.

◆ ◆ ◆

Coming to, I stretch and yawn. The room is dim, but around the edges of the curtains, there is a faint glow of morning light. I slept well—I wasn't troubled by pregnancy symptoms at all. I have Aidan and his skills in the bedroom to thank for that.

Talking of Aidan, the spot in the bed where he should be is empty. From the en suite, the gentle rush of shower water reaches my ears. I've half a mind to join him, but the sheets are soft and pleasant against my bare skin, and I'm cosy under them. I can't bring myself to leave quite yet.

Instead I stretch out, savouring having the entire mattress to myself. There's something peaceful about hotel rooms. They're tidy and minimal and aren't crammed full of personal possessions. My tiny flat is probably about this size, but it has a kitchen and all my belongings, and those make the space claustrophobic.

The sound of running water stops, and a minute later Aidan appears, clad only in white boxer briefs, his hair towel-dried but still damp. "Ah, you're awake." A smile brightening his features, he turns on the bedside lamp.

I blink a few times. "Morning."

Aidan brushes my cheek then leans over and presses a gentle kiss to my lips. His fresh skin carries a faint scent of soap, reminding me I, too, could do with a shower. Normally, I'm fastidious about being clean before going to bed—I have a strict night-time routine I hardly ever deviate from—but yesterday I didn't care at all.

That's one of the perks of staying in a hotel for a single night. It's a free pass to roll in the sheets with abandon and not worry about sweat or anything else. After all, we won't be sleeping here again tonight, and after we check out, the linen will be changed.

"What are you thinking about?" Aidan watches me with curiosity.

I smile naughtily. "Last night. We went at it like animals."

He laughs, the warm sound filling the room. "Aye, we did. I would ask if you enjoyed yourself but I reckon the whole hotel knows the answer to that. You really are loud when you come."

"Aidan!" Flushing, I swat at his bare leg. "You can't say that! Anyway, if anyone is to blame for the volume of my cries, it's you. Oh, and this thing."

With one finger I prod his penis through his underwear, catching him off-guard. He flinches but quickly recovers and grins.

"Well, I had fun too." He perches next to me and gazes at me with deep affection.

But at this closer distance, I notice something else in his eyes—a hint of unease? "What's wrong?"

Surprise registers in his expression, his brows rising. "What do you mean?"

"I know you well enough now to tell when things aren't quite right. Out with it!"

His forehead wrinkles and he absent-mindedly rubs his arm. "Wow, you're like a mind-reader. Hmm . . . how to put this? I realise you're keen to keep the mood light, and I get that, but . . . fuck, this is hard. Lass, there's something I need to say before I go back up to Bannock. It's . . . about your maw."

A queasy sensation settles in my stomach.

"I don't want to bad-mouth her, especially with her being ill, but—"

"Then don't," I say, an edge to my voice.

In an instant the atmosphere in the room changes. I swallow a lump in my throat.

What the hell? What exactly is his complaint against my mum? That the timing of her cancer is inconvenient for us? Jesus! I thought Aidan had matured, become less selfish, but this . . . this is unbelievable.

I sit up, pulling the duvet up too. I'm still naked under the covers and a sudden wave of self-consciousness washes over me.

"You're right," Aidan says stiffly. "This was a bad time to raise it. Sorry. You should be focusing on her health at the moment."

"Absolutely I should!"

He nods, his expression inscrutable. An awkward silence falls.

"Would you mind . . . er . . . while I go for a shower?"

My request isn't particularly well formulated, but Aidan understands and looks away as I slip out from under the covers and head to the bathroom. I desperately need some space from him.

In the shower my head spins. What the hell was he thinking? I don't know why he'd ever want to "bad-mouth" my mum—that's hardly going to get me on his side—but to do it now? I mean, what planet is he on? That's not okay.

I wash myself quickly. When I emerge, wrapped in a towel, he's already dressed. There's no kilt today—he's in jeans and a smart sweater, with a shirt underneath. His bag is packed and only his toothbrush, toothpaste, and winter jacket lie out.

"Grace . . ." He takes a step towards me.

I fix him with a steely stare and he freezes, sighs, then casts his gaze downwards.

"I'll . . . brush my teeth while you get ready."

I pull on some clothes but don't spend long on my appearance. I just want to go. Once I'm decent, I tell Aidan he can come out again, and he exits the bathroom with a solemn expression. Obviously, he's aware he's messed up. That's something, at least.

"I'm going to head to Mum's and have breakfast there," I announce.

Normally, I enjoy the morning offerings at a hotel, but I've been away from Mum long enough. Besides, I need some space from Aidan.

"Oh. I can see you to your maw's?" His eyes are dull, lacking their usual spark.

I shake my head. "No, I'll make my own way there. I could do with some time to myself."

"Right." He scratches behind his ear and offers a strained smile.

This is the worst. I glance around, checking I've not left

anything, then close over my bag. I've not even brushed my teeth yet but I need to get out of here. First, though, there's something I have to say and this is not going to be easy.

"I was thinking . . . with my mum and the baby, my head is all over the place so maybe it'd be good for us to put the brakes on for a while. There's only so much I can focus on."

He draws a sharp breath. "Fuck."

"I'm not ending things! I'm just saying . . . let me concentrate on my mum for a while then we can pick this up again later."

Aidan gives a small nod. "If that's what you need to do."

"It is. Mum's news came as a shock and it's made me realise she and I aren't as close as I'd like. I want to focus on that relationship for now."

Aidan swallows, his Adam's apple bobbing. "Of course."

His expression suggests this is the last thing he wants, but I'm grateful he's not making this more difficult than it has to be.

"Thanks. I'll be back in touch in a bit, okay?" I give him an awkward hug. "Oh, and let me be the one to decide when to reach out again. I might need a week or two. I really do appreciate your surprise visit but I'd rather this were on my terms."

Another nod. "Understood."

"All right, well . . ." I make for the door.

"Wait!"

Swallowing a sigh, I turn back. Aidan steps towards me. His gaze is pleading, his posture desperate.

"I know you're going through a hard time but I can support you through this. Isn't that what partners do? Grace, you've made me feel things I've never felt before and . . . crap, I don't have the right words but maybe this expresses it better than I can." Tentatively he takes my hand and says:

> I once was lost, but now am found,
> Was blind, but now I see.

"You're my Amazing Grace. I don't want to lose you."

Despite how this morning has gone, my heart skips a beat. The lyrics are apt—Aidan *has* changed since he met me—but the words also remind me of Mum, who named me Grace after hearing that song. She deserves my full attention at the moment.

I smile weakly. "Remember, I'm just asking to put things on hold."

His shoulders sag, disappointment weighing him down. "Aye. I'll wait to hear from you, then."

CHAPTER THIRTY-FIVE

GRACE

I open the box containing the pair of miniature red velvet cakes I picked up earlier. Each of the bright-crimson sponges is topped with white fluffy frosting, chocolate shavings, and an edible glitter heart. Today being Valentine's Day, they were naturally targeted at loved-up couples, but I decided they'd be a nice mid-morning treat for me and Mum.

I pop them on plates then grab two mugs, put in teabags—a decaf for me—and fill them with boiling water. My hot-drink consumption has definitely gone up these last seven weeks, but I enjoy the ritual of sitting down for a tea with my mum.

Opening the fridge, I take out the milk, and—oh, crap! Baby brain. I'd intended to pick up more when I was out, but I completely forgot and only a dribble remains. I split it between the two mugs, but there's not enough to turn our drinks the caramel colour Mum and I like. Well, we'll just have to make do.

On the work surface my phone buzzes. It's probably Aidan. Even though we agreed I'd be the one to decide when to resume contact, he's been messaging me a lot lately. To be fair, at the start of the year, I said I might need a week or two and . . . we're now halfway through February. I've left him waiting considerably longer than he was expecting.

I have sent him the odd message back, assuring him both the baby and I are okay, but I've kept them short and to the point. I know it's selfish and a little cowardly, but I'd hoped he might get the hint. That would have made what I need to do so much easier. Unfortunately, he's refusing to give up on me.

I pick up the phone. He's shared a cartoon depiction of the Loch Ness Monster with a tartan tam-o'-shanter perched on its head. Below, he's typed: *Happy Valentine's Day, Grace. You un-loched my heart. x*

It's a truly terrible pun, and yet not only do I let out a small giggle, a pang shoots through my chest. I still have feelings for Aidan, which is what's making this so difficult. I should have called him days ago, had an honest talk with him, and set him right. But . . . I didn't. I can't do it today anyway—not on the annual celebration of love. That'd be too cruel. But I also can't put it off forever.

He sends over another message: *Delivery on its way. You're at your maw's, aye?*

I groan, guilt gnawing at me. This is awful. I reply with a thumbs-up then pocket my phone.

In the month and a half since I last saw Aidan, a few things have changed. For a start, after staying with Mum on a temporary basis for a few weeks, I've now officially moved back in with her. The tiny flat is no longer my home. The son of a yoga client was looking for a place, and I was able to negotiate with the landlord to take him on as a replacement tenant and let me leave early.

It's not that Mum needs me around the house—she's

getting on fine—but it just makes sense. There's space here, and Mum is delighted at the prospect of living with her grand-daughter. Besides, after going through the initial testing process by herself, I want to support Mum through her treatments and checkups, especially as David has returned to Bannock. The great news is we now know it's been caught early and the prognosis is very good. I sat in on a recent appointment with a doctor and it was very encouraging.

I put the mugs and plates on a tray then take it through to the dining table. "Happy Valentine's Day, Mum!"

She glances up from her laptop and laughs at the heart-topped cakes. "Oh, lovely! Those look delicious."

A natural workaholic, she surprised me by arranging a leave of absence from her job. Physically, she'd manage fine, I'm sure, but mentally, she's been re-evaluating a few aspects of her life since the diagnosis, and I think she's realised there are more important things than work. She's currently designing a digital photo album for printing. She's got thousands of photos saved to the cloud and has always meant to get physical copies of the best ones but never quite got around to it. Now she's finally doing it.

"We were a bit low on milk," I admit. "I'll nip back out after this to pick some up."

"I can—"

"I'm happy to do it," I assure her, smiling.

Mum takes a break from the computer and we chat while enjoying our cakes. I'm savouring my final mouthful when the bell goes.

"Who could that be?" Mum wonders.

"I'll go see." I'm sure it must be whatever Aidan has organised but I don't say that.

I open the door to a delivery person who's carrying the most beautiful bouquet of red roses.

"Grace Adefope?" she checks.

"Er, yes. Thanks."

I accept the flowers and inhale their sweet, intoxicating fragrance. It's impossible not to be touched by the gesture—what's more romantic than red roses?—but I know that on Valentine's Day, they can be eye-wateringly expensive. I've been unfair to Aidan by dragging this out when I should have already ended things.

Closing the door, I check the card and see a message has been printed on it: *O my luve's like a red, red rose . . . A. x*

I tap the words into my phone. It's the opening line of an eighteenth-century poem by Robert Burns. Oh dear, he's sending me poetry now! He was perfectly happy as a single man. Have I ruined him? No, of course not. He'll get over this. He'll bounce back.

With a bit of distance from Aidan, I've finally been able to see clearly again. We had it right in the first place when we agreed to be platonic friends. Allowing romance to enter our relationship was a mistake.

I don't know what came over me towards the end of last year. I lost sight of things, I suppose, and got carried away. He's a very handsome man and charismatic too—I can't seem to think straight when I'm around him. I'd begun to dream of another life . . .

Of course, in Bannock there was also the magic of the snow, the beauty of the Christmas lights, the warmth of the wood-burning stoves, and the friendliness of the close-knit community. I'd got caught up in Emily's excitement as well, at the idea of us raising our babies there together.

But I was being ridiculous. I'll be a mother soon and London is what I've always known. This is where I built a career for myself from scratch, and this is where my mum is. My due date is nine and a half weeks away—the countdown is in single digits now. It'd be absurd to give up my stable life here to take a chance with Aidan in a remote Highland town.

"Well? Who was it?" Mum calls through.

"Oh . . ." Shamefaced, I return to the dining table holding the flowers.

She takes them in then tuts and shakes her head. "Have you still not ended things with that boy?"

"I'll . . . do it tomorrow."

"I've heard that before! Grace, we've spoken about this. You can't risk everything to move up north—not with a baby on the way, and not for a man with Aidan's reputation. You're not just making decisions for yourself anymore. You're making them for her too."

"I know. You're right. I really will call him tomorrow."

"Why not get it over with and do it now?"

"It's Valentine's Day! I can't do it today."

Her brow furrows. "Fine. But after this, no more excuses."

◆ ◆ ◆

I button up my winter coat over the curve of my swelling belly. It's hard to believe I've still got over two months to go. I'm already huge.

Opening the front door, I'm about to step out when I realise I've not got any cash on me. Baby brain—again! First, I forgot to pick up the milk, then I almost walked out of the house to fix that without taking money with me. *C'mon, Grace!*

I close the door and try to think where I left my purse. Normally, I'm good at putting everything back where it belongs, but recently I've been leaving items in the oddest places then been forced to hunt all over for them.

I ponder for a few moments then it comes to me. It's in a handbag that's hanging up—not such an odd spot after all. I take out the purse and slip it in the pocket of my coat. As I'm doing so, Mum's voice reaches me from down the hall.

"Roses? I told you to stay away from my daughter."

I freeze. What the . . . ?

Softly I pad closer, my heart thumping.

"You're making this harder for her than it needs to be. She's going to call you tomorrow to break up with you, so please let that be the end of this madness."

"Mum?" I enter the living room and stare at her in horror. "Who are you talking to?"

I know the answer, of course, but I'm so shocked I'm not sure what else to say.

Her eyes bulge and she hurriedly jabs the end-call button. "Oh, Grace, I thought you'd left. I was just—"

"Was that Aidan?" My voice wavers. "What do you mean, you told him to stay away from me?"

I recall Aidan's last visit and my stomach churns. He'd been desperate to talk with me about something. In the hotel room, he'd mentioned being hesitant to "bad-mouth" my mum and I'd taken great objection to that. I didn't let him explain but instead left abruptly, although not before telling him I needed some time away from him.

Now, though, I can guess what Aidan wanted to speak with me about. I can scarcely believe Mum has been sticking her nose in and meddling in things behind my back, but given how she's always been, I should have seen it coming.

She's still not answered me, although I'm sure her thoughts are racing, trying to figure out how she can come out of this on top.

"What the hell is going on?" I demand.

"Now, Grace, take a seat and let's discuss this in a civil manner. I won't have you raising your voice at me in my own home."

"Are you being serious?" My volume increases considerably. "Are you honestly trying to tell *me* off?"

"All I've been doing is looking out for you. You've got a baby on the way! When you and David flew back after Christmas, you were talking about leaving your job—leaving your life here—for some . . . outdoor instructor, and one who likes to sleep around. Well, I'm not having that!"

I inhale sharply. "Why do you think you have any right to make decisions on my behalf?"

"Because I know how hard it is to be a single mother. I've been through what you're about to go through. You'll need support, Grace. This isn't the time to leave London for a man who's obviously going to be unfaithful to you and who'll break your heart before the year is out."

I can't believe this, and Mum still isn't done.

"Mark—now *he* was husband material. He had a great job and excellent prospects. He'd have given you a good, stable life, but for some reason I will never understand, *you* left *him*!"

"Mark?" I howl, anger consuming me. "*Mark?* The man who barely gave a damn about me? Who treated me as his maid—as someone whose main purpose was to tidy up after him and make him his dinner? Mark, who wanted to have an open relationship with me so he could screw other women while I was ironing his shirts? You'd rather I'd stayed with him? Seriously, Mum?"

For once she's lost for words, her eyes wide. "I . . . I had no idea Mark was like that."

"Well, he was! And . . . and . . . oh, what a fool I've been!" I pace, my hands on my head. "When I was growing up, you were forever sticking your nose in my business. When I finally moved out, I felt such freedom, but then I met Mark and I gave up that freedom in return for . . . so very little. It took me a long time to realise I deserved so much more than what he was offering me. I vowed I'd never again get myself into that situation, that I'd always put my own needs first, and yet look at me! I've fallen right back into the old trap.

"Here I am with you, Mum, when up in Bannock is a man who loves me. And I've been ignoring him—I'd even talked myself into breaking up with him. But that's thanks to you, isn't it? You've been putting doubts into my head and subtly steering me to do what you believe is best. I could maybe forgive that—you're entitled to your opinion, I suppose—but contacting Aidan behind my back? No, that's unacceptable. You have no right to be that meddlesome.

"I realise you don't think much of Aidan but I do. He's a good man, Mum. I . . . I have to go." I turn and hurry away.

"Don't be ridiculous!" Mum calls after me. "I didn't know about Mark but—"

I yank the front door open and storm out of the house. Mum rushes to tug on shoes and grab a coat, but finally a bit of luck: a black cab is approaching and it's free. I wave it down.

"Grace Adefope, come back here!"

Ignoring her, I get in the taxi.

The driver—a middle-aged man with a thick moustache—turns to me. "Where to?"

"I'm not sure yet but just go, please. I'll figure out a destination later."

"Understood."

The cab pulls away before Mum can catch up. My phone rings—it's her. I reject the call. She tries again, and then a third time. After that, I block her number. I just . . . need some space to think this over, and if I let Mum talk to me and explain why she did what she did, she'll find a way of winning me around—she's always been good with words. She's been influencing my decision-making without my even realising it. I have to free myself of that, at least until I can get back on track.

I need to speak to *someone*, though. David is understanding but he has a special relationship with Mum and a tendency to overlook her wrongdoings. I try Emily instead but it goes straight to voicemail. I give her a few shots but I get her prerecorded message every time, so I ask her to call me then ring David despite my reservations. But . . . his phone also goes to voicemail.

I sniffle. I need them. Why can't I get through to them?

"Are you okay back there?" The driver glances at me in the rear-view mirror.

"Yes, thanks." I wipe at my eyes. "It's just . . . been a bad day."

"I'm sorry to hear that. Have you made up your mind where you're going?"

"Er, I'll get back to you on that."

"That's fine by me, but just so you're aware, the meter is running."

"I know."

I open my contacts list and immediately see Aidan's name at the top. I hesitate. He's the person I really need to speak to and yet . . . I doubt a call is enough to sort this.

For the last few weeks, I've been trying to forget all the great things about Aidan and to convince myself that staying in London is the right decision. Now, though, I can't hold back the memories—they come to me unbidden.

The way he carried me through the woods when I went over my ankle. The themed video calls he organised to get to know me better. The cullen skink he prepared, surprising me with his culinary skills. And the fancy restaurant he took me to with the incredible view across the Thames to St Paul's.

More than all that, though, it's the way he makes me feel when I'm around him. He opened his heart to me, and in return, I've been neglecting him.

Oh God. I need to see him. In person.

I look up flights on my phone then hesitate. Can I even travel by air this far through a pregnancy? I check that first, and yes, I'm safe to go on a plane up to thirty-six weeks. There's a flight today with tickets still available, so I book a seat then tell the driver to take me to the airport.

Despite everything, guilt twists in my gut at the thought of leaving Mum down here on her own, so I shoot off a message to a neighbour that Mum's friendly with, explaining I'm having to go away for a while and asking if she wouldn't mind putting her head in Mum's door and checking she's okay. I don't mention we've had an argument. Mum, who's all about appearances, would hate that.

For now, though, I need to focus on myself—or rather, more importantly, I need to focus on Aidan. I don't have any belongings with me. My go bag for the hospital, which I've kept ready just in case, was sitting in the hall, and with hindsight I could have grabbed it on my way out. Oh well, too late. Even without so much as a toothbrush, I have to see him. Today. I have to sort this.

CHAPTER THIRTY-SIX

GRACE

When I arrive at Inverness Airport, I again try Emily and David, praying one of them may be able to come and pick me up. But I still can't get through to them and neither has responded to the messages I've left. It's like fate is conspiring against me. The day I need them most, they're both unreachable, mysteriously so. I don't understand it.

I've no choice but to take a taxi—another one. Between a flight and two cab rides, today is really eating into my savings but I don't care. All that matters is I get to see Aidan.

When I reach Bannock, it's just gone half past four. At Christmas it would have been dark at this time, but it's still light, sort of. The sun is obscured by gloomy grey clouds that release a constant drizzle.

I point out Elspeth's house to the driver and he pulls up outside. The fare is steep, as he warned me it would be. As well as the forty-minute journey here, it has to cover his return to the city. I pay up, tip him too, then get out.

He does a three-point turn and, with a wave, drives off back the way he came. I approach Elspeth's door, my arms and legs trembling with nervous excitement. I reach out and ring the bell.

When Aidan showed up on my doorstep without warning, he wore a kilt. My heavy winter coat can't compete but hopefully he'll just be happy to see me.

I wait.

And wait.

Nothing. No sounds from inside. No footsteps drawing closer. Only rain pattering on my hood and the splash of a puddle as a lone van drives by. Otherwise, Bannock is quiet.

This is not at all going to plan.

I'd assumed Aidan would be in or, if not, that Elspeth would be around. As a chef, she works most evenings but the Bannock Hotel's restaurant is closed on Mondays and Tuesdays, and it's Tuesday today. If she's not at home, I'm not sure where she might be, and nor do I have any idea where I'm likely to find Aidan.

Oh God. I came from London to see him face to face. I'd hoped to surprise him like he did me, but I suppose I'll have to call him and arrange a meet-up. It's not how I imagined it.

I take out my phone and tap his name. I wait but . . . it rings out. It doesn't immediately go to voicemail, like when I try Emily or David. Instead he simply doesn't pick up.

Bloody hell, what's going on today? Where is everyone?

Emotions bubble up in my chest but I push them back down before they can overwhelm me. I won't cry—I refuse to. I'll remain composed, no matter what.

Turning, I gaze across the road at the Bannock Hotel. I could go in there and see if I can speak with Emily, but there's a good chance I'd bump into one of the McIntyre boys first or maybe even some hotel guests. I don't want to break down in front of them, and right now I'm only just managing to hold myself together.

No, I decide to try my brother instead. At his, the only other person I might have to deal with is Johnny and I can cope with that.

I head to their pretty little cottage on the lane by the river, but David's car is nowhere to be seen and there are no signs of life from within. Even though my gut tells me no one is home, I try the brass knocker. Their place remains still and quiet.

Tears sting my eyes but I brush them away.

Stay in control, Grace. You'll just have to go to the hotel.

I trudge back, trying my best to avoid puddles. The journey up here and the argument with Mum have drained me completely. I'd hoped Aidan might wrap me in his arms and make everything okay. It seems it's not going to be that easy.

As if to kick me while I'm down, the hotel's reception has been decked out for Valentine's Day. Fairy lights twinkle on the walls, a beautiful floral arrangement sits on the front desk, and heart-shaped balloons float on either side of the entrance. These bob and sway when the door swings closed behind me.

The decorations drive home to me what a fool I've been. Aidan and I should be together right now, celebrating our romance just like other couples across the country. Instead, earlier today, I was seriously considering breaking up with him, thanks in no small part to Mum's subtle but persistent interference. I've been so blind.

There's no one at reception but behind the desk is a door to a small office. I know Emily and the McIntyre brothers sometimes work there so I call out, "Hello?"

Several seconds pass. Then, "Grace?"

I'm so busy staring at the office door I don't notice Jamie

appear from the restaurant. I turn to him and do a double take. His chestnut hair is neatly styled, and he's dressed in a kilt, waistcoat, and jacket, topped off with a crimson cravat. I associate the youngest McIntyre brother with practical jokes and winding people up—I forgot he scrubs up well when he wants to.

"Jamie! Why are you looking so smart?"

He glances down at himself then grins. "Aye, not too shabby, right? We're opening the restaurant tonight, even though it's normally closed on a Tuesday. Emily suggested we put on a special Valentine's menu and charge a bit more than usual. To justify the additional cost, we're throwing in a few extras here and there, and since I'm waiting tables, I thought I'd get my legs out as a wee bonus for the diners. That wasn't actually one of Emily's suggestions but it's a good idea, don't you think?"

Even though I'm damp and dishevelled from the rain, and at an emotional low, I let out a soft laugh. "You're just hoping it'll get you some decent tips, aren't you?"

He winks and I manage a smile, but then—as if from nowhere—a sob bursts from my lips.

"Shit! What's wrong?" Jamie steps closer, his brow furrowing. There's no sign of his usual playful demeanour. He's all seriousness.

"I'm sorry." I sniff and attempt to pull myself together. "Everything just got a bit much there. Is Emily about? I was hoping to speak with her."

Jamie grimaces with regret. "Er, I'm afraid not. Let's get you a seat. Come on, through here."

He beckons me into the office, drags out a chair from under the desk, and gestures for me to sit. I do, small tremors shooting through my body. I sense that a full-on breakdown is imminent but I'm trying my best to hold it back. This is so embarrassing. I don't know Jamie well enough to cry in front of him.

"Right," he says in a low voice, "so . . . Emily isn't here but Elspeth is. She's in the kitchen with Lewis, getting things ready for tonight. She always knows what to say and she's a great hugger too. I'll go get her."

"Wait!" I swallow down my emotions. "Can you and I just chat for a while?"

As awkward as this is with Jamie, I'd like to compose myself before seeing anyone else, especially Aidan's mum.

He's already set off for the door but he stops and raises his eyebrows. "Er . . . sure. If that's what you want. I mean, to be honest I am a wee bit out of my depth here but . . . aye, let's talk." He perches on the desk, fidgets with his hands, and attempts an encouraging smile.

Normally, Jamie would sooner tease someone than reassure them. There's something sweet about his discomfort, and strangely it helps to calm my nerves, even though he himself is far from relaxed.

Wiping at my eyes, I meet his smile with a weak one of my own. "Thanks. And sorry about the tears. It . . . hasn't been a great day." I take a moment to gather myself. "So . . . Emily. If she's not here, where is she?"

"Oh, she and Ally have gone away for the night as a treat to themselves for Valentine's Day."

A memory comes to me. A week or two ago, on a call, Emily did mention she'd be doing that. I should have remembered but my thoughts have been so scattered today, it slipped my mind. But . . . it still doesn't explain why I've not been able to get through to her.

I pull out my phone. "I've lost count of the number of times I've tried her but it's gone to voicemail every time. Any idea why that is?"

Jamie nods. "Her phone is off, as is Ally's. Before they left this morning, Ally took me and Lewis aside and told us not to try contacting them. He said, even if the hotel goes on fire, they don't want to hear about it until they get back tomorrow."

I chuckle quietly. I can imagine Ally saying that.

"So . . . aye, they got us to open the restaurant on a day it's usually closed and made us put on an extra-special menu. Meanwhile, they've buggered off to have a night of sex and romance. All right for some, eh?"

He winks to show he's not seriously criticising them. I get the impression he's actually quite looking forward to serving diners in his kilt.

"That explains that, then," I say, "but I've not been able to get through to my brother either. It's so weird."

"Er, not really—that's got a simple explanation too. Elspeth bumped into Johnny yesterday and he told her about his Valentine's present for David, which your brother wouldn't have found out about until this morning. They're also away for the night, off to a luxury cabin a wee way up north. It's the kind of place you go to escape everything: it comes with a hot tub but no mobile phone signal. No wonder you can't get through to him."

"Ah."

If David had realised he wouldn't have reception, I'm sure he'd have given me a heads-up. As the trip was a surprise, he might not even have known where he was going until they got there.

So . . . I've travelled up from London, and not only is my

best friend not here today, neither is my brother. That's fine so long as I can see Aidan. He's the one I'm really here for.

I put my phone down on the desk. "When I got to Bannock, I went to Elspeth's house, looking for Aidan, but no one was in. I tried calling him but couldn't get through. What's the deal there? Has he also gone away for the night?"

Jamie frowns. "Nah, he should be about. But . . . he doesn't live with his maw anymore. Don't you know that? He's got his own place now."

This news is like a sucker punch to my heart. He's . . . moved out? Aidan didn't mention that to me. We're having a kid together—isn't that the kind of thing he should tell me? Then again, I suppose I have been avoiding him for quite some time.

But . . . oh shit, that house on Boxing Day, the isolated property I absolutely hated, he wouldn't have . . . ?

Dread settles in my stomach. He was really keen on it at one stage. If I've not even been answering his calls, maybe he decided to push ahead with it? Crap, crap, crap!

"Jamie, where are you?" Lewis's voice rings out.

"Er, just coming!"

"Well, hurry up! You're supposed to be decorating the restaurant. The first customers will be arriving soon and we're fully booked until close. It's going to be a busy night."

Jamie rolls his eyes. "I'll go and have a quick word with him. You chill here for a wee bit. You can take your coat off, if you like. Can I get you a tea or something?"

"Er . . . a glass of water would be great."

"Sure, I'll be back in a minute or two."

With another reassuring smile, he leaves. No sooner does he do so than I realise I can't just sit around here. Jamie, Lewis, and Elspeth are putting on a special dinner tonight—I don't want to distract them and take up even more of their time. Besides, it's Aidan I need to speak with and I now have an idea where he might be. If I can't get through to him on the phone, I'll have to go see him in person.

Standing, I head out of the office. The reception is once more empty, so without a word to anyone, I slip outside, back onto drizzly Main Street.

I aim for the bridge, cross it, then pass the church, all the while bracing myself against the weather. Aidan said a path runs from Bannock Woods to the town of Duntreath and that it goes past the house. That makes things easy—I should have no trouble finding it. Except . . . he also said it takes the best part of an hour to walk there.

Already the sky is darker than it was when I arrived in Bannock, and it'll only get darker still as the sun sets. But there's dusk too, right? An hour . . . I'm sure I'll be fine. Besides, what choice do I have? Everyone I know in this town is either away for the night or working at the hotel. And yes, I took a taxi here from the city of Inverness, but I've no idea how you'd go about arranging one from this end.

This is okay. Sometimes love requires a grand gesture. Well, this can be mine. I'll hike to Aidan's on this cold, rainy evening—a feat not many women would consider while seven months pregnant—and I'll throw myself at his feet and beg him to forgive me for ignoring him. I'll explain I didn't know about my mum's meddling and somehow I'll fix everything.

Yes, that's how this is going to go. Some might claim it's a terrible idea—reckless, even—but I only have myself to blame for having to do this. If I hadn't pushed Aidan away, I wouldn't be in this pickle.

I reach the woods and head on in, soon finding and taking the footpath marked DUNTREATH. In the summer, when I fell here, the forest was vibrant and beautiful. At Christmas, when everything was covered in a layer of white, it was also stunning, though in a different way. Now the atmosphere is eerie and foreboding. On either side of me, trees rise tall and menacing, their bare branches reaching for the darkening sky like long skeletal fingers. The shadows they cast stretch across the woodland floor.

I shiver but press on, venturing deeper and deeper into what increasingly feels like a wild and perilous environment. Bannock and civilisation fall further behind me with each step I take. The sight of snowdrops offers my nerves some distraction—their pristine white petals are a promise that spring is on its way and winter will soon be over. But with night approaching, the delicate flowers are closing up.

The drizzle from overhead becomes heavier until large droplets of rain are pelting down on me. I trudge on, pulling my coat tighter around me and tugging my hood down further. Maybe I've made a mistake—I consider turning back—but no, the thought of seeing Aidan again and of making things right fuels me. It gives me the strength to take another step, and then another.

Unfortunately, the weather only gets worse. Soon it's pouring down hard and relentlessly, and the occasional gust of wind that finds its way through the trees sprays drops into my face. My coat does little to protect me from it, while beneath my shoes, the path quickly turns to mud. I squelch on but . . . God, what the hell am I doing? I'm carrying a baby. It's still winter. I shouldn't be out in this—this is madness.

With each passing minute visibility decreases and soon I'm

squinting to see through the gloom. I don't want to get my phone wet but I'm going to have to use its torch feature just to light my way. I reach into my pocket and—

It's not there.

Oh, shit.

I stop, frantically patting my other pockets, heavy rain continuing to strike me. But my phone isn't anywhere. With horror I realise what's happened. In the hotel's office, when I was talking with Jamie, I put it down on the desk. When I left, I didn't take it with me.

Despair washes over me, as chilling as the rainfall saturating my clothes. I'm out here alone without any means of calling for help. How could I be so stupid and irresponsible? Earlier today, when I was at the shops and forgot to pick up milk, that was kind of cute. *Oh dear! Baby brain. What am I like?* Now, though? This is serious. I've put myself at risk—my baby too.

And for what? I don't even know if Aidan's at that house! What if I get there after walking for an hour only to find the property still and locked up? I'll then be miles from Bannock without shelter.

I should never have come out here. This is utterly idiotic. I need to go back. And yet . . . my breaths are coming quicker, my heart pounding faster. Panic bubbles up inside me, threatening to boil over, and though I try to stop it, I don't know that I can.

I lean against a tree and think of the breathing exercises I teach my yoga students. Closing my eyes, I attempt to put them into practice but my pulse is reverberating in my ears, and the baby—as if sensing my distress—wriggles.

Focus on the rise and fall of your diaphragm, I tell myself, but it's no use. My anxiety is spiralling out of control.

I either need to go on or turn back—staying out here

exposed to the elements won't solve anything—but my heart is going like the clappers and my legs are weak. I need to get a grip and calm myself, but instead my head is telling me what a fool I've been.

You came out here in the dark and the rain without your phone? You're going to be a mother, Grace! You should be more responsible than this. What were you thinking?

A sob escapes my lips, my tears mixing with the raindrops trickling down my face. I sink to the mud-soaked ground and hug my swollen belly.

Then, from somewhere far off, my name reaches me on the breeze. Is it just the wind playing tricks on me or is someone really calling me?

I sit up and strain to listen against the pounding deluge.

"Grace?"

There it is again. It's still distant but clearer now, and it's definitely not my imagination. I recognise that low, deep tone.

"Aidan!" I shout, scarcely believing he could be here.

"Grace! Thank God!"

His familiar voice pierces through my panic, soothing my turbulent thoughts and restoring some of my strength. With a struggle I clamber back to my feet. Wiping at my watery eyes, I squint through the curtain of rainfall.

"Aidan? Where are you?"

"I'm coming!"

Through the murkiness of the woods and the thick sheets of rain, a light appears. It draws nearer and soon the shadowy blur of a figure emerges from the gloom.

"Aidan!" I stumble towards him.

His shape becomes more defined, his features coming into focus. Sheltering under a golf umbrella and carrying a torch, he strides through the trees with purpose. I hurry forward and fling myself at him, burying myself into his chest, not caring that I'm getting him wet. It doesn't bother him one bit—one of his arms encircles me and presses me even closer to him, while the other holds the umbrella above us, protecting us from the downpour.

"I'm so sorry!" I blubber. "I'm sorry I've not been in contact more. I'm sorry my mum's been calling you behind my back—I'd no idea until this morning. Have I messed everything up?"

He pulls away from me, his gaze raking over me, searching for signs of harm. Apparently satisfied, he fixes me with a stern stare. "I'm furious with you, Grace. It's the second time you've come into these woods without your phone, and I'm telling you, it better be the last. But as for the other stuff? Forget about it. You have nothing to apologise for."

He draws me to him once more. Tension ebbs from my shoulders, the weight of worry lifting from me. I inhale deeply and release a sigh of relief.

"But bloody hell, you're soaked through. We need to get you out of this rain and warm you up. Are you okay to walk?"

"Y-yes." I sniff. "Now that you're here, I am."

"Good. Now, take your coat off."

I do as he asks. He removes his own winter jacket and gives it to me. It's not intended for city life, like mine, but to provide genuine protection against extreme weather in the great outdoors. It's roomy at the shoulders and too long at the arms, but I don't care because, to my delight, it zips up over my bump, even if it is a tight squeeze. It feels like being wrapped in a cocoon of warmth.

"That should help but I still want to get you inside as soon as possible. Hook your arm through mine. I'll carry your coat and the umbrella. Can you manage the torch?"

I nod and take it.

"Good. If I go too fast, just say, but let's not delay longer than we need to."

Guided by torchlight, we set off at a brisk pace but I find I'm able to match his speed. Now he's by my side, as if by magic, all my anxiety is gone. I don't have to worry because I know he'll do everything in his power to keep me safe—tonight and always. This realisation hits me with a certainty I can't question. I know it to be the truth the same way I know that cream and jam taste good on a scone or that Emily and I will be best friends for life. I'm not sure why I ever doubted him.

"We're heading to Bannock?" I ask when it occurs to me we're retracing my steps. "I'd thought you might be at the house you showed me at Christmas. Jamie said you'd moved out of your mum's, and I assumed—"

"Aye, I know what you assumed. Jamie called me and told me you arrived at the hotel upset then disappeared into thin air. When he mentioned the last thing he said to you—that I've got my own place now—I put two and two together, and thank God I did. What's that phrase?" He glances sidelong at me, and despite the obvious concern in his expression, that lovable cheeky grin breaks through. "To *assume* is to make an *ass* of *u* and *me*?"

I let out a sound that's half gasp, half laugh. "Aidan Stewart!" My voice is still finding its strength again but I push on. "Are you calling the mother of your child an ass? And on Valentine's Day!"

He grins and gazes at me like I'm the most precious thing in the world. "Fuck, you're beautiful, Grace. I've missed you."

My heart skips a beat, even though I'm sure he must be lying—it's dark and I'm a wet, bedraggled mess. And yet . . . something in his eyes tells me he's being perfectly serious.

I swallow. "I've missed you too."

We press on through the woods, back towards Bannock.

Suddenly a thought comes to me. "Wait, how did Jamie get through to you? I tried calling you but you didn't pick up."

"Ah. Sorry about that. I was doing some work in my new place and my music was on pretty loudly. Jamie got lucky: I heard my phone going in a break between songs."

I'm in no position to tell him off, not after what I've put him through, but even so, I say, "Well, listen out in future, okay? When I call, you answer. I need you, Aidan. We . . . we're having a baby together."

He nods. "How about we make a deal? You stop going for walks without your phone, and I'll always pick up when you ring. Agreed?"

"Agreed. So, er . . . you *didn't* buy that house we saw on Boxing Day?"

He chuckles. "No. You made it quite clear you hated it. I got a place in Bannock."

"Oh. Right. I . . . feel pretty stupid."

"You shouldn't. I don't like that you put yourself in danger, but I am flattered you were so desperate to see me you set off through the woods. Am I that irresistible?"

"Yes," I answer honestly. "You are. I . . . want you in my life. I want us to raise this child together, if that's something you'd like too?"

Aidan doesn't miss a beat. "Of course it is. I love you, Grace."

He says it so bluntly and with such conviction I'm caught off-guard.

I hesitate, but not for long. "I . . . love you too, Aidan."

He stops, turns to me, and presses his lips against mine. Despite the cold and wet, they're soft and warm, and they ignite a fire inside me. I lose myself in the kiss, every nerve in my body tingling.

Eventually he pulls away again and grins. "Sorry, I couldn't resist but we really should get you back. C'mon!"

The journey to Bannock feels only half as long as my lonely walk out. When we get there, we pass the church and cross the old stone bridge, then Aidan turns down my brother's lane.

"David and Johnny are away for the night," I say. "We can't go to theirs."

"I know." Aidan keeps going anyway, passing their home and continuing past four others that back onto the river until he reaches the cottage at the end of the cul-de-sac. "Here we are."

A warm glow radiates from the property's windows, cosy and inviting on this rainy night. The door is painted a bright blue, the colour standing out prettily against the grey stone walls.

"You . . . live here?"

"Aye. Let's get you inside."

He opens up and beckons me in. Just like at Johnny's, the main living area is open plan. Embers smoulder in a wood-burning stove, around which a plush brown couch, two armchairs, and a small wooden coffee table are arranged.

Aidan hangs my wet coat up then helps me out of his jacket and hangs that up too. He heads over to the stove, opens the door, and tosses in a couple of logs. A comforting, smoky scent fills the room.

"Grab a seat and get warm. I'll fetch you a towel, plus some joggers and a hoodie of mine for you to change into."

I don't move from the entrance. I'm too stunned. "I . . . don't understand. This place . . . is yours?"

"Aye, do you like it?"

"Of course I like it. It's beautiful! But how . . . ?"

"I'm happy to fill you in but not until you're out of those damp clothes." He gestures to an armchair. "Sit!"

I shake my head and cross my arms. "Nope. I want the tour."

"Grace, I really think—"

I silence him with a stare. "I'll be fine for a few more minutes. I'm already warming up. Before I do anything else, I need to explore this place, and I strongly recommend you don't refuse a request from a woman who's seven months pregnant."

He hesitates for a moment then grins. "I suppose I can quickly show you around, but then you're sitting your bum down by the stove, okay?"

"Deal."

He leads me to the main bedroom and then to the bathroom. Everything is in really good nick, which is a surprise. That house he showed me on Boxing Day needed a lot of modernisation, but this place is pleasant and charming. The worst thing I can say about it is it's maybe a little bland—it could do with some touches of personality here and there—but that's easily fixed.

"What's the story?" I want to know. "How did you end up moving here?"

"An old friend of my maw's has been renting it out as a

holiday home for years. A while ago she mentioned to Maw she was thinking of selling up—she's getting older and could do without the hassle. I had a chat with her and . . . well, we were able to arrange a private deal, which meant no estate-agent fees. That saved us both a bit of money.

"As for the mortgage, Da agreed to be my guarantor, which helped. Don't get me wrong, I'll be making the monthly payments myself, but since Bannock Adventures is still new, the bank insisted on a fallback, just in case."

"Wow. And the furniture?"

"It was pretty much all already here. As it was a holiday home, it's not like she needed any of it—she'd have sold it or given it away—so we made it a part of the deal. The only room I've really worked on so far is this one."

He guides me to what, in David and Johnny's cottage, would be the spare room. "It's still a work in progress. If I'd known you were coming up today, I'd have tried harder to get it finished."

"Just hurry up and show me!"

He smirks and pushes open the door, and I can't help but gasp.

It's . . . a nursery. The walls have a fresh coat of pale-yellow paint. A mobile dangles above an oak cot, while a nursing chair sits in one corner beside a bookcase. There are a few books on display already, including the Paddington title I gifted Aidan at Christmas. On the floor is a toolbox next to some partially constructed flat-pack furniture—it looks like it's going to be a changing unit. That's what Aidan must have been working on when I tried calling him.

I can hardly believe what I'm seeing. "This is amazing!"

"You like it?" A relieved smile tugs at his lips. "Good. A lot of the stuff is second-hand but it's all in great condition. Folk around town had things they didn't need anymore, which helped because, after buying this place, my funds were a wee bit . . . limited. I hope that's okay. If there's anything you want to change, just let me know and—"

"It's perfect. I absolutely love it."

The care he's put into this room warms my heart.

He scratches his head. "And . . . you're not annoyed I asked Emily and David not to mention it to you? I wanted to be the one to tell you about it, but it hasn't been so easy for me to get a hold of you lately."

"Of course I'm not annoyed." I find his hand and squeeze it. "Not even slightly."

"I'm glad. Well, any time you're up from London, the baby can stay here—as can you, if you fancy it. And . . . I don't want to put any pressure on you, but if you'd ever consider moving in with me, then—"

"Yes! Of course I'll move in with you, Aidan. Yes, yes, yes!"

There are things I need to figure out, like what to do about Mum. She may have hurt me, but even so, she's going through a difficult time and needs my support. For now, though, I have to think about what's best for me and—even more importantly—what's best for my baby. That means having Aidan in the picture, despite Mum's attempts to push him out of it.

"This has turned into an okay Valentine's Day after all, hasn't it?" Grinning, he pulls me into a hug then winces. "Shit, you really are soaking. Let's get you back to the stove."

He leads me into the living area, and while I thaw out by the fire, he closes the curtains.

"It's a dead-end road so it's not as though anyone will go by, but still, you should have privacy while you're getting changed. I'll grab you a towel."

"Wait! First, come over here."

He raises an eyebrow but does so.

I reach out and touch his jumper. "Oh no! Your clothes are damp too. They'll have to come off as well."

"Don't worry about me—the brolly kept away the worst of it. All I care about is you."

I roll my eyes. "You're missing the point." I tug his jumper up and over his head and toss it aside.

"Ah, I see what's happening here. Gotcha." He begins to remove my clothing.

I smile, unbuttoning his shirt. "Before you get any ideas, I'm tired. This isn't for sex—at least, not for now. Maybe you'll receive a Valentine's treat later on. What I want to do is hug you while the fire warms our bare bodies."

Aidan considers this then nods. "Sounds good to me."

With ease, I pull off his shirt, drop his jeans, and slide down his underwear, while—with a little more difficulty—he peels my wet things off me. Soon, though, we stand facing each other, naked, the stove flickering and crackling beside us, its glow highlighting every curve and muscle of our figures.

Carefully he draws me to him and runs his hands up and down my back, rubbing warmth into my chilled skin. My protruding belly gently presses into his firm, toned abs. His pubic hair lightly tickles the underside of my bump. Between us, the baby squirms and shifts.

"Love you," I say for a second time tonight, trying out the phrase again, testing how it feels on my lips and sounds in my ears.

"And I love you, lass." His words are as comforting as the touch of his body against mine.

CHAPTER THIRTY-SEVEN

GRACE

The murmur of the river is like a lullaby, soothing and calming. I awoke a while ago but I'm in no rush to get up. I'm content to lie on my side and become acquainted with the sounds of my new home. Aidan is cuddled up against me, an arm around me and a hand tenderly resting on my bump. I can't imagine anywhere I'd rather be right now than here.

He's still asleep, his breath softly caressing the nape of my neck. Although I trained him to wear pyjamas when he stayed with me in London, he's reverted to his old ways but I'm not complaining—far from it. His bare skin radiates heat, keeping me toasty on this February morning.

Unlike Aidan, I'm not naked, having borrowed a baggy T-shirt of his to sleep in. Apart from the clothes I wore yesterday, which I left by the stove to dry, I don't have anything with me in Bannock—no pyjamas, sleep scarf, toothbrush, or fresh outfit to change into. It's not ideal but it's a worry for later on. At the moment I'm happy and that's all that matters.

He murmurs something unintelligible, a whisper of dreams, then snuggles even closer to me. I remember that night in London when we lay like this, our bodies connected like jigsaw pieces. He didn't sleep at all because I mischievously rubbed my bum against him. I half consider trying that again—he'd probably think it a pleasant way to wake up—but no, I don't have the heart to disturb him. I let him rest, comforted by the steady rhythm of his breathing, which I feel through the gentle rise and fall of his chest.

My phone sits on the bedside table—Jamie handed it in last night after the restaurant closed. Careful not to rouse Aidan, I reach for it then open a chat with the woman who's due to cover my yoga classes during my maternity leave. I fire off a quick message to see if she'd be interested in starting a little earlier. I'll wait for her reply before asking what she thinks about taking over from me on a permanent basis.

There are a number of things I'll have to sort out. I'll need to go back to London to complete some admin and collect my belongings, but that'll involve seeing Mum. So long as I'm lying here with Aidan's arm around me, I'm not going to think about that. I can't avoid it forever but I can put it off for a while.

As I'm returning my phone to the table, it rings. My first thought is it's my maternity cover getting back to me straight away, but no, it's Emily's name on the screen. I answer, Aidan stirring behind me.

"Hi, Emily."

"Grace! My God, I've just seen your messages and missed calls. Is everything okay?"

"Er . . ."

Sitting up, I gaze down at Aidan, who's blinking, his hair tousled, one side of his face slightly flattened by the pillow. Somehow he manages to be both utterly adorable and irresistibly attractive at the same time. I don't know whether to stroke his cheek or kiss him.

"Grace?" Emily prompts.

"Oh, yeah, everything is okay. Actually, things are great—sorry if I panicked you with those missed calls. Guess where I am?"

"First, I'm glad to hear you're all right. You had me worried for a moment. And as for where you are, well, since you're asking, I'm guessing you're not at home. Are you . . . in Bannock?"

"Correct! But also wrong. I am in Bannock but I'm home too. This *is* my home now."

Emily lets out a gasp, quickly followed by a squeal. "You're moving to Bannock? Seriously?"

"Mm-hmm."

Reaching down, I glide my fingers over Aidan's chest, brushing the light hairs there and tracing the definition of his muscles. He smiles up at me sleepily.

"I'm in bed with my Highlander right now, in our new place, which is just a few doors away from David and Johnny's and only a few minutes from the hotel."

"Oh, Grace, that's amazing news! It's such a beautiful cottage. I was desperate to tell you about it but Aidan insisted I keep my lips sealed. Now, I've actually got some news too. Seeing as you made me guess where you are, why don't you try guessing where I am?"

"Hmm, I know you went away for the night but I've no idea where. You'll just have to tell me."

"Gretna Green."

Emily and I were there earlier this year—it's where Ally went down on one knee. The village is famously associated with runaway weddings, harking back to a time when young English couples crossed over the border into Scotland so they could be married without their parents' permission.

"Wait! Did you and Ally . . . elope?"

At this Aidan props himself up and rubs the sleep from his eyes. His expression becomes alert and curious.

"We've not told anyone else yet," Emily admits, "but . . . yes! I'm Mrs McIntyre now."

"Oh, Emily, that's fantastic. Congratulations!"

A flicker of surprise passes over Aidan's face then he breaks into a grin. He leans close to me and says, "Aye, congratulations, Mrs McIntyre! Can you pop on loudspeaker so I can say a few words to your husband?"

"Ha! Thanks, Aidan. I didn't know you were listening in. Of course!"

I turn on loudspeaker too and the four of us spend the next ten minutes catching up, filling each other in on our Valentine's Days, although mainly I let Emily and Ally do the talking. I don't want to bring down the mood by going over all that happened yesterday. There are a few details that can wait until we see them in person.

They're heading home to Bannock today, so we agree to meet up once they're back then we say our goodbyes.

"Wow!" Aidan says after the call is over. "They're married. That gets me thinking . . ." He sits up next to me, our backs against the headboard, and reaches for my hand. "Grace Adefope, there's something I want to ask you." He looks deep into my eyes and there's no playfulness in his expression now—it's serious and intent.

My heart lurches and I swallow. "Wait, you're not going to—"

"Let me finish." Tenderly he grazes my cheek with his fingers. "Grace Adefope, will you do me the honour of agreeing with my da's advice that we shouldn't rush into marriage?"

"Aidan!" Gasping with indignation, I slap his bare chest, hard. "That was mean!"

He grins, wraps his arms around me, and pulls me closer to him, nuzzling his face against mine. "But I do love you, Grace, and I can see it happening one day. For now, to make up for my wee joke, how about breakfast in bed? Or we could go out to the Coffee Bothy?"

"Or I could cut off your willy to teach you a lesson? What do you think about that?"

His laughter echoes through the room. "Okay, I get the message—pretending to propose to you is not a prank you find funny. Noted. Anyway, as I'm not too keen on your suggestion, why don't we go for my first proposal of breakfast in bed?"

I slide my hand under the covers and take a hold of his penis. "Hmm . . ." I say, considering. "Fine, you can keep it. This time." I give it a squeeze then let go.

He chuckles, pecks me on the lips, then slips out of the bed, his skin glowing in the gentle morning light that filters through the curtains. He yawns and stretches, his muscles flexing, and I openly admire his naked form. From a wardrobe he produces a pair of joggers, which he tugs on, not bothering with underwear, apparently. He puts on a T-shirt too then leans over me, gives me another kiss, and leaves to prepare breakfast.

I close my eyes and gently rub my bump, happily listening to the sounds of Aidan humming away to himself as he rustles something up. I'm so relaxed I'm drifting off again when there's a knock at the door.

"I'll get it!" Aidan calls.

His footsteps pad through the living area, the door creaks open, and then . . . nothing. Aidan doesn't say anything.

"Who is it?" I ask.

"Er . . . Grace, you may want to come out here."

Puzzled, I get out of bed and search Aidan's wardrobe for a dressing gown. Not finding one, I instead pull on a pair of shorts and a hoodie then head through. When I see who's at the door, I freeze.

"Mum?"

She stands stiffly in the doorway, a small suitcase by her side. "Hello, Grace."

I don't know what to say or even what to think. I'm still so hurt by what she did, but at the same time, she travelled up to Bannock? She should be taking things easy!

"You . . . you'd better come in," I offer eventually.

"Thank you." With a forced smile, she steps inside.

Aidan, his jaw tightly set, closes the door behind her.

"Er, over here. Take a seat." I gesture to an armchair, while I sit on the sofa.

Aidan hovers, unsure whether he's meant to stick around for this conversation, so I pat the spot beside me. I'm done with excluding him and speaking with Mum in private. He deserves to be a part of this and hear everything.

Mum lowers herself into the chair, having left the suitcase by the entrance.

I glance over at it. "It looks like you've brought a lot of stuff with you."

"Oh, those are your things. You left in such a rush yesterday you didn't have time to pack anything. I thought you might need some supplies."

I'm taken aback by this. "Er . . . thanks."

We're getting off on the wrong foot. I'm supposed to be annoyed with her but instead I'm thanking her. I'm also concerned about her. It's a confusing mix of emotions.

An awkward silence settles.

"Grace, I . . ." Mum begins, but then her breath hitches. She blinks.

Wait, are her eyes growing watery? As if in answer to my question, a tear slips down her cheek.

I'm stunned. I don't know that I've ever seen Mum cry before. She's always been . . . unshakable. Yes, since the diagnosis, she's shown another side of herself—she's opened up, confiding in me how hard it was for her as a single mother. But actually seeing her teary shocks me.

"Mum?" Already my anger is melting away. I couldn't hold on to it if I wanted to. This is the woman who gave birth to me and raised me. How can I stay annoyed with her when she's upset like this?

"I'm fine. I'm just . . ." She gulps. "I'm so, so sorry, Grace. I've been so troubled by what you said about Mark. I'd no idea. Obviously, I don't know what's best for you and I need to trust you to make your own decisions. What I did—calling Aidan behind your back—was unacceptable.

"I can't bear the thought of losing you or of not being a part of my granddaughter's life. And Aidan"—her attention turns to him- -"I'm not sure how you and I are going to get past this, or even *if* we can get past this. Have I ruined any chance of the two of us getting along?"

Aidan glances at me and raises his brows. It seems he's deferring to me to decide how to handle this, which is understandable. She is my mother, after all.

"Mum," I say carefully, "I appreciate the apology. But

you're right: you do have to let me make my own decisions. I can't go through the rest of my life with you believing you know better than I do what's best for me. I don't want to hear that I could have done 'more' than become a yoga instructor or that I should be with this partner rather than that partner. Why can't you love me for who I am instead of trying to mould me into who you'd like me to be?"

Mum's voice breaks. "Oh, Grace, but I do love you for who you are. I . . . I can only apologise again. I'll try harder. I promise I will."

I nod then I stand, as does she, and we hug. I hold her for a long time. I'm about to become a mother myself and have a daughter of my own—I don't want to lose Mum's support in my life. Sometimes a little shake-up is exactly what a relationship needs to grow stronger. Hopefully, that's what happens here.

When I finally let her go, we return to our seats and she shifts her focus back to Aidan.

"I'm afraid I've driven a wedge between us that may be difficult to remove. I don't suppose you'll be able to forgive me?"

Aidan scratches his head. "Well, I'm only just beginning to mend my relationship with my da, which was strained for too long, so . . . I'm in no rush to fall out with anybody else. Aye, I can forgive you."

Mum's face brightens but Aidan holds up a hand to show he's not done.

"I need you to understand, though, that I'm in love with your daughter, and I'm going to love our bairn just as fiercely. I won't tolerate anyone trying to put themselves between me and my girls. I'm willing to give you a second chance, but not a third."

It's a threat—something I'm not used to hearing from Aidan's lips—but strangely, a look of respect crosses Mum's face.

"I understand."

"Then let's say nothing more about it." Just like that, Aidan's serious expression morphs into his usual boyish grin. "You timed things well, Viola—I was in the midst of rustling up some breakfast. Why don't you and Grace move over to the table and I'll put on extra? Can I get you a tea or a coffee?"

EPILOGUE
AIDAN

"Och, just look at the pair of us, Aidan," Maw says with a laugh. "Me with Ru, you with Callie. We're a fine sight, aren't we?"

We're in the snug of the Bannock Hotel, sitting around a table with Jamie and Grace. My daughter, Callie, is peacefully snuggled up against me, fast asleep. Maw, meanwhile, is gently bouncing Ally and Emily's wee one, Ruairidh, who shows his appreciation with a gummy smile. Both bairns are now a little over three months.

"Your son suits having a baby in his arms," Grace comments to Maw. "When I first met him, I never would have imagined I'd one day say *that* about him."

Maw's laughter fills the small room. "Until you came into his life, I'd never pictured Aidan as a father, but I'm so proud of the man he's becoming thanks to your influence." She beams at Grace then gives Ru an extra-big bounce, producing a delighted gurgle.

I'll concede he's a pretty cute baby, even if he's no patch on my daughter, of course. He's in a onesie featuring Roo, his namesake character from Winnie the Pooh.

Ally and Emily are off on a walk, enjoying a bit of child-free time. Viola, David, and Johnny, meanwhile, are away on a day trip to the Black Isle. Despite its name, it's not an island but a peninsula. It's a great place to see dolphins—especially at Chanonry Point—and David is hoping to spot some.

At every opportunity, I've been keeping the promise I made to Grace at Christmas to show her around the Highlands. We were planning to join the others today, but Grace suggested we have a chill day instead and that was a great call. It's been exactly what we both needed after some interrupted nights and a busy period at Bannock Adventures.

We've been lucky to have had a lot of help from Viola and Maw, and we're so grateful for it. Viola has been travelling up regularly and utterly dotes on her granddaughter. Her treatment has, thankfully, been a success. She's been talking about going part time at her job—not that she needs to for health reasons but so she can come up even more often. That's fine by me. After a rocky start, she and I have been getting on well.

Across the table, Jamie lowers his face so it's the same height as Ru's. Picking up a muslin cloth, he hides himself with it. "Where did Uncle Jamie go?" He lets the cloth drop. "Here I am. Boo!"

Ru's eyes widen and he giggles joyfully.

Jamie smirks. "Even wee Ru knows I'm the funniest guy around here." He pats his nephew's head. "Good lad."

"Mate, that boy chuckles at anything," I object. "My Callie, though? She's got a sophisticated sense of humour. She prefers the funny faces her daddy pulls."

I gaze down at her in her Paddington onesie and can't resist brushing a finger across her adorably chubby cheek. She's angelic when she's asleep, although I am slightly disappointed she's not awake. I'd quite like to show off the incredible laughs I've been getting out of her lately.

She stirs, her mouth opening in a sleepy yawn, and my heart melts. She's already got me wrapped around her little finger. I'd do anything for her.

I steal a quick glance at Grace and we share a smile. She's the most amazing mother to our wee lass, as I knew she would be, and seeing her care for Callie has only deepened my love for her. Our journey here may not have been the most traditional way of starting a family, but I can honestly say that if I could go back in time, I wouldn't change anything. Grace's unexpected pregnancy turned out to be the best thing that's ever happened to me.

"Oh, it's lovely to see the Bannock Hotel with young ones in it again," Maw says. "I've so many fond memories of when Aidan and Iona ran around here with Ally, Lewis, Jamie, and Cat. Talking of Iona, isn't it just wonderful that she's moving back up to Bannock?"

Behind the bar, something smashes—a bottle of wine, I think.

"Shit!" Lewis says.

"Correct me if I'm wrong," Jamie calls, "but aren't you supposed to count things during a stocktake, not break them?"

Lewis stands, coming into view above the bar. He's been busy working while the rest of us have been chilling. He fixes Jamie with a glower. "I won't bother answering that." Turning his attention to Maw, he says, "Elspeth, did you just say Iona is moving back?"

"Aye. A position came up at the vet's and she got it."

Lewis's expression brightens, his lips lifting at the corners.

"Richard is coming up with her," Maw quickly adds.

The smile on Lewis's face falters. We all notice but Maw pushes on regardless.

"He's starting a new role as a wind turbine technician. Apparently, Bannock is a great spot for him to be based."

"Ah." Lewis nods. "Right. Aye, of course." He hesitates then grabs a pint glass and pours himself a lager.

"Drinking on the job?" Jamie questions.

"Like you don't always do it. Besides, stocktaking is thirsty work. Fancy grabbing a mop and bucket and cleaning up this mess?"

"Nah, I'm sure you're on top of it. Anyway, I've got my hands full trying to cement myself as Ru's favourite uncle." He lifts the muslin again then drops it. "Boo!"

I chuckle, feeling a bit bad for Lewis, although not bad enough to give up holding my daughter to help. Besides, it's not really the spillage he needs assistance with. It's his obvious affection for my sister, even though she's with another man. Unfortunately, there's nothing I can do to fix that situation.

But I am excited that Iona is returning to Bannock after spending several years in Glasgow. I found my way home after travelling the world, and now she's being drawn back too. With Grace and Callie here, and my relationship with Da better than it's been in ages, it's clear I've entered a brand-new stage in my life, surrounded by family and friends. I'm looking forward to all that lies ahead.

In my arms Callie wriggles and cries out.

"Oh dear, what's wrong?" Maw asks her. "Are you hungry? Is it milk time?"

"Maybe she just needs Daddy's special dance." I stand, hold

my daughter close to my chest, and do the bouncy motion I've been perfecting over the last few months.

Callie soon calms to a whimper and then, finding her thumb, she settles against me.

"Och, would you look at that!" Maw beams with pride. "What a good da he is."

"He's wonderful." Grace rubs my back. "And next year he'll get to spread the love, what with another little one on the way."

I freeze. Maw's eyes widen. Jamie's jaw drops, while Lewis almost spits out his lager.

"You're . . . joking?" I say.

Grace stares at me seriously for several seconds, then she chuckles. "Yeah, sorry. You once told me I needed to practise my teasing. Am I getting any better?"

Jamie claps his hands together and howls with laughter. "Your face, mate! She got you so good."

My cheeks flushing, I grin.

Maw clucks her tongue. "You're obviously spending too much time with these lads, Grace. The last thing we need in Bannock is another practical joker." But the corners of her mouth turn up, showing she does see the funny side.

"Well," Grace adds, "maybe one day we will have a second, but for the moment I think we've got our hands full."

All the commotion wakes up wee Callie. Her eyelids flutter open, and she gazes up at me with those inquisitive dark-brown eyes that are so like Grace's. I smile at her then pull her favourite silly face and am immediately rewarded with a giggle. The sound warms my heart.

Aye, Grace is right: maybe one day we could have another. For now, though, I'd say life is pretty damn perfect as it is.

A NOTE FROM THE AUTHORS

We hope you enjoyed *The Highland Fling*. Want more of Aidan and Grace? Subscribers to our free email newsletter can download a bonus epilogue featuring the pair.

The *True Scotsman* series continues in *The Highland Crush*, Lewis and Iona's story. Haste ye back to Bannock for this friends-to-lovers romance.

For more information about the bonus epilogue and *The Highland Crush*, visit amymcgavinbooks.com.

Bonus Epilogue   Next Book

The True Scotsman Series

The
HIGHLAND
CRUSH

AMY McGAVIN

13482535R00184